PRAISE FOR ***LUCIFER'S GAME***

Lucifer's Game is enjoyable and insightful. It entertains with wit, sophistication and great characters. I couldn't put it down.

SYLVA DVORAK, PHD, Co-Author of NY Times Bestseller
Your Hidden Riches: Unleashing the Power of Ritual to Create a Life of Meaning and Purpose

Through a most beguiling story, *Lucifer's Game* invites you to take a peek under the covers, as it were, to acknowledge, and perhaps embrace, your disowned and rejected selves that are calling out for attention and healing, opening your soul to the possibility of true transcendence and spiritual balance.

DANNION BRINKLEY, NY Times best-selling Author of
Saved by the Light and *Secrets of the Light*

A fascinating novel that leaves no reader untouched, *Lucifer's Game* is a spellbinding tale that delves into the human struggle between our often hidden shadow and our capacity to live in the light. A must read for everybody inquiring about the True Self, spiritual Wholeness and wanting to develop a life of Self-Realization.

SIEGMAR GERKEN, PHD, The Core Evolution Institute

Will Schneider invites us on an exciting journey that takes us to the cliff's edge of temptation and darkness in the ultimate game of good and evil and the triumphant human spirit.

BRENT N. HUNTER, Social Media Pioneer,
Author of *The Rainbow Bridge*

Lucifer's Game is so visual it feels like a movie. The story is powerful, intriguing and entertaining. It's loaded with life-changing insights, leaving us with a banquet of food for thought.

DEA SHANDERA-HUNTER, former Executive Vice President,
MGM Worldwide Television

Lucifer's Game takes us on an unexpected wild ride revealing much about the shadow side of life. The contrast between the light in Jackson Trent, the main character and the dark in the very colorful Lucifer results in a story that is truly unforgettable. This book has major motion picture written all over it.

MICHAEL BERLIN, PH.D, Executive Producer/Writer,
Bass Clef Bliss

Lucifer's Game is a brilliantly woven metaphysical 'guide book' to higher conscious awareness. It is cleverly crafted to illuminate the Light and show the Shadow within us, revealing a path to true spiritual growth.

JEFF HARMAN, Spiritual Counselor, Astrologer and Filmmaker

An engaging, thought provoking page turner with an intuitive sense of humanity's innate need to constantly transcend itself. The utter originality of this book is that no other fiction writer managed to figure out that Lucifer also has to evolve with the times and cannot do it without our help. This book validates the old adage that the Devil can't do much damage without individuals inviting him into their thoughts or experiences either wittingly or unwittingly.

PARTHENIA GRANT, PHD, Host of Divine Love Talk on crntalk.com

A touching companion to the psyche, *Lucifer's Game* poetically taps into the spiritual and the humane, the light and the dark, offering a deep, smart, and playful dialogue of paradox. A deep seeker myself and a lover of new perspectives, this book landed in my lap at just the right time. Bravo! A wonderful, endearing, and playful read.

ANDI STARR, Musician, Singer Songwriter

Lucifer's Game is a fun, fast-paced read that takes us into the depths of the shadow side and the heights of the light. Truly a must-read!

TEMPLE HAYES, Unity of St. Petersburg, Florida,
Spiritual Leader, Author, Radio Host, Difference Maker

Lucifer's Game

Lucifer's Game

You're playing it,
whether you know it or not

BOOK ONE: THE REALM OF SHADOWS

Will Schneider

This book is dedicated to all those who are attuned to the echoing call of Spirit from deep within...

Editorial Director: Rick Benzel
Editing: Rick Benzel and Susan Shankin
Art Direction and Design: Susan Shankin & Associates
Cover Art: Thierry Gentil
Interior Art: Tim Kummerow

Published by Over And Above Press
Over And Above Creative Group
Los Angeles, CA
overandabovecreative.com

First edition
Printed at Bang Printing in the United States of America
10 9 8 7 6 5 4 3 2 1

Distributed by SCB Distributors

Library of Congress Control Number: 2015911459
ISBN: 978-0-9907924-5-1

If you liked this book, let others know. Please review it on your favorite website.
Connect with us at:
SnapOutOfItBlog.com
LettersToLucifer.com
Look for upcoming events and workshops at LucifersGame.com

Acknowledgments

THE UNFOLDMENT OF WRITING A NOVEL IS, BY DEFINITION, a singular experience. A story that wants to be told bubbles up from the depths of the imagination. But then, as the tale takes shape and form, there's nothing more valuable than sterling feedback, constructive criticism and helpful suggestions from the voices of intelligent and trusted friends. In that light, I want to express my thanks to a few in particular.

First and foremost, a source of incalculable input has been my great compadre, Brian Weller. Part wizard and with a fertile, brilliant mind that has decades of metaphysical development lodged within it, Brian's enthusiastic support, exceptional suggestions and sheer delight in the concept of the story's exploration of the Light and the Shadow is so appreciated. Brian's stamp is clearly etched into this tale . . .

Deep gratitude goes to Shivaun Mahony, a woman of profound depth and wisdom with a nose for keeping a story from losing its way. Shivaun has been the greatest of 'sounding boards', seeing to it that the flow of the narrative remained honed with a keen, intriguing edge.

Then, there's Richard Lang, the best friend a man could ever have. It was my humorous conversation with Richard, over a bottle of wine, which sparked the original idea of inventing a conversation with a 'Lucifer' of my own creation.

My profound appreciation to Constance Blake, a graceful, beautiful Spirit of love and light, who, over time, has ceaselessly been encouraging me to exercise more fully my gift of writing.

I'm very grateful to Rick Benzel and Susan Shankin, my publishers from *Over And Above Press*. With steadfast patience and resolve, they've brought their collective experience to bear, guiding the manuscript through the maze of the publishing arena and into the fruition of an actual book; well-edited and beautifully formatted. Now, for all of us, may it go out and multiply!

Lastly, I'd like to acknowledge the incomparable Debbie Ford, who has left us all a legacy of tremendous depth and transformation. Debbie's clear-eyed and fearless encouragement to bring the light of awareness down into our darkness was a powerful motivating force for me in writing this tale.

Contents

We're creatures of habit. We crave the familiar patterns.
Given the choice, as the poet Rilke put it,
we tend to lean towards the easiest side of easy.

We do our best to shape life to be predictable
until it's not; until the day the unexpected rolls in
and explodes open that cozy illusion.

First Contact

Pleased to meet you, hope you guess my name.
But what's puzzling you is the nature of my game.
—The Rolling Stones

Dawn was cracking open across the Hawaiian sky like a fresh egg, the golden yoke rising out of the sea to the east. God, I love this little piece of the islands. It's far enough off the main *tourista* track to lose most of the vacation crowds, and stunning in its lush tropical beauty. This must be where they come to take those travel agent poster shots.

Pulling the brim of my cap down to shade my eyes, I stopped to take in the panorama, enjoying the subtle pleasure of the gentle, incoming waves swirling around my ankles. The sea was aqua today, reflecting the clear blue sky and early morning light, the surf rolling in with an elegant curl. This particular Hawaiian beach was one of those wilder stretches, full of graceful curves, in and out, like a long, sandy snake.

A line of tall, stately coconut palms graced the back edge of the sand, stretching their elongated, curved trunks skyward and leaning out towards the ocean, as if the sea was beckoning them. They provided welcomed shade and I dropped my daypack, and then myself, down onto the warm sand to rest. The small boutique resort where I was staying, the *Mahana Kai*, was just around the curve of the beach and I was in no hurry to get back.

Taking a swig of water, I delighted in watching a family of four walking along the water's edge, the youngest son tossing a stick into the surf as their handsome Golden Retriever joyfully bounded into the shallow waters to fetch it. As they approached, the father snared the dog's collar and snapped on the leash. Although appreciating his concern, I would have preferred he allow that big, friendly pooch to scamper over to say hello. I've never met a dog I didn't like and this one was so happy, with that big laughing grin of a Golden who's in his element.

"Can I pet him?" I asked. The owner nodded and unhooked the leash. The dog bounded into my lap, as if I was his long-lost best friend, bowling me over with his energy. An expert licker, he covered me with wet kisses of unbounded affection, his dripping tail wagged fast with enthusiasm. He looked up at me with those soulful eyes and gleeful expression that said: *Do you have any idea how much fun I'm having out here?* "C'mon Farley," said the father, leashing his collar again and pulling him away. "Sorry, he doesn't know what a big goofball he is."

I laughed. "May we all find a way to be that high on life!"

The family moved on another 100 yards up the shore, unfurling a blanket and setting up for a snack. I noticed that Farley had abandoned the fetching stick as he had quickly developed a new fixation. Sitting perfectly still at the edge of the blanket, he stared ever-hopefully at their picnic basket that his twitching nose could tell was full of exciting possibilities.

Rolling onto my back on the soft sand in utter contentment, I gazed up at the shimmering palm fronds swaying hypnotically in the breeze. The magical rustling sound they made was soothing to me and I dozed off. When I awoke, yawned and looked around, I saw a few people collecting shells.

Far to my left, way up the beach, a dark figure was approaching. As it got closer, I could finally see it was a man. Even from a distance, he caught my attention by his odd gait—*shuffle, shuffle and a dip of the neck; shuffle, shuffle . . . dip of the neck.* As the man neared the family, Farley pried his eyes off the basket and his tail stopped wagging, freezing in mid-air. Slowly, he rose up on all fours, the hair along his spine standing on end. I couldn't hear his low growl but I could feel it. I recognized the unmistakable rigid body language of a dog on high alert.

In a flash, mild-mannered Farley lunged forward, his cheerful face now snarling and baring fangs. He dashed straight at the man, who was about thirty yards away. I sat bolt upright, cringing at what was about to befall the unsuspecting walker. The man looked up to see this large, powerful dog bearing down on him with serious intent, yet he just kept shuffling along without altering his strange pace. When Farley was perhaps fifteen feet away and closing in fast, the man raised his left index finger up and pointed it straight at the charging dog.

It wasn't as though Farley stopped in his tracks. It was more as if the dog hit an invisible shield and literally bounced off of it! Unhurt but startled, Farley shook himself, and barking wildly, tried again and again but could not penetrate within five feet of the man. By this time, the father had raced over, dragging the dog away. Whatever profuse apologies the father was uttering, the man seemed oblivious and just kept shuffling forward, eyes down as if nothing had happened.

How weird. I've had big dogs all my life and thought I'd seen damn near everything but I'd never seen that. Who was this guy? Resting my chin on my knees, I watched him draw closer until he was directly between the sea and me. For the first time, he stopped, looked in my direction, turned and began walking right towards me. I sat up a bit straighter and, as he drew near, I was able to visually take him in. He was a very large figure, by that I mean borderline obese, with a prodigious, protruding belly. He reminded me of a bumper sticker I saw a few days ago on a car driven by a big woman with a sense of humor: *I'm in shape. Round is a shape.*

Sitting atop his massive, curved shoulders rested a gargantuan head. Black hair with a mind of its own and a four-day beard growing with wild abandon gave him a scraggly look, as though he had just fallen out of bed. An iconic earring dangled from his left earlobe on a two-inch chain. His eyes were concealed behind a pair of *Maui Jim* wraparound shades. And if Hawaiian shirts can be loud, the one he was sporting was screaming. His bad taste was made even more apparent by the clashing plaid of his baggy shorts. His fingers looked like Polish sausages—short and plump with thick tufts of hair between the knuckles. A large, gold medallion hung from what little neck he had left, the oval disk almost lost in the matted forest of chest hair that spilled out of his half-buttoned shirt.

Without so much as a "How do you do?" he chose a spot right next to me, his enormous derriere plopping down on the sand, hitting the ground with a distinctive thud as he let out a wheezing "Ooph." Whipping out a handkerchief, he dabbed his forehead, drenched with the signs of a body overdoing it. He just sat there, staring forward at the sea.

"Water?" I offered, thinking dehydration wasn't far off.

He grabbed my plastic bottle in his big mitt, guzzling it all down in one unending glug-glug and wiped his mouth with his massive ham of a forearm.

"You're welcome," I muttered dryly to myself, as he handed me back the empty without a word. I had to ask:

"So tell me, do you always have this delightful effect on animals?"

He snorted with laughter and looked at me. "So you saw that. Yeah, no one's ever gonna confuse me with St. Francis. I've just come to expect it. Dogs, especially, don't seem to like my vibe." He must have heard my stifled chuckle, as he added: "Okay, a bit of an understatement, I'll admit."

I was about to ask him how he did that thing to protect himself from Farley when he blurted out:

"You're Jackson Trent, aren't you?"

My head swiveled as I turned to eye him closely. "Do I know you?"

"Definitely not. Let's just say I'm a fan of your writing. Your blog, *Snap Out of It*, has become a big hit and I've been reading it with great interest. Some of your points of view I even agree with."

"Wow, I'm deeply touched," I murmured, my sarcasm leaping out before I could muzzle it. That was odd, as I'm not usually derisive with a perfect stranger.

The man scratched the stubble on his neck as he looked me over. "In my view, there are two kinds of smart people: those who can take something simple and make it complex, and those who can grasp something complicated and simplify it."

"And which one of those are you saying is me?"

"You're the latter," he replied with a knowing air.

I thought about his comment for a moment before responding. "Some perplexing things are actually simple, in essence. We just make them complicated." I then faced him directly. "And your name is?"

"Look, I'm dyin' for a cold beer and I hear one calling me. I can pretty much assure you I'm someone you want to meet. How about rendezvousing with me at your hotel bar in an hour? We can chat in comfort. My ass is getting scorched on this hot sand."

"You know where I'm staying?" I asked, somewhat alarmed.

"Relax, I know where everyone's staying. Look, I realize I'm being a bit cryptic, but just meet me there. I'll explain everything."

Somewhere deep in his baggy shorts pocket, a cell phone started ringing—the ring-tone an annoyingly piercing siren of a fire engine. He yanked it out and glanced at the screen: "Damn. I gotta take this. I'll see you on the outside deck, under the banyan tree. In an hour."

Hauling himself up with a grunt, he brushed the sand off his expansive backside, much of it sprinkling down on me. Off he shuffled with that eccentric amble, phone pressed to his ear, heading back up the beach the way he'd come. I was relieved to see that the family and the dog had moved on. Still, I was rattled . . . questions swirling. Who was this pushy guy? How did he know where to find me? And what made him so sure he was someone I'd want to meet? Besides, did I want to meet with him?

I sat with that for a bit until I could feel an answer emerging from within. I had to admit, my curiosity outweighed my apprehension. He struck me as a real character; odd, yes, but not boring. I was intrigued. After all, he couldn't be all bad if he was reading my blog. Curious? Yes. I suppose he seemed harmless enough. What could possibly go wrong?

"Ha!" I blew out a hollow, mirthless laugh to that question. It would be more accurate to ask what else could go wrong? My life had already gone off the rails. This morning was my third day on the island and I had arrived an emotional wreck, my *mojo* running on empty, reeling from a one-two punch that life had delivered. The very core of my Being had been pummeled. But after a brief time on this stretch of paradise, I was starting to feel the bleak winter in my heart thawing out, the sap slowly starting to flow through the branches of my soul once again. This part of the island was big medicine, as the shamans say.

Time seems to move at different speeds. It felt like only a week had passed, although it was closing in on a year since my world had come crashing down. I shut my eyes and let my mind drift backwards, allowing the memory of what happened on that fateful day to float to the surface of my awareness.

It had begun as an exceptionally fun afternoon. The Sonoma coastline north of San Francisco has some great beaches and we were on a long, sandy cove called *Portuguese,* arguably one of the best along the California coast. It was a classic summer day for my daughter, Francesca, and me. She was having a blast, sketching her name in the sand with a stick and collecting small pieces of driftwood in a little yellow bucket for a science project. At ten years of age, an evolving individual had begun to emerge and I was enjoying her company in a fresh, new way.

One of the pleasures of being a father is watching your child in a state of delight. My heart smiled as I walked the beach behind her, letting her roam freely along the sand, as she skipped lightly. If I had been looking out to sea at that moment, I might have seen what was incoming and, just maybe, had a chance to react in time. With no warning at all, a massive wave hit our beach with a roar that thundered. It's called a 'rogue wave,' a single breaker of gigantic proportions. A rogue is very rare, but when one strikes the coastline, the swell is huge.

What had been a safe distance on the beach all afternoon was now slammed with a foaming, white wall of seawater, eight feet high, and, as it swept ashore, my last terrifying thought was of my daughter. Before I could whip my head around to attempt a warning yell, I was blown off my feet, haplessly spun around underwater, completely at the mercy of this swirling force. As the wave receded and my head broke the surface, I gasped for air and screamed, "*Francesca!*" Frantically scanning the beach, my daughter was nowhere to be seen. She had vanished, swept away by this monster. All that remained was her little yellow bucket, half buried in the sand.

"FRANCESCA!!"

Racing along the water's edge as a man possessed, my wild shouting yielded nothing. The stiff wind blowing in from the sea snatched my desperate cries and threw them back in my face. About twenty yards offshore, a tall spire of rock jutted straight up out of the surf line.

Diving into the surging currents, I swam to it, powering through the choppy breakers and clawing my way up its jagged, crumbling mass. From the vantage of a small ledge near its top, I could peer down on the churning surf below. There was no sign of my daughter. I bellowed out her name over and over, until my voice was a hoarse croak... choking on tears.

From a Zodiac boat, the Search and Rescue team did find her. The Captain who orchestrated her recovery eventually located me behind a sand dune, curled up in a fetal crouch, convulsed in the deepest, darkest place of grief. There's a level of pain beyond the veil of tears and I had free-fallen into it. When my heart could no longer contain one more drop of hellish anguish, it didn't stop there. I felt myself simply dissolve and become pure, distilled anguish itself, now boundless in the depths of its bitter torment. I vaguely remember the man's gentle touch on my shoulder: "Sir, you're gonna have to come with us. *Sir, can you hear me?*"

My wife, Chloe, from whom I was separated, had called and pleaded with me to do something else that day with Francesca who had been at my house for the night. Maybe it was Chloe's intuitive hunch . . . who knows? But that morning, I didn't want to hear it and we'd argued. I had adamantly insisted on keeping to my plan. Francesca had inherited my love of the sea and she was begging me to take her there. A day by the ocean was our favorite adventure together and I didn't want to let her down.

In the aftermath of this gaping hole in our lives, Chloe and I fell apart. Our relationship had crumbled completely. What had initially been a gradually widening gap, now eroded into a deep chasm between us. My overwhelming sorrow was compounded by the gnawing guilt of having been powerless to do anything to save my sweet child in her moment of peril.

Chloe, her heart crushed as only a mother could fathom, was dealing with bereavement in her own way. She, understandably, had turned her inconsolable loss into a towering inferno of anger. Her repetitive accusation, “I *told* you not to go!” stabbed at my heart. Rage mixed with truth is a harsh cocktail to swallow, and it left us no room to grieve together. The very sight of me caused the nightmare of losing our precious child to rear up for Chloe all over again. It was clear she wanted me out of her space. Her eyes blazed with “Go away.” I had lost the two most important women in my life.

So go away I did. Unfortunately, there’s much truth in the old adage: “Wherever you go, there you are.” I moved out and got my own apartment, but my heartache followed me like a thunderstorm overhead, blackening the sky with dark, roiling clouds. Blinding bolts of lightning would flash in the form of unannounced, jagged memories. These were followed by the rolling thunder of ‘if onlys’ dripping in regret. Sheets of rain poured out of my bloodshot eyes.

This smothering sadness was unfamiliar to me. I had never realized there was such a bleak state of mind. My nature had always been, more or less, irrepressible optimism. My heart leaned towards being a source of joy, a spring from which my natural *joie de vivre* bubbled up. Like anyone, I’ve had my own trials and tribulations, but those rough patches would always be nudged aside by the resurfacing of my upbeat buoyancy. Previously I’d looked at people who suffered from depression with a kind of naïve empathy; I had no idea how black the sky of one’s inner landscape could get. All this changed for me on that afternoon gone horribly wrong.

Like a stranger lost in a strange land, I ended up taking several wrong paths in my lame attempts to deal with it all. The first dead end I wandered down came in the sound of a clinking glass. Never much of a drinker, but in the hurting place I was now mired in, the bottle ‘came a callin.’ What do you want? I muttered morosely. The bottle answered, full of assurances: *You know that devastating wound? Well, I’m here to ease those sharp edges and smooth things out. Try me. Bottoms up!*

It was a persuasive offer and I took it. For a while, we got along just fine, the bottle delivering on its promise. Late at night, drinking alone in the isolation of my living room, sitting in an old creaky rocking chair, I'd sip the liquid fire, feeling it slowly spread throughout my bloodstream. Gradually, as the liquor took hold, my anguish would begin to soften into something more akin to nostalgia, my heart feeling brave enough to stir up recollections of fatherly moments with Francesca. There was the proud soccer dad cheering from the sidelines, or us camping in the Sierras as she caught, and released, her first trout. Those kinds of sweet, joyous memories would rise up to the surface.

I'd rock and rock, eyes closed, clutching the bottle to my chest as if it were precious. Pouring myself another, I'd feel warmer and fuzzier, encouraged to open the door of my memories wider. Well, one thing I learned about booze—if you don't know when to stop, it's not going to warn you. It got to a point in the evening that, as the haze thickened, the coziness of it all would turn on itself. Nostalgia would take a nasty dive and dissolve into its ugly cousin, self-pity, and a whole new level of torment would roll in: *Why her? What'd she do to deserve this?* Then, trying to chase those demons away and submerged in that alcohol-dulled state of mind, there was only one logical thing to do . . . pour another one. *Well thas not workin too well . . . mayb anuthr . . .* until, I was slip-sliding into the abyss of *blotto.*

Too often, I found myself cracking open eyelids that felt like sandpaper to the harsh morning light, having passed out in the wee hours of the night. My mouth had been replaced by a ball of thick cotton, my head splintered into a thousand shards of glass. You'd think the mournful moan of 'never again' escaping my parched lips might have had real staying power, but that's not the pattern of self-destruction. Come the next evening, all was forgotten. As darkness fell across the land, a similar shadow spread out across the terrain of my inner world, that dreaded sense of sinking stirring in my battered heart. Before I knew it, it was rocker time. It took the assistance of a close buddy to pull me out of that downward spiral, as, for the life of me, I just couldn't help myself.

Other friends, wanting to lend a hand, turned me in the direction of a medication designed to blow the turbulent clouds away. I tried that route. Chemistry has definitely come a long way. They have a pill for every conceivable kind of mental state and I know it's been a godsend for many. But how do you put a finger on what was eating away at this soul of mine? Is there a pill for tremendous guilt, mixed with devastating loss, leading to deficient emptiness, and swinging from anger to indecisive helplessness—all topped off with a crushing sadness that stuck to me like glue? Got something for that, Big Pharma?

In the end, I did try the suggested medication. It knocked out the real lows of my sense of despair. That, in and of itself, was a relief. It helped me stabilize. But over time, my experience was that, in canceling out my profound despondency, this particular drug simply took away my ability to feel, altogether. I was anesthetized and that wasn't what I wanted. I had just lost my daughter, my darling little girl, and swept away with her went the tattered remains of my marriage. I'd forfeited everything of true value in my life. I realized that going numb was not the answer, not for me.

Finally, I got introduced to grief counseling, in a group where everyone had lost big-time. I dragged my sorry ass to this gathering and found a place to land—a supportive environment where I was no longer flying solo. There's nothing like helping others who are equally in the grip of despair to pull yourself out of a ditch. The group experience was useful, but at the same time, I knew my anguish would not be completely healed through this process. It was too deep. So I took my great wound, carefully placed it in a protected, hidden chamber of my heart, and locked it away.

One meeting, someone in the group suggested that I consider 'getting out of Dodge' for a bit, going somewhere warm and friendly, some place that would nourish my soul. I thought about her suggestion long and hard. Part of me was against it: *You're running away, Jackson*. Yet another voice within sensed it was a good idea: *Go. Let some beautiful nature work its magic*. Eventually, I opted to listen to the latter voice. So, in truth, I hadn't come to Hawai'i to vacation. I had staggered here, deeply scarred, in order to let myself heal. I was still raw and vulnerable, wanting to come up for air.

With a shiver, my eyes fluttered open from my memory. Sitting on the warm, white sand, I was relieved to find myself back in this Polynesian paradise. Part of why I'd specifically chosen to come to yet another beach setting, of all places, was to make my peace with the ocean. I could feel it starting to happen. The sea is as majestic as it is ruthless and unpredictable. To engage with it must be on its terms, not yours. If I could forgive the ocean for snatching my Francesca, perhaps, just maybe, I could forgive myself.

As I gathered up my things to go, I noticed the large indentation in the sand where my visitor had been sitting. What a peculiar dude! I wish I'd been able to see his eyes behind those reflective sunglasses. The eyes of a person say so much. And how did he stop that charging dog? And why would a sweet retriever 'go off' like that on him? Goldens love everyone. Who is this guy? It wasn't too late to back out of the rendezvous, but there was something curiously irresistible about the way he had said with such confident conviction: "I can assure you I'm someone you want to meet."

I've never considered myself to be psychic, to have that particular kind of sensitivity and yet I am fairly intuitive. Something is rolling in on me. A kind of premonition seems to be trying to get my attention. What's the message? I'm listening . . .

Be careful.

Duly noted. I jumped to my feet, scooped up my daypack and headed back to the resort.

CHAPTER
2

I Am the Prince of Living Large

When you sup with the Devil... use a long spoon.

—George Gurdjieff

UPON RETURNING TO MY COTTAGE AT THE MAHANA KAI, I showered off the salt and sand and changed into some fresh clothes. A glance at the clock told me it was time to go, so I grabbed my wallet, phone and daypack. I headed out along a path thick with tall bamboo. It meandered in the direction of the resort's central structure, an open-air, grass-thatched *hale.*

Arriving at the outside patio bar, a quick look around revealed that my acquaintance had not yet arrived. I took a small table on the raised deck off to the left, in the shade of a giant banyan tree. Relieved that he was running late, it allowed me to fully appreciate this marvel of nature. A mature banyan is like no other tree on Earth, so Tolkienesque that it defies description. Expressions like enormous and spectacular are woefully inadequate. My vantage point along the edge of the deck also treated me to a sweeping view of the beautiful grounds below. The acreage was a pleasing balance between wild plant life, manicured grass and tropical gardens, as the three forms co-mingled effortlessly. Plumeria trees loaded with fragrant blossoms rubbed elbows with wild orchids, everything bursting in the temperate island air. Looking further out, I could see the royal palms swaying on the white sand beach and the sparkling sea beyond.

"*Aloha*, sir. Will you be ordering the brunch buffet?"

The voice startled me. I turned around to see a lovely *wahine* with a dazzling, dimpled smile, black, shiny hair cascading down her left shoulder. A fresh hibiscus flower was tucked behind her ear. Her figure was wrapped in a colorful sarong. What a beauty!

"Hello! Yes, I think I'll be doing the brunch, but I'm waiting for someone to join me."

"Something from the bar in the meantime?"

Hmm, alcohol? I hadn't had a stiff drink in months. I could hear a warning bell clanging, *Go easy.* But hey, this was supposed to be a vacation, right?

"A Mai Tai sounds kinda touristy. Maybe you could suggest something more exotic, some classic Hawaiian drink?"

"Are you familiar with a *Haupia*? That's my favorite, white Crème de Cacao, rum and coco syrup, mixed as a smoothie over crushed ice."

"That sounds really good. Sign me up!"

"Excuse me?"

"I mean I'll take one . . . So, are you from this island?"

"No, I was raised in a small town, Kaunakakai, on the south shore of Moloka'i."

"Moloka'i, that's where the leper colony was, right?"

Her smile faded fast, like a flower closing up after sunset. Whoops. "I'm sorry. Did I say something wrong?"

"No, not really. It's okay."

"Yeah, I did. Forgive me."

She glanced over her shoulder to see if she could speak freely, and then stepped a bit closer: "This island is beautiful, but my island is breathtaking. When outsiders hear the name Moloka'i, all they think about are the unfortunate lepers from years ago. If you only knew! Moloka'i is the true old Hawai'i, a wonderful community and *aloha aina,* 'love of the land.' It's been left alone, unspoiled by development. It's the island where the ancient traditions are kept very much alive. So, frankly, Moloka'i is unparalleled."

I felt like an idiot—the classic 'open mouth, insert foot' misstep. How easy it is to be insulting if you don't understand a culture.

"Sorry I sounded like such an ignorant *haole."* I made a stab at repairing the damage. "I know a little about your home. It's called the Friendly Island, right? I've heard about the fantastic Kalaupapa Reserve and the mystical Halawa Valley with its wild rain forests and steep waterfalls."

She drew in a deep breath, lips pursed. It was clear that there was no redemption for me in her lovely eyes. I was just a tourist spouting facts about places I'd never experienced. I tried again:

"I also know that there's not a single stop light on the entire island! And the sea cliffs on the north shore are the highest in the world... and that there isn't one building on Moloka'i taller than a palm tree."

Still no response as she fiddled with her order pad.

"I even know about the *Ka Hula Piko* festival."

"Really?" Finally something had clicked, as her face was suddenly wreathed in light. "*Hula*'s my greatest love. My grandmother, as a young *wahine*, was known all over the islands for her *hula* skills. She taught me everything, starting when I was just this big." With a lithe flick of her wrist, she indicated a child about three feet tall.

"*Hula*'s the language of the heart. It's our way of storytelling."

"May I ask you your name?"

"Nalani."

I held out my hand. "Jackson. Nice to meet you, Nalani. Maybe someday I'll have the chance to see you dance. I'd love that."

"Maybe," she said, her demure shyness returning, yet there was a sweetness to her smile that wasn't there before. "Come to the *luau* tonight on the beach. That's why I'm here at the *Mahana Kai.* They've brought me to this wonderful resort for my *hula.* Working at the bar just gives me a little extra cash."

Whatever feathers I may have ruffled had settled down as she stood there, eyeing me for a long moment. I had the slightly uncomfortable sense I was being studied. Finally, she said softly:

"Are you okay?"

Whoa! That took me aback. "Okay? What do you mean?"

She held her gaze. "You have kind eyes, but there's such sadness in them."

I shifted in my chair. "It's obvious, huh?"

"Yes," she said simply. "I'm sorry. Didn't mean to pry."

"I've . . . had a rough year."

She gave my forearm a light touch. "Well, Jackson, I think you've come to the right place."

It's amazing how the slightest gesture can convey so much. I felt a wave of tender compassion ripple through me. How lovely and soothing, the touch of a woman. I could tell I was starved for it. Nalani scanned the deck.

"You said you're waiting for someone?"

"I am, but chances are he won't show up."

She turned towards the bar. "Okay, then I'll go ahead and put your drink order in now."

A voice bellowed from behind her. "Hey, not so fast, little lady! Bring me a *Fire Rock* pale ale, will ya? Make sure it's plenty cold."

It was him—clashing attire, shades and all. He dropped heavily into the chair across from me, the rattan creaking alarmingly under the strain. After some squirming around to get settled in, he leaned towards me with a whispering leer, as Nalani walked away.

"I see you're wasting no time hitting on these cute native girls. Good man! Get her number?"

"No, I didn't get her number. What I got was an education."

"How so?"

"Never mind. By the way, did you pick out that, uh, colorful aloha shirt yourself? That's a real classic. I can see why you wear sunglasses." Again, my sarcasm was leaping out, but I didn't know why. Apparently oblivious to it, he beamed proudly:

"Oh yeah, I always pick out my own wardrobe. On sale, too. Half price! Hard to believe, huh?"

Hard to believe they finally found a customer, I thought. We sat in awkward silence for a moment until I asked: "Okay, so here we are. I've got a few questions for you, if you don't mind."

"Fire away, my friend."

"For starters, what's your interest in me? Are you a reporter? Oh shit! Are you with the I.R.S.? Look, I'm working out a payment sched . . . "

"Relax! I'm neither. It's your writing, in general, and you, in particular, that interest me, Jack."

I winced. "Hold it right there. Let's get something straight. Please don't call me *Jack*. Reminds me of an earlier part of my life I'd prefer to forget. It's Jackson, okay?"

He gave me a dismissive wave. "Whatever. As I was saying, it's your writing. You touch into metaphysical areas I've never come across before and I'm a voracious reader of that arena. Where did you learn all that stuff?"

I watched a bright red *liwi* bird alight on the balcony railing as I mulled over how to respond. My blog, *Snap Out of It,* had been launched just prior to losing Francesca. Despite my life suddenly coming apart at the seams, the message I've been attempting to convey had attracted a wide following and the blog had really taken off.

"Where did I learn all that? That's a complicated question, so let me give you a simple answer. Let's just say I've paid my dues. Like a lot of people who are searching for greater understanding, I've invested a serious chunk of my life into spiritual teachings that I've been drawn to. If you clocked in the commitment that I did, you're bound to absorb a certain amount of insight over time. As for my writing? Everyone's gifted in some way. Expressing myself has always come easily."

"But why do you write? What's your motivation?"

This felt a little invasive, so I chose my words carefully. "At the risk of sounding sappy, I write because I feel like I want to give something back."

The man looked puzzled. "Give something back . . . to whom?"

"To anyone who wants to listen! Look, the world's a screwed-up mess, and getting progressively worse on all fronts. My take on life is that you can't just sit on your ass, anxiously wringing your hands. Everyone has something to offer . . . to contribute."

"You think so?"

"Yeah, I think so. If everyone does something, things can change."

"No offense, of course, but that strikes me as a rather juvenile notion about the world."

His retort pushed a button of mine. "Really? Well, have you ever heard it said: 'Those who say it can't be done shouldn't interrupt those who are doing it'?"

"Have you heard: 'Naïve optimists end up full of disappointments'?"

"No, never heard that one."

"That's because I just made it up, but it's true," he snorted.

"So, we disagree. But I'd rather be optimistic and do something than to be part of the problem. Speaking of quotes, there's one by Einstein that says it well. Something along the lines of: 'It's everyone's obligation to put back into the world at least the equivalent of what they take out of it.' At some point in one's life, giving back can become a necessity and a joy, and it can take any number of forms."

"Like what?"

I thought for a moment. "Okay, I'll give you an example. I have a good friend whose contribution to the world is one-on-one. A month ago, I went along with her into the rough Skid Row Tenderloin district of San Francisco where her small group gathers on Saturday mornings, sets up some tables and feeds the hungry. People were lined up around the block—the destitute, the underbelly of the city, the ones a notch or two below 'downtrodden,' driven to the mean streets by addiction or circumstance. One at a time, my friend handed them a sandwich and a drink. She looked each person directly in the eye, into their ravaged faces, those haunted, hollow eyes that pleaded: 'Don't you judge me, too.' She beamed back loving compassion from her beautiful, warm heart. Not a word was spoken and yet, most of those people walked away with the sense that they'd truly been seen. That experience moved me to tears."

"Okay, whatever. But do you think her little contribution makes a damn bit of difference in the big picture for those poor wretches? They're still out on the streets, huh?"

"Why don't you ask the homeless alcoholic who was able to push back that constant gnawing hunger for a few hours, who felt a ray of kindness come his way? People are showing up all over the place to help the world. I have another friend who's a successful ophthalmologist. Every summer, instead of kicking back and relaxing in a place like this, he spends his vacation window flying off to Tibet, where he fights his way through the tricky Chinese bureaucracy and sets up a temporary hospital camp, way up in the Sitsang Plateau region. More than half the locals over the age of sixty in that area have been blinded by cataracts from a life under that intense, bright sun. Once his 'eye camp' is set up, word spreads and villagers come from far and wide, bringing in their elderly blind. After a short, delicate operation, these seniors walk out of his tent with their sight restored. Tell me, how cool is that? That's Marc's contribution."

My acquaintance still seemed unimpressed. "And you?"

"As for me, I write. And if, as you said, you read my blog regularly, you know that I never profess to have the answers for someone else. If you don't understand that, then you didn't understand my message. All I know for sure is what's worked in my life, what I've found to be true and useful for me. If I can articulate that in a way that might be of help to someone else, that's great, that's my intent. But if nobody gets it or wants it, that's fine, too. It's simply my contribution. Who it impacts, if anyone, is out my hands."

"You seem to be impacting quite a few. That's why I found you."

"Okay, you found me. So what can I do for you?"

"Your drinks, gentlemen."

Nalani placed the glasses on our table with sacramental grace. I could clearly see the dancer in her, camouflaged behind the façade of a barmaid. A whiff of jasmine oil from her thick hair wafted by and I found myself turning to follow the delicious aroma. My God, she was pretty. Is there anything more attractive to a man than a natural beauty who's comfortable with herself?

My portly companion grabbed for his drink. "Where ya from, honey? This rock or one of the others?"

"I'm from the island of Moloka'i."

"Oh, the leper island." He leaned backwards. "No offense, but you're not contagious, are ya?" letting loose a snort of a laugh.

Nalani gave him a level stare and said evenly: "You say 'No offense' before you insult me? How very thoughtful of you."

"Hey, where ya going? I was kidding! Whoa, no sense of humor!"

I was appalled and ready to stand up and walk away. The glare I delivered across the table must have conveyed it, as he quickly changed his tune.

"Hold on, Jack! Didn't mean to offend the little lady. Just my way of flirting."

"Really? I see you have the same deft gift with women that you have with dogs. Look, I've been doing most of the talking, instead of asking questions."

"You noticed."

A wiseass. I was getting annoyed. "Okay, I'll give you two minutes to fill me in on who you are and why I should be spending this glorious day . . . with you." I glanced at my watch for effect.

"Okay Jack, I'm gonna get to the point, but you may not be ready for what I'm about to say."

"Try me."

"Alright, so you're a writer and you must have an affinity for metaphors, true? Well, here's my card."

It was black with small white type. I held it up close to my eyes:

I was named after the Morning Star
Yet I am one with the darkest of night.
A Guide into the subterranean.
The Keeper of your hidden Inner Cavern.
Master of the Shadow World.
Holding the torch for the Rejected Ones.
The voice of the forbidden fruits, ripe for the plucking.
I am the Prince of Living Large.

"What the hell is this supposed to mean?"

"Read it again, this time more slowly."

I did and then pulled out my cell phone and Googled: named after the Morning Star. It made me laugh. "This is weird. It says: *Lucifer.*"

I looked up and my drink mate was stock-still, clearly not laughing with me. Then he slowly reached up and, for the first time, took off his sunglasses, revealing his eyes. Whoa! Very strange. His left eye was sky blue and his right, a deep green. But the primary thing that jumped out at me was the powerful intensity behind the eyes, as if they were burning with red hot coals. Holy shit! My jaw dropped stupidly as the realization was rolling in.

"Are you telling me . . . *Lucifer, as in the Devil?!*"

He made a slight bow of the head. "That's right, the one and only. I've noticed mothers don't name their children after me. No little snot-nosed Lucifer's running around, last time I checked. But don't jump to conclusions, Jack. Sure, I've been technically labeled, uh, let's make that libeled, 'the Devil' but that's a long story. It's a sad fact that the people who know the least about me always have the strongest opinions."

"Lucifer?" I felt a shudder shoot up my spine. "Prove it!"

"Like how?"

"I don't care, but make it convincing."

The big man scanned the bar patio. In the far corner was some fellow reading a newspaper, hidden behind the sports page he was holding up. Glancing my way, Lucifer folded his chubby hands on his immense belly and focused his attention back to the man. Within a few seconds, a wisp of smoke began to rise from the very center of the newspaper. Moments later, it burst into flames, the guy screeching in terror and dumping a pitcher of margaritas on the blaze to put it out. I was stunned. Goosebumps broke out all over my body and I leapt to my feet, heart pounding.

"Alright, pretty damn convincing! So what do you want with me? What did I do?"

"Sit down, Jack. Nothing is wrong, if that's what you mean. Take my visit as a compliment. Sit, sit. Let's chat."

A compliment? That was a bit much. Terrific. Now I've attracted Lucifer into my life. Still standing, I asked him: "If you're who you say you are, why don't you go drop in on someone who's more interested in your line of work."

"Which is?"

"I don't know and I don't really care to know. Nothing personal but you're on the same par as the Grim Reaper as someone I'd least want to meet."

"Aw, Jack, you say the sweetest things. You warm the cockles of my cold, black heart! Fortunately, I've got a hide as thick as a buffalo, although you'd probably never guess that. Why do I want to talk with you? The answer to that will reveal itself in time. For now, just understand that there's something about you that interests me."

"Well there's something about you that alarms me."

"Oh, relax. Come on, sit down. I can appreciate how my dropping in like this would scare the bejesus out of anyone. But, here I am and, well, frankly, you're still listening. And let's be honest. You're getting a chance to talk to me, Lucifer, Prince of the Darkside himself. You're a writer who craves intrigue, not one to miss an opportunity, right? Underneath your shock, you're actually kind of curious, aren't cha? And thanks for not freaking out any more than you have."

"Other people you've dropped in on have panicked?"

He bent forward, his whole body jiggling with mirth.

"That's putting it mildly. You'd think I'd lit their hair on fire!"

With wary trepidation, I let myself sink slowly back into my chair. Lucifer leaned towards me, a little too close for comfort and continued:

"Let's start by agreeing to this. I'm not going to twist your arm to converse with me. It's entirely up to you. One thing that's overlooked about me is that I never force an issue on someone. Suggest? Yeah. Cajole? Sure. Manipulate? Guilty as charged. Tempt? Oh boy! Definitely known to persuade, but I never force. It's true that humans have free will to make their own choices. That's 'The Law' and whether I like it or not, I've gotta follow it. This conversation is entirely up to you. So, Jack, it's your call . . . are you in or out?"

As I sat there, staring across at him, I felt the clammy grip of fear creep under my skin, starting to wrap itself around my heart. I let my gaze settle on the great banyan tree to calm me down and draw from its strength. What to do? Was I flattered by his visit? Possibly, but what, exactly, was he after? It hadn't escaped me that I'd yet to get a straight answer from him. Still, it was a daunting decision, continuing a conversation with Lucifer, for chrissake! My solar plexus was quivering.

On the other hand, I do have confidence in my sense of the world. I'm clear on what I value, what I've verified to be true, and I can defend the positions I believe in. But could I hold my own against the likes of *him?* There was also the fact that I was feeling so shaky and vulnerable in my life right now. I swallowed hard. As I was gathering my thoughts, I could see a scale within my mind, balancing my options. I felt the measured weight on both sides of this strange offer presenting themselves, making their case. Finally . . . the scale tipped:

"Okay, I'm in."

"Fantastic! I've earmarked this entire day for you. You've got me till the wee hours. Or you can bail out anytime sooner. Cool?"

"I guess we'll see, won't we?"

"Great," he smirked as he rubbed the expansive terrain of his mid-section. "Let's get some grub. I'm so hungry I could bite the leg off a low-flying sea gull!"

I gave him a sidelong glance. "I'm gonna assume you're kidding."

The Sunday buffet at the *Mahana Kai* was legendary and did not disappoint—the very picture of lavish abundance. Every conceivable offering was laid out with elegant presentation. Lucifer had a few large plates balanced on his massive right forearm, as he enthusiastically shoveled food onto them, expertly piling up at least one of everything and two of most. Watching him work the buffet was a display of pure, unadulterated gluttony. I noticed the tourists behind us in line staring at him, aghast, and thought: *Oh man . . . if you only knew who this is pigging out here next to you!*

Back at our table, we both focused on consuming the incredible meal before us. Nalani responded to my wave and brought us another round of drinks. Taking in her sleek fluidity made me think of a Neil

Young line: "I used to order just to watch her float across the floor." Lucifer scarfed his food down so fast that we both finished our brunch around the same time, although he had twice as much. I noticed him eyeing the buffet table with the unmistakable intention of going back for round two. But before he could get up, I looked hard at him and heard myself say:

"You're reviled you know; I mean, really hated."

He beamed. "I certainly hope so. To be hated shows that people still keep me in mind. I'll take that."

"You mean, like what they say in Hollywood: 'There's no such thing as bad publicity.'"

"More or less. In their case, a nasty exposé of a celebrity gets their face in the news, which still makes for good PR. As for me, people hate what they fear. I'm greatly misunderstood."

"I don't see how you're misunderstood. You're hated for what you stand for. Aren't you the archetype of evil?"

"Jack, that sounds so dramatic. Evil is a matter of interpretation. Actually, I'd define myself as a figure who's been grossly misperceived, shafted with a bad rap by history. Someone once said: 'Apology to the Devil. It must be remembered that we have only heard one side of the story—because God wrote all the books.' Perfectly put! I couldn't have said it better. Don't laugh, but I just might be here to help you."

My expression was incredulous. "That's hard to believe. What do you mean help me?"

Lucifer's big head rocked from side to side, as if the question was rolling around inside his skull like a marble. "There are things you simply don't see. I'm here to lead you out of your ignorance."

"You're assuming I want your help. But be honest. You do have nefarious intentions for humanity. Your focus *is* on evil, right?"

Leaning forward closely, Lucifer peered into me, not just with his eyes but with his intense energy. His whisper was a kind of wheeze: "Who's to say what's evil?"

"Religion emphatically claims that you're the very source of villainy in the world."

He let out a short snort. "Yeah, right. Go on . . . "

"And that your entire MO is to corrupt people's moral code. According to one highly accepted view in the Western world, you, Lucifer, for reasons of your own, want to lure people into sin."

"Really. And what is sin? And why would I wanna do that?"

I chewed on his questions for a moment. I definitely had my own thoughts on this topic but I opted for a more generic answer. "I'd say that sin is defined as disobeying the spiritual laws laid down by God. As to why you'd want to lure people into sin? The way I heard the story, you're pissed off at God because you got booted out of Heaven for being, well, an over-reaching jerk."

Lucifer eyes rolled in their sockets. "I beg to differ."

"And, as the story goes, now you're fighting tooth and nail against God's will, trying to pull human souls down into the Hell *you* were cast into. As they say: 'Misery loves company.' No pun intended, but am I warm?"

"No, you're not warm at all. That's another stereotype. You believe this propaganda?"

"Do I believe in Hell? Personally, no, I don't. That piece of dogma never stuck with me. I think Hell's a chilling story concocted by some patriarchal old farts many millennia ago. This is strictly my take on it and I'm obviously cynical in this area."

"So what do you believe about Hell, Jack?"

"Me? I think the spiritual power brokers around the 3rd century were drawing up rules for the new religion they were constructing. It was supposed to be based on the simple, extraordinarily beautiful and spiritually enlightened teachings of Jesus. These guys probably figured a horrifying Hell story would terrify the uneducated masses. They wanted people to think: *Holy crap! If I don't toe the line, I'll roast in everlasting Hellfire!* In my view, this was designed to keep the faithful obedient and shaking in their sandals. But you tell me, Lucifer, does Hell exist or not?"

Lucifer's wide face split into a grin. "I recently heard the best answer to that: 'Heaven is where the police are British, the lovers Italian, the mechanics German, the chefs French, and it's all organized by the Swiss. Hell is where the police are German, the lovers Swiss, the mechanics French, the chefs British and it's all organized by the Italians.'"

I stifled my laugh. "C'mon, does Hell exist or not?"

He picked up his fork and twirled it for a moment. "Well, that's a big question. The short answer is no, but also yes. Hell is real, but it's nothing like what people think. It's not at all what was concocted by Dante's feverish imagination in his book, *Inferno*, which is, by the way, one of my all-time favorite novels. Great illustrations! But Hell's not that at all. It's not a place where people are tormented eternally. Hell is something else, somewhere else. You might be in it right now and not even know it, Jack!"

His statement startled me. "What do you mean?"

"Because you wouldn't recognize it." He paused, and then: "I'll give you a big hint. Hell is primarily the absence of Heaven. Once you've tasted Heaven, anything short of that is some level of Hell. And speaking of Heaven, I'm heading back to the brunch table!"

Lucifer left me alone to ponder while he refilled his plates. Sitting back down, he immediately began loading a few heaping forkfuls into his cavernous mouth. As he chewed loudly with a wolfish joy, he seemed to be looking me over.

"You're a peculiar combination, Jack. Do you consider yourself a religious person?"

Damn. The way he ate was revolting. "Hey, do us both a favor and stop talking with your mouth full. I hate that. And no, I'd say my interest is more in the direction of the spiritual than the religious."

He paused long enough to swallow. "What's the difference?"

I took a moment to answer. "It's said that religion is for those who don't want to go to Hell, while spirituality is for those who have lived through it."

Wiping his mouth with the back of his hand, Lucifer seemed to find that amusing. I wanted to pick up on his intriguing thread that Hell is the absence of Heaven, but got distracted as Nalani walked past us, leading some new buffet guests to a table. Returning, she gave me a subtle smile, which made my heart skip a beat. I could still feel the warmth of her touch on my arm. A snicker came from across the table.

"That woman's so hot, she's even making me sweat! Look at you. You're practically panting."

My head whipped around. "Can't a man appreciate a woman without having it turned into something seedy?"

Lucifer leaned back in his chair, giving me a cynical look. "You're pathetic, Jack."

"Pathetic?"

"Yeah. Take a look. You won't admit that you desire this woman in the worst way. And yet there you sit, trying to be polite, respectful and oh-so nice."

"Okay, I find her attractive, I'll give you that. But I can't feel much of anything these days. There's something broken inside me."

"What's broken? Tell me about it."

"What's broken is none of your business, Lucifer."

"Well, here's what I see, Jack. Denial. You're systematically denying this lusty creature inside you, this wild panther, pacing back and forth in a cage where you have him locked up. You've got him buried down so deeply you're not even aware of this ravenous, powerful beast. You think he's outta sight, outta mind. Ha! He's coming out through your hungry eyes. So why not go for her? You're free to do what you want."

I sat there in a brooding silence. Yeah, he was right. I am free to do what I want. Since we split up, Chloe had started dating, but I hadn't yet tried. We'd been together for so long and some bonds don't evaporate overnight, at least not for me. Sure, I longed to hold a woman in my arms again, ached to experience the closeness of connection, but I was feeling way too vulnerable to let anyone in. My heart still hurt, as if it had been badly bruised and wrung dry. Adding to my reluctance was the ever-lurking guilt in the side aisle of my mind. Its message was: "Do I deserve love again after everything that's happened?" As for Lucifer's point, it's true that all through my marriage I'd remained loyal. I didn't feel obliged to admit this to him, but that brand of loyalty had, indeed, come at a price. I had pushed my wild panther way down and caged it.

"I'm not ready to engage with a woman yet. I can't seem to get my motor running."

Lucifer pinched the bridge of his nose, shaking his head in disbelief.

"For chrissake, Jack, if ignorance is bliss, you must be orgasmic! Did you just say you're not ready? Let me see if I've got this straight. Here you are, all by your lonesome on this romantic, tropical island, licking your wounds like an injured coyote. Everywhere you look, you're surrounded by beautiful women, in general, and this one, in particular. And what do you do? You bury your head in the sand. You're shutting yourself down, keeping a tight lid on your powerful erotic energy, sitting there passively neutered and passing up the chance of a lifetime with a gorgeous native girl, all because you're just not ready? As I said, there's a word for that . . . *pathetic*."

Ouch. That stung. "Oh come on, Lucifer. Don't hold back. Tell me what you really think."

He shrugged. "Hey, no one's ever going to accuse me of being polite. I tell it like I see it. Deal with it."

I was trying to. If I could get past his harshness, there was some truth beneath his blast, but I was struggling to admit it.

"What makes you think Nalani has the slightest interest in me?"

"See? That's exactly what happens when you cut yourself off from your panther. You're in your head, making up stupid, lame excuses."

"Stop insulting me."

"I'm not insulting you, I'm describing you! I could tell instantly that there's a mutual buzz between the two of you. If you'd stop living between your ears, and allow yourself the freedom to get in touch with it, to actually sense into your animal maleness, you'd know it. And here's a tip, pal. This woman is just as hot for you. Oh, I'm sorry, I forgot—you think it's far more honorable to limp along, keeping that wet blanket smothering your life force. Are you a man or a rodent? Don't make me guess. What's the problem? Is your brokenness getting in the way of your panther?"

"Back off! I can see that your idea of personal growth is an erection."

It seemed to be his turn to stifle a laugh. Another long, pregnant silence dropped down between us. I didn't know whether to be pissed off or to burst out laughing. Finally, I muttered: "You're a sarcastic blowhard, you know."

His thick lips curled into a sneer. "Oh, you have no idea the depths I can go. You know that little voice inside your head that keeps you from saying things you shouldn't? Well, I don't have that."

Nalani was clearing off a vacated table close by. She set the tray of empty glasses down and pulled up a chair to join us.

"I'm going to be off my shift in a few minutes. Anything else I can do for you two?"

Slowly, Lucifer scanned her up and down. "Yeah, but it's not something on the menu . . . "

I kicked him under the table. "Sorry, Nalani, I'm not with him. We just met." She gave me a slight grin that conveyed: "Don't worry.

I deal with cretins like this all the time." Our eyes met once again, only this time I didn't feel as though I was being studied; it was just sharing a pleasant visual exchange. Lucifer let out the soft, throaty growl of a jungle cat. His implication didn't escape me. I scanned my 'inner terrain' but still couldn't seem to locate the panther within. But, nonetheless, I was definitely enjoying taking in the captivating gaze of a woman who seemed so at ease and collected. Finally, Nalani broke the spell and asked: "Did you enjoy the brunch?"

"The brunch was great. I think we're okay." I looked over at Lucifer. "How about a change of scene?"

"Fine with me."

Sifting through her stack of tabs, she pulled out ours, setting it on the table. Making a point not to reach for it, I glanced across at him: "Split the bill?"

"Sure." Lucifer reached for his back pocket. Then, with a feigned frown, he started pawing at his other pockets.

"Let me guess . . . Nalani, please charge the bill to my cottage. Thanks for taking great care of us."

I slipped a nice tip under my empty glass and gathered up my things. Lucifer was busy struggling to eject his enormous torso out of the uncooperative chair that was apparently designed for a derriere two sizes smaller. When he was finally on his feet, I stood up, feeling the pleasant effects of the drinks, and followed behind him as we walked across the patio towards the exit. Not surprisingly, he was as massive from the backside as the front. His eccentric walk gave me the impression that I was in the shadow of a lumbering prehistoric creature. No doubt, not too far from the truth!

What added to the strangeness was, for lack of a better word, the vibration he was emitting. Lucifer's energy field was palpable. It felt like I was close to a high-voltage generator—intensely powerful and somewhat disorienting. I could hear the rising whine of a warning voice within me starting to kick in with its cautionary alarm: *Jackso*n . . . *Jackson, here we go again, you nitwit! Another fine mess your curiosity is getting us into.* And yet, hell yes, I was curious! My inquisitiveness still outweighed my fear.

I turned and looked back to the bar. Nalani was leaning against a wall, watching us leave. I was treated to the sweetest smile imaginable. Once outside on the lush grounds, Lucifer stopped and turned to me.

"So, I see you opted not to pursue the opportunity."

"Call me pathetic, but I feel . . . well, I guess shy kind of says it."

"Try hopeless." He poked me with his pudgy finger. "Tempting though, huh?"

"Oh yeah, very."

"Too bad for you, pal. Right now you could be off somewhere, well on your way to making passionate love to that island goddess, instead of standing here looking at my ugly mug."

"You're right . . . especially about the ugly part."

Lucifer took a step back. "Now who's being sarcastic?"

"Oh, you have no idea of the depths I, too, can go."

"Ah, so you're a smartass, too. I like that. Okay, where are we heading, Jack?"

I took a look around. "How about hanging out poolside for a while? I'd like to take a dip . . . or do you and water not mix well?"

"Don't worry about me. Let's go."

As we got on the walking path, Lucifer's cell started ringing, its fire engine siren piercing the serene calm. Glancing at the incoming number, he muttered: "For chrissake! I told her to handle that one. Do I have to do everything?" He barked into the phone. "What is it?" A long pause was followed by an ominously quiet tone of voice. "This happened when? And you let them go? All of them? Hang on a sec." He turned to me: "Jack, I gotta deal with this now. Dicey situation. How about I meet you at the pool a little later?"

"Fine . . . just curious, though. Care to share what your situation is all about?"

Lucifer stared me, as if pondering my request. "No, I don't want to share. Believe me, this one, you're better off knowing nothing about."

His focus returned to the phone. In a low tone, he growled: "Yeah? Well here's my response to him: 'Two words . . . one finger'!"

Ambling off, deep into a heated discussion, his left arm flailing, emphasizing some point he was fuming about, Lucifer disappeared around the bend on the path adorned by an explosion of flowering hibiscus. I could swear they wilted as he walked by, but when I turned for a double-take, they were back to normal.

What Do You Want With Me?

I can resist everything except temptation.

—Oscar Wilde

THE POOL AT THE MAHANA KAI WAS A LOVELY AFFAIR. It curled and curved all the way around itself, as if sculpted and shaped by nature. Comfortable chaise lounges were scattered around, a plush towel neatly folded at the foot of each. In the far corner of the pool area, I could see a quiet spot. Pulling a couple of lounges together, I rummaged in my daypack for my swim trunks and slipped in and out of the nearby changing room.

Settling back into the comfort of a chaise, my eyelids drooped and I found myself letting go, that beautiful release of sinking into the magic of the place and the simple pleasure of being alive and present to the moment. The air was perfect. To call it mild would be selling it way too short. Smooth as silk, the soft breeze that caressed my face was lightly toasted around the edges, yet cool, moist and utterly refreshing. Flush with flowers, the surrounding landscape perfumed the airwaves with a delicate sweetness. I could feel the gentle approach of bliss tiptoeing in until a loud belch rudely jolted me out of my tranquility. Irked, I opened my eyes to see Lucifer with a towel draped around his bull neck and decked out in neon lime trunks splashed with blobs of pink.

"Jack, you look way too comfortable," he said, scratching his bottom. Shading my eyes, I lifted my head up off the chaise.

"Damn it, Lucifer, stop calling me *Jack!* Every time you do, it annoys me. The name's *Jackson.*"

Yawning. "Sure."

"Yes, I was comfortable. Is comfort something you disapprove of?"

A heavy sigh. "I don't have time for comfort. In my world, there's no rest for the wicked. Way too much to manage. My mission never, ever stops."

"I suppose talking with me doesn't qualify as wasting time in your book, does it? Because you have some agenda, something up your sleeve with me, don't you?"

Lucifer grabbed the empty chaise next to me and plopped down on it, his rotund body reminding me of a beached walrus. He scoffed, "My, my, aren't we suspicious. Can't a guy carry on a conversation without having ulterior motives? I just want to get to know you, Jack . . . *son.*"

On that note, I sat up. "Stop jerking me around. I still don't know why I'm talking with you. If you want me to stay, quit dodging and weaving. If you're interested in a real dialogue, then do me a favor and don't take me for a moron."

Lifting his sunglasses up onto his forehead, Lucifer trained his fiery eyes in my direction. Damn! I had to steel myself from the intensity. It took all my will power not to visibly lean back and away.

"Alright, Jack. The truth is, I do personal interviews every so often. I like to check in with a real person, preferably someone who's developed an actual point of view on life. In this case, you're the lucky winner. The writing from your blog has told me enough about your slant on things to make you qualify. I want to hear from a relatively intelligent human what it's like to be alive these days."

He was flattering me and I knew it. "Because?"

"Because you people are constantly changing! Believe me, some things always remain the same about the human race, exactly the same, as far back as you go. But in other ways, damn it, you change on me, shifting with the times. I have to keep up, put my finger on the current pulse. I'd like to pick your brain and, well, I'll let you pick mine . . . to some degree. That's the deal."

"Why would I want to help you?"

"Don't look at it that way. Take this as a unique opportunity. Talking with me isn't just a strange and curious experience. Anything is possible here."

I stared at him, not sure what he was getting at. "Meaning?"

"Well, just imagine if, through our conversation, you could change my mind about something. What an impact you'd have on the world! Wouldn't that make you proud? You, who wants to 'give something back,' as you put it."

Now it was my turn to snicker. "You do know how to lure, don't you? The one thing I'm a sucker for, you dangle it. But I'm on to you."

"Okay, you're on to me . . . or so you think. Hey, you're a big boy. You can stop this dialogue anytime you want. In the meantime, c'mon, let's talk! Open up. Don't worry about the 'what.' It doesn't matter. Good conversations generate a flight plan all their own."

Lucifer snared my bottle of sunscreen off the side table and started slathering it all over his massive torso. "So tell me, why'd you come to this beautiful place alone?"

"I came to get rebalanced. Hawai'i is very healing."

"Healing? You look perfectly healed to me."

I thought for a moment. There's no way I would trust this character with the story of my shattered world. On the other hand, I could choose to discuss an area that was one step removed from my great losses and still be true, although he'd already seen fit to ridicule me about it.

"I came to the islands to refire my *mojo.*"

Lucifer yawned. "Big deal. Everybody comes here to recharge their battery."

"No, it's more than a recharge. To me, *mojo*'s something deeper. It's not just that I'm fried, burned out and need a vacation, although that's true enough. My *mojo* is my fire, my passion and life force. It's the high-octane fuel that ignites my soul. What happens with me is that sometimes my inner world gets out of balance; too much *this,* not nearly enough that. My *mojo* becomes *slowjo*. Eventually I find myself depleted, with nothing left in the tank. That's the sorry condition I've been in lately, and why I've come here."

"So, is it working, this place?"

"What's working for me is what you call wasting time. I'm free from having to accomplish anything in particular. Unhooked, unplugged, unfettered. I've got nothing to do and all day to not do it. I'm letting my time unfold with a natural flow, no agenda. I suppose recharging one's *mojo* is something else you disapprove of, Lucifer?"

"Hell no! I prefer a human being fully energized. Where you and I differ, I suspect, is the direction I want to see that *mojo* pointed towards."

"What do you mean?"

Lucifer pointed his chubby index finger at me. "Take you, for example. When you get all fired up about something that you think is important, your impetus is to want to reach out with it, right? You're looking out into the world, trying to, what you called, 'make a difference' with your blog, instead of looking for ways to cover your own ass."

"I cover my ass all the time. But last time I checked, we don't live in a vacuum. I hold to what I said earlier about offering something back to the world. My *mojo* powers that drive in me to contribute."

"That's exactly my point. You've got your energy directed outward instead of in. That do-gooder mentality of yours is so ridiculously naïve. You should be amassing, accumulating for yourself. Instead, you're dispersing and pissing away your precious *mojo* on wanting to be helpful to others. You ought to be focusing on taking care of *numero uno*, on getting what's yours!"

"And getting what's mine . . . does that entail, in your view, stepping on the backs of others?"

Lucifer cocked his head, his eyes narrowing into thin, little slits.

"That depends. Maybe. Sometimes. Doesn't have to be that way. But don't miss the point. There's only one truly important person in your life, and that would be you. Ever been in the jungle? What's the rule there? Survival of the fittest! The biggest, the baddest or the most cunning, the shrewdest or the cleverest, those are the ones who get what they need. In case you didn't notice, the idea is to be the predator, not the prey. The predators are the ones who exercise their power every chance they get. They don't just survive, they thrive. Is it at the expense of the weaker? You bet, but so what? That's the law of the jungle. So do you think it should be any different with humans?"

I burst out laughing. "Do you have any idea what a selfish, greedy bastard you sound like? Such a warped view: What's mine is mine . . . and what's yours is mine, too."

"Why is greed such a bad thing? Didn't you see the movie *Wall Street*? 'Greed is good.' Where do you think that line came from?"

"Yeah I saw it, but you seemed to entirely miss the point of that movie. Greed is a question of degrees. We all have a desire to want more. You have to know how to take, but you also need to know how to receive. I'd agree that life is what you make it. For most of us, no one hands you anything on a silver platter. You have to be clear on what you want and go out and make it happen. Sometimes, taking more than you need allows you to save for the proverbial rainy day. That's just being prudent. But it can be a very slippery slope and it's a perfect example of a different law . . . *the law of diminishing returns.* Do you know it?"

"Of course, I'm familiar with that. But why do you think greed is a diminishing return?"

"Because greed doesn't know when to stop. Here's my understanding of that law. Something you gain can be a good thing. Receive more of it, and it can be even better. But at a certain point, it peaks. If you just keep adding more after that, it begins to go downhill, your 'returns' start diminishing."

Lucifer looked exasperated. "So you see greed like a hill that ends up bringing you down? That's ridiculous! My rule of thumb is simple: 'Understand what you want in life, what you're hungry for, what you feel you deserve, and go out and just take it . . . as much as needed, and then some. Grab what you can, when you can. More is better!'"

I held my ground. "What I said is that, in life, you have to know how, and how much, to take. At some point, enough is enough. When greed far exceeds need, it starts becoming something else. Something guzzling, piggish."

"That's what you say! Me? I'm advocating being self-centered to the hilt. Nothing wrong with that. I call greed 'the intelligent pursuit of self-interest.'"

"Oh, please. You can frame it any way you want, but, as they say, you can put lipstick on a pig, but it's still a pig."

Jamming a wadded-up towel behind his head, Lucifer countered: "The weakness with humanity, and one that I constantly play on, is that people are not forceful enough in the pursuit of their own goals. And what's the solution to that? *Stop putting yourself last!* Quit sacrificing your desires and dreams! Greed should flourish! Any successful entrepreneur is greedy. I describe this trait as having your priorities lined up right."

I sat up straighter, warming to his challenge: "You're missing my point, again. I don't confuse greed with the healthy drive for success, which is a great human quality. Sure, the entrepreneurial spirit, by definition, is steeped in self-interest, as it should be. But then there's Wall Street, the real one, not the movie. Look at what those greedy money guys did when left to their own corrupt devices in pillaging the economy. How many countless 'little people' get financially crushed by the scams perpetrated by those too-big-to-fail bankers, by the cutthroat traders and their company execs?"

Lucifer's eyes sparkled! "I give it up for Wall Street! Those guys are gifted, real Olympians in my book! They take greed to dazzling new heights and they go by a simple creed: Money is the root of all wealth. Maybe some of your little people need to learn a serious lesson about the hazards of their own greedy nature. You mentioned the last economic crash. Let me ask you something. How many of those little people said to themselves: I'll buy a house I can't afford because it'll be worth double its value in no time at all. I'll beat the system! That became the fast lane to countless foreclosures, so don't just blame the smart guys on Wall Street."

I didn't entirely disagree. "There's some truth to that, but these small investors were played for suckers by the power brokers who invented the game. The deck was stacked against them from the get-go. These modern-day corporate pirates have no conscience at all. You call them smart, but their intelligence gets channeled all in the name of greed."

Lucifer was having none of this. "Those little people were saps, just like you're being now. All I'm saying is that greed is a basic human instinct.

Maybe you're muffling yours, just like you're sitting on your wild panther. You may have buried it, but it's in there, my boy. Just because you're not in touch with your own greedy streak, doesn't mean it's not wired into your psyche. When you stifle your greedy nature and smother it with something silly like 'conscience,' you seriously dilute your power. Like I said, it's survival of the fittest. Are you predator or prey?"

I inhaled deeply to settle myself before replying, gazing up at the gorgeous cloudbank gliding by. "No, you've got it backwards, Lucifer. We weaken ourselves when we close off from the voices of the heart. I think you have to seriously 'dumb yourself down' to be able to tune out something as incredibly powerful as your conscience. In order to become a truly self-centered, selfish prick, you have to refuse to feel anything that doesn't support grabbing what you want. That makes you numb, narrow and myopic, dangerous to yourself and to others. But you think the end justifies the means, huh?"

"Absolutely, Jack! It's the payoff for having your priorities straight. 'Me first, everyone else . . . get in line!' What do you achieve by being benevolent, charitable, and kind? I'll tell you what you get! You get mushy. Your personal power gets bogged down in a sticky mishmash of gooey feelings that have nothing to do with securing your own goals. I say, don't just be a prick; be a *conscious* prick!"

I broke out laughing. "That's priceless! What exactly is a conscious prick?"

"It's when you're fully aware that you're being a total jerk, and you just stay with it. It's when someone takes a stand and says, 'I may be oozing with greed but, screw you, I'm thriving!' Or, 'I'll shove the weak out of my way, but that's what I choose to do to get what I want, and, besides, that's what they deserve for being weaklings.' That, my boy, is being a conscious prick, a bonafide sonuvabitch, with intention!"

"Aw . . . so touching! Just what I would expect Lucifer would say." I raised my arm in a grandiose mock toast. "Come all ye gluttonous, avaricious, miserly, insatiable, grubbing, grasping takers; all you war profiteers, crooked politicians, polluters and exploiters of children! Joins hands with the corporate shysters and financial crooks! For we are the enlightened ones, the conscious pricks, unencumbered by the excess baggage of conscience and the useless sense of decency and fair play that comes with it."

Lucifer waved his hand, dismissively. "Hey, so we disagree. Damn, I'm thirsty as hell. Hang on a minute . . ."

A poolside waiter walked by with a brisk pace, expertly balancing a tray on his shoulder with a tall pitcher of an iced beverage and stemware. He was hurrying to deliver the drinks and as he passed, Lucifer stared intently at the young man's back and gave his left index finger a slight twirl. The waiter spun around on a dime, walked directly up to us and graciously presented the drinks:

"Your *pina coladas*, sir. Shall I just put this on your room tab, Mr. Collins?"

Lucifer squinted up into the sun in the general direction of the waiter's voice.

"Yeah, do that. Oh, one more thing. You won't remember any of this."

The young waiter set the drinks down on our little end table: "Thank you, sir. Excuse me, but remember what?"

"Never mind, Junior. I think you were heading that-a-way."

The waiter took his leave and wandered off, having lost the bounce in his step. He had a puzzled look on his face, as if he was struggling to recall something important. I crossed my arms. "Somewhere, a Mr. Collins is going to be none too happy about this."

"Yeah, well, it'll be somewhere else and I don't have to think about. Ah, my thirst is about to delightfully disappear. Ask me which of these two factors I care more about, him or me? That, by the way, is being a conscious prick. You'll notice I walk my talk!" Lucifer filled both glasses and handed me one. "Salut!"

I had to admit this was the best *pina colada* ever. Could it be that what made it taste so exceptional was having obtained it through illegitimate means? After all, I could have offered to pay for it. I was starting to get a sense of Lucifer's worldview, or at least the little slice he was revealing to me. What a piece of work this guy was!

The pool beckoned and a few laps in the cool water felt incredibly invigorating. Resting my forearms at the edge near the deep end, I could feel the direct tropical sun on my back. Somewhere above me, I heard his voice:

"They got a hot tub at this place? I could use a soak. How about you?"

I knew the way, so I climbed out of the pool. Threading us around the backside of the swimming area, we passed through a beautiful alcove, arched with bougainvillea. The expansive Jacuzzi was a lovely surprise. It was one of those classy infinity pools. When you looked out, the edge of the water line was designed to blend perfectly with the distant horizon and ocean view. The effect was seamless. It gave you the visual impression that the pool and the sky merged in some magical way. The only other sign of life was a young couple in the far left corner of the Jacuzzi, entwined in a sweet, romantic embrace. With just their heads above the water, they were the picture of two lovers sharing a tender, intimate moment. My instinct was to not disturb them. I whispered: "Let's come back later."

Lucifer kicked off his sandals. "Nah, they're just leaving."

I glanced again at the lovers. "No, they're not!"

"Yes, they are." As Lucifer shuffled past them along the edge of the pool, the woman suddenly pulled back from a swooning kiss and gave her lover a hard whack across his face.

"What'd ya that for?" he sputtered in shock.

"You swore you'd never see her again, that's why!"

"Who? You can't be talking about . . . C'mon honey! That was two years ago! What made you think of her?"

"I don't know. It doesn't matter. You promised!"

"I can't believe you'd bring that up!" The man rose up out of the water, stomped out of the pool and grabbed a towel off his lounge chair. "Are you ever going to let that go? And why now?"

As he stormed off, she cried out: "Fredrick, wait, I'm sorry!" Rising hurriedly out of the pool, the woman was startled to see us sitting there. A look of embarrassment crossed her face. Lucifer reached over and handed her a fresh towel.

"Thank you, sir. You're so kind. So sorry for that little scene," she murmured, somehow feeling the need to apologize.

"No problem, sweetheart, but you'd better hurry," he advised. "Freddy looks pissed."

As she disappeared through the alcove, racing after the wet footprints of her lover, all I could do is shake my head. "Nice. You're a peach."

Lucifer shrugged and waded in. I followed and we both sat down, soaking up to our neck as the soothing waters worked their magic. Finally I broke the silence. "For someone who doesn't value relaxing, you look pretty damn comfortable."

"I'm just thinking . . . contemplating something you said. I've always been a firm believer in helping humans tune out that annoying inner voice of conscience. There's nothing worse than having a nagging sense of morality. It just gets in the way. It weakens one's resolve to snag what you want."

I chuckled. "Nothing like the guiding principles of scruples, values and ethics to screw up someone's self-indulgent plans, right?"

He gave me a dry look. "What I'm reflecting on is your comment that you have to 'dumb yourself down' to tune out your conscience. I've always been of the opinion that weeding out conscience makes you smarter, more powerful, not less. So I'm mulling that one over."

"Well, I can see where stifling the voice of conscience can make someone more powerful."

He perked up noticeably. "So you agree?"

"Sure. What *is* a conscience, anyway? It's our internal moral compass, a sense of right and wrong, according to one's own belief system. So the voice of conscience can and will put the brakes on all kinds of things. It's like saying to yourself: *I'm not going to go out and burn and pillage today.*"

Lucifer interrupted. "Please, Jack, get it straight! It's *pillage and burn!* All through history, I have to keep reminding so many dim-witted invaders across the planet: Boys, remember, it's pillage, then burn! Idiots!"

I continued. "My point is this. Without listening to your conscience, you can be unstoppable, just steamrolling over anything and everything in your way. I'll grant you that there's a certain blunt power in that. Look at the Nazi High Command. Sure, they were powerful but there couldn't be a more clear case of 'dumbed down' humans than Hitler and his evil circle of fiends. Eventually, that mentality destroyed them."

Lucifer absently toyed with his earring. "Okay, so those characters overplayed their hand, I'll grant you that."

"When you live without conscience, it shuts off entire parts of your psyche that are expansive in nature. The voice of conscience expands you outside of the little box of yourself. It takes others into consideration. Turn off that switch and it makes you smaller, not bigger. And when you're thinking small, you become weaker, not stronger."

Lucifer's eyes widened and he stared at me for a long moment." "Damn. You could be right about that one, Jack. Well, that flies in the face of my Basic Agreements!"

"Which are?"

"Okay, here's '*Lucifer's Five Agreements.*' Very simple:

One: Be slippery with your word so that any promises made can be quickly revised;

Two: take everything personally, so that you can know exactly how and when to retaliate;

Three: always make assumptions in order to stay one step ahead;

Four: always do your best to get an edge over everyone else; and

Five: be skeptical, very skeptical and thus never swayed by listening to your inner heart.

That, my friend, has been my blueprint to becoming powerful."

I found his list appalling. "So wrong! If that blueprint of yours creates anything, it's weakness."

"Because?"

"Because underneath what you call this 'powerful' self, you're operating from a core that's based in fear. It's screaming: *Gotta get more! Not enough to go around! I, me, mine!* It's packed full of insecure agitation. So in that sense, it makes you thicker, denser. Sounds a lot like dumb? Real power is the ability to expand one's consciousness. The more light you let in, the more you see. So, in your case, Lucifer, if I heard you right, you want someone to become a conscious prick, right? That's your benchmark. Well, shut down conscience in a person and all they become is a run-of-the-mill garden-variety prick. They may be sociopathic, perhaps, but not conscious at all. So you see, your premise is completely faulty."

Lucifer sat there motionless with a furrowed brow, his fingers steepled together, deep in thought.

"This is good. This is why I need to do this."

"What are you talking about? Do what?"

"Have these kinds of conversations with thinking people like you. I get way out of touch! I can see that humans have changed. You're much different now than, say, the Middle Ages. The perfect strategy for one era becomes clunky in the next. So tell me, is this 'take' of yours on conscience what you call 'New Age' thinking?"

"Hardly. Developing a sense of conscience goes back a helluva lot farther than New Age thought. It sounds to me like you've been steering people wrong for centuries."

Lucifer slowly leveled his gaze. I braced, expecting a harsh response for my having chided him. Instead he said simply: "How would you like a job?"

I spit out the ice cubes I was chewing on. “What!? You can’t be serious.”

“Do I strike you as someone who likes to kid around? Yeah, a real job. Let’s call it an advisory position.”

I laughed nervously. “Let me guess. You want my help to redesign your strategy with us. Like what? Instead of shutting down conscience in people, you’re wondering how you can incorporate it, yet helping them become even more powerful conscious pricks?”

“Yeah, something like that, for starters. You catch on quick, Jack. I’m thinking, ‘Conscious Prick 2.0,’ to use your terminology. So, are you going to help me? It could be great fodder for your blog.”

“Count me out. I’ll have this conversation with you today, as I kinda like the challenge of a sparring partner. But otherwise, no thanks. Don’t try to draft me onto your team. Helping you goes against everything I believe in.”

“Correction, it goes against everything you think you believe in.”

“What do you mean by that?”

“Listen, Jack, buried deep underneath that familiar nice-guy persona of yours is a ‘shadow world’ of entirely different voices, far more in tune with me. But maybe I’m just talking to the wrong part of you.”

The wrong part of me? What was he referring to? I suddenly began feeling very uneasy. “I’m not interested, got it?”

“Okay, I’ll drop it . . . for now.”

We both went quiet. Lucifer held up his stubby hand, studying the hair on the back of his knuckles.

“So, you’ve got issues with the I.R.S.?”

I laughed mirthlessly. “*Issues?* That’s one way to say it. For years, I completely trusted the wrong accountant and his creative bookkeeping. That was my greed in action, come to think of it. You know, turning a blind eye to all those questionable write-offs. Well, now it’s all come back to bite me in the ass. So yeah, I’m locked into a major dispute with Internal Revenue.”

He smiled expansively. "Oh? And who's winning that argument, pray tell?"

"Very funny, Lucifer. They're actually being pretty cool, all things considered."

"How big a number?"

"Big . . . for me, anyway."

"Hmm, sounds pretty stressful." Lucifer now toyed with his earring. "So, how'd you like that entire headache to go away, just disappear? You know . . . " He snapped his fingers. "Vanish."

I let the implication of his offer sink in and gave him a long, hard stare: "Listen to me. Exactly what part of the word 'No' don't you understand?"

"Alright, but think about it. The job offer stands."

He rose out of the Jacuzzi, his massive body steaming like a lobster. "I'm cooked! What's next?"

I got out, too, and toweled off. "Before I met you, I was planning to visit a very cool place not far from here. You can come along if you're interested and won't embarrass me in some way."

Glancing at his cell, Lucifer began reading an incoming text. Whatever it was, his face darkened, the atmosphere suddenly crackling with electricity. I noticed the hair on my forearms was standing on end. Without taking his blazing eyes off of the text, he answered:

"Sure, I'll join you. I have some private business to attend to first. I'll meet you in the main lobby at the top of the hour."

As he waddled away, I was again struck by the power of his energy field. Once he was gone, a stillness returned to the air around me, whereas, in his company, there was that oddly strong hum of vibration. I was unsettled by the offer he had wafted under my nose. What kind of idiot did he take me for, anyway? How would I like a job? Yeah, that'd look great on my résumé: "Consulting and Business Development for The Prince of Darkness." But, oh man, it was tempting to imagine that entire tax ordeal just vanishing!

CHAPTER

4

An Invite Declined

Footfalls echo in the memory, down the passage
we did not take, towards the door we never opened...
—T.S. ELIOT

I HAD TIME TO KILL SO I LET MY FEET TAKE ME WHEREVER they wanted to go. I ended up walking a path that led alongside the resort's bocce ball courts, with a game in progress. I stood off to the side as three older men, focused and in deep concentration, were in the midst of a match. I figured they must be from Europe, given the precision of their ball placement that comes from a lifetime of playing this ancient sport.

"Hello Jackson."

Startled, I turned and was met by a lovely, dimpled smile. "Nalani! What a nice surprise. Do you play bocce?"

"No, I never understood the rules." Looking at the threesome, she added, "The players always look so intense!"

"It's a great game of strategy. Takes five minutes to learn and years to master. Want me to explain it to you?"

"No thanks." Then after a pause: "I was actually looking for you."

"Really?" Only half-joking I said: "Whatever it is, I hope you'll give me a chance to explain!"

"No, it's me who wants to apologize. When we talked earlier, I didn't mean to pry into your life."

"Pry? You mean back on the bar patio . . . when you asked me if I was okay?"

"Yeah. I intruded on your privacy. That wasn't cool of me."

"And why's that?"

"It's hard to explain. I'm not sure I understand it myself. There you were, this very pleasant, handsome man, relaxed and with an easy, disarming smile. And yet, when I looked into your eyes, I saw pools of grief. When a person's suffering, that's like sacred ground. Their private sorrows should be left alone."

I was floored. Struggling to find words to respond, I said, "I'm surprised it was so apparent."

Nalani bit her lip. She seemed to be choosing her words carefully. "I think when someone is grieving in their own life, they can recognize that state in another. They're attuned to it. I've been going through a rough time myself. So, it's given me insight where I can, at times, recognize the heartache in others. Does that make sense?"

"You're a very sensitive woman."

"Sometimes I wish I wasn't." She smiled. "Wanna walk for a bit?"

I glanced at my watch. I still had some time. "Sure, and feel free to ask me anything you want. I'm glad you found me."

We stepped back onto the path. I let Nalani take the lead, as she knew her way around the grounds. After a few minutes, she surprised me by taking my left hand and lifting it up.

"So, no ring. Can I assume you're not married?"

"Separated. And you?"

Her facial expression took on a faraway look. "I lost my husband in a surfing accident."

Now it was my turn to see loss reflected in her eyes. "Oh God, how devastating that must've been for you."

I got quiet, giving her the space for private reflection. Eventually, I said softly: "Accidents . . . they're such a shock. They give you no time to prepare. The blows come completely unexpectedly, and your world, as you knew it, just explodes. It leaves you in pieces, trying to glue some semblance of life back together."

"Sounds like you've been there, Jackson."

"The ocean stole a loved one from me, too . . . my daughter."

"Oh no! I'm so sorry. Do you want to tell me?"

It amazed me that, yes, I did want to tell her about my loss. We took a seat on a grassy spot in the shade and I slowly opened up that tender memory. I shared my story of how the sea had snatched away my little girl. I described the irrevocable repercussions this emptiness had created, and my separation from Chloe.

As I spoke, I felt her warm touch on my arm. I realized I'd been so immersed that I'd been telling my story with my eyes closed. Blinking open, I looked into the sympathetic face of this alluring woman, whose soft expression conveyed her condolence more clearly than words. Nalani's presence was like a soothing balm and it encouraged me to open up even more to her. I told her how that calamity had sent me spiraling downward into my soul's dark night. As much as it hurt to relive those memories, it felt wonderfully cathartic to share the devastation of my past year.

"And so how are things going for you now?"

I brushed away a tear. "I'm much better, thanks. But to be honest, I still feel weak at times. My passion seems to have wandered off, but I've learned a lot about letting go of things I can't control."

She leaned in, encouraging me to say more. "Such as?"

"Well, I'm much more accepting of 'what is.' A man instinctively wants to 'fix' things. But there's no fixing this loss, there's only coming to terms with it. I'd say I'm somewhere mid-stream in that process. I'm getting there, Nalani. It's very humbling to feel so helpless, so exposed and emotionally vulnerable. It's not the way a guy wants to feel, let alone admit. Hey, enough about me. Would you be willing to share your story?"

Now Nalani got still, taking a moment for herself. She seemed to be experiencing her version of opening up a painful memory. Her husband, Kekoa, had been a champion big wave surfer, an expert capable of riding the giant swells that roll into the north shore of the island after Pacific storms. She explained how that sport had undergone a dramatic change, increasing its thrilling challenges but making it much more dangerous. It used to be that the truly enormous swells were simply unrideable because a surfer, no matter how skilled, couldn't paddle fast enough to catch the top crest of the wave. But now, with the aid of jet skis, a surfer could be towed, just like a water skier, and then, with that kind of speed, shoot out onto the face of the huge breaker. Kekoa had paddled out on a day when the swells were so enormous, even his highly skilled friends were backing off.

"I begged him not to go out that day. I sensed the danger, as though I could smell it in the air. But there was no keeping Kekoa from his passion. He wiped out on a monster wave. They think he was knocked unconscious on a shallow coral reef. No one really knows for sure what happened."

We sat there in a shared, pensive silence, both of us gazing out to the deep blue waters beyond, this ocean we loved so much. Ironically, the sea had taken from both of us our most cherished loved one. I was struck, once again, by the uncanny intuition of women. Both Nalani and Chloe had clearly sensed the peril lurking on those fateful afternoons. Reaching for her purse, Nalani slung the strap over her bronze-skinned shoulder. "Will you be coming to the *luau* tonight?"

"I think so, although my day's been, well, strange, to say the least. I'm definitely planning on coming. I'd love to see your *hula* dancing."

After a long pause, Nalani tilted her head. "Would you like to tell me about your strange day over dinner at the *luau?*"

I looked into her beautiful eyes, lit up with a subtle expectation. As the invitation sank in, I felt my heart lurch unexpectedly, my chest contracting inwardly... tensing, like a subtle spasm. I could hardly breathe! My heart space, which had been open and flowing throughout our lovely conversation, now suddenly felt like a tight little muscle, squeezing off that flow. Oh God. Is this the best I can do to protect my raw vulnerability?

Nalani seemed to read my thoughts. "I understand. I'll see you around." She gave my shoulder a soft squeeze. "Take care of yourself, Jackson." With that, she stood up, straightened her sarong and headed off. I watched her go with mixed emotions: her undeniable allure dueling with the reactivity of my internal protective shield.

As she vanished at the end of the path, I was suddenly aware of another presence. Whipping my head around, I saw a large figure with arms crossed, leaning casually against a tree. Lucifer was taking it all in. How long had he been there? Annoyed, I jumped to my feet, but when I looked back, he was gone. How he had disappeared that quickly, I didn't even want to know. I had a few minutes to spare and made a beeline in the direction of my cottage to change and pick up a few supplies.

As I walked, my mind returned to Nalani. I couldn't believe I had turned down this beautiful woman's offer! Her invite had caught me by surprise, but what response had jumped out of me? Did I just make a big mistake? I was suddenly hyper-aware of how wobbly my heart still was. Is it ever going to heal?

The Realm of the Shadowlings

When walking through the valley of shadows,
remember... a shadow is cast by a light.
—Austin O'Malley

I broke my commitment with myself to stay unplugged all week. Sitting on the edge of the bed in my cottage, I took out my phone and got online to review the comments and questions that were coming into my blog. I then stole a peek at my emails. Not a good idea. It's amazing how much relaxation can quickly drain away when a wave of reality rolls in—troubles with Chloe that made my heart sink, notifications regarding my upcoming audit, each calling out for my attention. The Internet ensnared me in its usual time suck. When I glanced at my watch, I was late. I found Lucifer sitting on a lobby couch, engrossed in an iPad. I plunked down next to him.

"Writing home to mom?" I queried.

He didn't look up, still absorbed in reading. Finally he shook his head: "You people are so clueless. What would you do without me?"

"Say what?"

"People, they're so conflicted about everything."

"What are you talking about?"

He pushed back his tablet and stretched. "The last person I had a decent conversation with, like what we've been doing today, was from the deep South, a real southern belle." In an Alabama drawl, he quipped, "'Well now Lucifah, honey, why, ah do declare, yo style a' reachin' people is so yestahday. Y'all jus' have ta get with the times, Sugah! Work smartah, not hardah! Y'all jus' got ta get social.' I had no idea what she was talking about, so she showed me this Facebook thing and walked me through how everyone is networking these days. Whoa! She definitely had a point. I saw how I needed to modernize. So, with her help, I took a stab at it, starting up my own online advice column. It's called *Dirty Laundry—Letters to Lucifer.* It took off like a bat outta . . . you know. I get almost three million hits a day on this thing." He glanced my way. "Is that a lot?"

"That's impressive. Who writes to you? Give me some examples."

"All right, here's one I just responded to:

Dear Lucifer,

I work in business development for a Fortune 500 firm. I recently became privy to some top-secret inside information regarding a particular company we do business with. This info will very soon make their stock take a huge jump. I'm considering buying in early, as I can make a ton of money on the deal! On the other hand, my actions would be illegal. I'm a religious man and am agonizing over what to do. Should I refrain or just go for it?

Tempted in New Jersey

"So of course your advice was 'Go for it!' Right?"

Lucifer wore a look of insulted disdain. "My reply:"

Dear Tempted,

Damn, I really empathize with your dilemma. Tough call. My suggestion to you is very simple. Hold everything! Instead of acting swiftly on this incredible financial opportunity apparently being wasted on you, my advice is to go out and buy a boot, preferably for the left foot, size 13 DD. Then I'll come over, put it on and kick your ass around the block a few times to knock some sense into where your brains seem to be lodged. Being a religious man and all, you must have forgotten that all-important line: God helps those who help themselves. Jump on it, you imbecile!

Yours, Lucifer

I rubbed my chin thoughtfully, "I like your sensitivity. Helpful, yet discreet. Encouraging, but with a light touch. Lovely."

With a raised eyebrow he scrutinized me, searching my face for signs of sarcasm. I just blinked twice and smiled sweetly.

He grumbled: "This is a lot harder than I thought it would be. To give the best advice, I often need more information. When you showed up a few minutes ago, I was mulling over this one:

Dear Lucifer,

I'm having an affair with my boss, who also happens to be the wife of my best friend. I'm savoring the best sex of my life, yet find myself wracked with guilt! Should I just keep my mouth shut and enjoy the ride, so to speak, or do you think I should come clean? Help!

Conflicted in Kalamazoo

"See what I mean, Jack? Do I advise him to carry on in the thrill of juicy adultery? Or is it an even better idea to tell him to secretly seek revenge against this best friend for some reason yet to be revealed, and give him a little encouragement to go that route? Or, should I up the ante? For example, is he capable of using the affair to blackmail his boss in order to advance his career? So many avenues for my guidance!" Lucifer smacked his forehead with his palm. "See the dilemma? What would your advice be?"

"Well, how about: Come clean?"

"What! Why do that?"

"Well, I realize he'd run the risk of salvaging his integrity and possibly saving a friendship, but just imagine the firestorm that coming clean would spark in all directions . . . the boss being fired, bad publicity for the company, and more."

Lucifer strummed his fingers on his tablet. "Hmmm. Great idea. Why didn't I think of that?"

"Oh, I'm sure it would have occurred to you in due time. You were just busy focusing on the obvious—cheating, blackmail, revenge. Okay, enough. Let's go."

As Lucifer stood up, I had to marvel at his latest choice in attire. Just when I was thought he had already reached the pinnacle in incompatible outfits, he surprised me by outdoing himself. He was truly gifted, hopelessly color blind and with a sharp eye for the hideous. He caught me staring at the intensely gaudy pattern of surfing armadillos on this latest aloha shirt, but mistook my look of disbelief for envy. His posture expanded a bit, preening. "Not bad, huh? And guess what?"

"Half price?" I ventured.

He stepped back: "Are you psychic or something?"

"Or something," I muttered under my breath. I slung my daypack over my shoulder as he handed me his tablet.

"Here, stick this in your pack. Where are we off to?"

"There's a place near the resort I want to explore. It's supposed to be very cool."

The Leikona Arboretum was a veritable pristine tropical jungle. Twenty-seven acres of what Hawai'i must have looked like before bulldozers and *haole* 'improvements' changed everything forever. The path we followed through its grounds surrounded us with a wide variety of spectacular flora. An explosion of blossoming plant life abounded, with a thick canopy of trees overhead, filled with a diverse assortment of colorful birds enthusiastically chattering away in various South Pacific chirping dialects. We stopped alongside a small, elegant waterfall lined with ferns. Fat orange *koi* gracefully swam in the pool at its base. Lucifer was totally unmoved by such natural scenic beauty. I commented on his ambivalent attitude:

"Not much of a nature lover, are you?"

"Me, love nature?" He glanced around. "What I see is exactly what's here—a bunch of trees, some noisy parakeets splattering bird shit all over. To me, nature isn't something I romanticize. The nature of *things* is what I focus on. That's what I'm up against, and it's rarely pretty."

"How sad. You're missing a lot."

He snorted, "Stick with me and you'll see how much you've been missing."

Within the thick leafy cover of a treetop, two small green parrots were busy chitchatting and looking down at us as we passed below. Suddenly they went dead silent. Then, without hesitation, they both simultaneously dive-bombed, taking a bead at Lucifer's head. Their piercing squawks had alerted him and he ducked just in time, razor sharp claws missing his pate by inches.

"Bastards!" he seethed, raising up his index finger and pointing it at them in a menacing manner.

"Don't," I shouted.

Lucifer glared up at the offending birds. "I hate nature!"

"Well, I'd say it's a safe bet that nature hates you right back. Have you ever considered making your peace with the natural world? A different approach, maybe?"

Taking the sullen look on his face as a 'No,' I started down the path. "I want to see the rest of what this Arboretum has to offer. You can sit here and stew if you want. I'll be back in a bit."

I wandered through the property, quietly enjoying the verdant abundance and imagining how stunning old Hawai'i must have been. When I swung back around, Lucifer was gone. I found him in an open clearing, his left arm pointing to the sky and twirling his index finger in a figure eight. I looked up in the direction he was pointing and saw something remarkable. A dozen or so of those green parrots were hovering just above us and gliding back and forth in the precise pattern he was moving his finger, like kites on invisible strings.

"What are you doing?"

"Like you said, I'm trying a different approach with nature."

"Well, it's a start. How do you do that?"

He kept the birds moving in a synchronous flow. "Hard to put it into words that you'd understand. The simple answer is, it's mind over matter. What looks like magic to you is just plugging into a concealed power source." He paused for a few beats, and added, "I can teach you to control a lot of things much more useful than this child's play. Just say the word, Jack."

Dropping his arm, the birds instantly scattered.

I let his comment sink in. Another offer, and I didn't doubt him for a second. I dabbled with the mental picture of having access to newfound powers. What would it be like? As I entertained the idea of unlocking and controlling a hidden energy field, I felt a tingling of excitement. I allowed my imagination to play with the notion. I may be refusing this offer but something deep within was highly stimulated. I finally let the image go, though not without a hint of regret.

"No thanks. I have a hunch your price is a lot more than I want to pay, if the *Faust* story was any indication of what you charge."

"That story is inaccurate. Faust was dyslexic. Turns out he sold his soul to Santa."

Just as I got his joke, Lucifer continued, "Jack, you don't know what my price is. You might be pleasantly surprised. People like Faust are fools, terrible negotiators who end up getting what they deserve. He was both greedy and shortsighted, a bad combination. But greed isn't your primary predilection. You have other desires we can light a fire under."

"Such as?"

Lucifer grinned wickedly but ignored my question, saying: "Think about it. It's a great opportunity that I rarely offer and you shouldn't pass it up. A smart woman recently said: 'The minute you settle for less than you deserve, you get even less than what you settled for.'"

Well, that line zipped right over my head. "Can you run that by me again . . . . No, never mind. I'm still gonna pass."

We started meandering wherever the path was leading. On our left, we came upon an elderly Hawaiian man sitting on a bench, peacefully reading a book. As we passed him, his smile was so warm it invited me to say hello.

"Hi. Are you reading something good?"

"Ae man, is da true good book, bruddah," he beamed, showing us the cover of his Bible. He flipped open a page he had bookmarked and recited it to us with his eyes closed:

"Da Boss Above, he takes care me, Jus like da sheep farma takes care his sheeps. He gonna give me everyting I need.

He let me lie down whea da sweet an soft grass stay. He lead me by da water whea I can rest.

He give me new kinda life. He lead me in da road dat stay right, Cuz I his guy."

I looked over and noticed that Lucifer's discomfort level had increased a notch. Best to keep moving. Once we were out of earshot, I asked him, "Why the scowl?"

Lucifer spit into a bush, as if getting something distasteful out of his mouth.

"These islanders have always bothered me. They tend to be way too warm and friendly for my taste. Give me a short-tempered, pushy New Yorker any day. Now there's someone I can work with. I've never had that much luck getting a foothold around here. Didn't care for his reading material, either."

"You have issues with that particular book, I assume?"

Lucifer's eyes flashed with intensity. "I have issues with the way I'm portrayed in that book. And keep in mind, it was written by the same people who said the world was flat! Anyway, it's a touchy subject, so don't get me started about that. You have no idea how I can get."

That gave me an involuntary shiver. "Alright, but I'm curious. How do you want to be portrayed? You obviously care. If you're not the devil we think you are, who are you?"

"Let me put it this way. If you take something and twist it a quarter turn, it can become totally different from the original, barely recognizable. Come on! The current portrayal of me is embarrassing, like a cartoon version of who I really am, as if I have no complexity."

"I get your point. Most people think of you as some buffoonish character in red tights with horns and a pointy tail, waving around a pitchfork."

"Exactly. And I'm surprised they haven't updated that image, with me trading in my pitchfork for a high-voltage cattle prod to goose people with. Ridiculous!"

"You still haven't answered my question. So if you're not *that*, then who or what are you?"

Lucifer slipped into a silence, his face impassive, like granite. "Okay, so we're finally getting to the good stuff, Jack. Let's open this conversation up. Who or what am I, you ask? That's an impossible thing to understand . . . for you, at least."

"Impossible for me? Why?"

"Because a lower consciousness can never understand a higher one. It's an irrevocable Law of the Universe. Just as a baboon can't possibly comprehend a human, a human can't comprehend me. I have access to an entire realm that you, from the human perspective, are completely unaware of. It's right under your nose, but invisible to your sleepy eyes. You see the world through the lens of your ego. Any reality beyond that, of which there are many, you're utterly oblivious to! The human thinks, *If I can't see it, smell it, touch it, hear it, taste it, or mate with it . . . it ain't there.* How utterly quaint. Just forget who I am for the moment. A better question would be: What's my Game? Know that and it'll reveal a lot about me."

"*Lucifer's Game?* Tell me about it."

"My Game? It's a complex strategy, lots of moving parts. But I'll tell you what. I'll reveal one layer at a time as we go today, assuming you stay in this conversation."

"I'm in it already. I agreed to this dialogue with you, didn't I?"

"Yeah, I figured you would. That's one of the reasons I chose you from the mountain of souls I could have spent today with. So let's begin by understanding something basic. Humans tend to associate games with playtime; you know 'fun and games.' In my case, I'm dead serious about my Game with humanity. Granted, it's endlessly entertaining and amusing to me, but I also have a mission. So, let me start you off with a hint: I'm a creature of the night."

I looked him over. "With your choice in clothes, I'd say that's an excellent idea."

"Smartass. Let me explain and stop me if you get lost. So, here we are on this beach in the middle of the day. Now picture that we're still sitting right here, but it's 4:15 a.m. What would be different?"

I scratched my head. "Hmm, an aptitude test. I think I got this one. The obvious answer is, it would be night."

"Exactly. Same beach, same everything, only now it would be dark. You'd accept that as true and natural. Nothing strange about it, right? Well, human nature is set up in essentially the same way, with two basic, completely opposite shades. You've got your Light and your Dark side, too. The big difference is that human beings desperately try to stay in what they think is the Light, which feeds right into my Game. You people get so caught up in wanting to generate a positive self-image—a rosy mirror that you hold up to yourselves and to the world. At the same time, you push away and disown certain characteristics that you consider to be unacceptable. Are you tracking me, Jack?"

"Yeah, I'm following. So where're you going with this?"

"Okay, here's the real kicker! These undesirable qualities you push away don't just disappear. They get shoved 'underground,' into the unconscious, down into the darkness, below the surface of your awareness. And what happens? These 'unwanted' aspects become your 'Shadow' side. They remain alive and well, buried down deep in the hidden dark world of the psyche."

"I get it. The unwanteds get exiled and go subterranean."

"So, your precious little ego ends up embracing only a carefully filtered assortment of qualities from the Light, all the traits where you proudly think: *Oh yeah, this is me!* Meanwhile, your ego separates out and pushes away a collection of all your rejects, the flip sides of yourself, the unsavory characteristics that make you cringe, and they go to the Dark."

"You're saying we 'rearrange the furniture' within?"

He shook his head. "No, it's more like you stick some pieces of furniture down in the basement. For instance, in your Light assortment, you might put, say, your honesty, while in your Shadow, you stick your deceitful side. Into one goes your sweet forgiving nature, and in the other, your mean-spirited vengeance. One has your confidence; in the other you bury away your deep-seated insecurity. The Light gets your cheerfulness, the Dark your depressive grey gloom.

This separation process is constantly ongoing. Gentleness, understanding and thoughtfulness up here . . . and violence, jealousy and belligerence down there. *Comprenez, Jacques?*"

"And you're saying you're behind all this, that this is your Game?"

"Hell no, not at all! That's the big misconception. Humanity is always blaming me for their own quirks and peculiarities. It's the other way around, Jack! This is the way you people are designed. It has nothing to do with me. It's simply what everyone does."

"Okay, so you don't create that separation process we go through of 'keepers' and 'rejects,' but you sure take advantage of it, right?"

"Precisely! You grasped this quicker than I thought, dude! That's my Game and I take full advantage. Luckily for me, that false separation from your unwanted qualities is a lame strategy that doesn't really work at all. Those cast-off abandoned selves might be pushed down and away, out of sight, but they're not out of your psyche. Trying to hide away these disowned characteristics is as foolish as if you were to sit here, way after sunset and insist that there's no such thing as night! Ridiculous because there is the night. It's exactly the same with the Shadow. Well, guess what? You're looking at the Champion of the Dark and I'm damn proud of it. Remember my card?

Yet I am one with the darkest of night.
Master of the Shadows World.
Holding the torch for the rejected ones.

"I'm the Master of that Shadow World, Jack. That's my terrain, my medium, my milieu, holding a torch up for all those castaways that I affectionately call *Shadowlings.*"

"Shadowlings? I know a bit about the human Shadow."

Lucifer's voice dropped a notch and was suddenly oozing with derision. "Well then, tell me something. Why is there no mention of the Shadow realm in your *Snap Out of It* blog? Like most of you 'spiritual seekers,' you've conveniently chosen to ignore that area of consciousness, and that makes you ignorant. Have you ever really explored your Shadow and seen what's down there? No. So don't make me laugh."

Whoa! His intensity was flaming . . . and he was right. I'd studied about the Shadow but never really delved into that world. My blog is about developing awareness of the Light. It focuses on how to deal with obstacles we all share, like the harsh voice of the Inner Critic or snapping out of the drowsy, hypnotic state we're stuck in, for example.

"So, what exactly is it you do with these Shadowlings that everyone has buried?"

Lucifer's posture seemed to swell. "I help them stay alive and kicking! You humans reject Shadowlings and I embrace them. It's dark in the Underworld, so metaphorically, think of me as the 'fire keeper.' Use your imagination and picture a large crackling hearth, with all the rejected selves gathered around the blaze, trying to stay warm. I tend to the fire. Look closer. Who would you see? Maybe Pride and Envy, standing next to Greed, who's swapping strategies with Revenge. To their left are Lying, Hatred and Manipulation, who are all laughing at Gluttony who's busy warming his hands alongside Judgment. And those are just a few."

"But if I've pushed these Shadowlings out of my consciousness, it's for a reason. I want them out of my life! If I've declared that I don't identify with these unacceptable energies as who I am, why do I have to claim them as mine? I got rid of them for a reason!"

Lucifer found that comment very humorous. "You don't have that choice, man. They are part of you! Try as you might, you can't cherry-pick your human traits, keeping these and rejecting those. They don't disappear, Jack. Sure, you try your damnedest to let these Shadowlings live out their entire existence in that dark Underground realm. But believe this," he added, poking me hard with his finger, "they'll creep back up to the surface and, shall I say, *express themselves* at a time when you least expect it."

"So we push them down under and you encourage them back up? The bottom line then is, you're still a destructive influence, which is how you've always been perceived."

"Jack, you just don't get it. I don't create the Shadowlings . . . humans do! Try to picture this . . . Imagine that you have a spiral staircase concealed within your psyche. If you were to stand at the top of those stairs, you'd see the steps circling down, down and down . . . eventually disappearing into the darkness below. Well, that's where you've exiled all your rejected Selves. Each one of your individual Shadowlings, you've banished it down those stairs. Every person has their own specific list of particular disowned Selves that they've ordered to the basement below. Well, get this! That spiral staircase works both ways. Given half a chance, and with my expert guidance, these Shadowlings sneak back up those steps at some point!"

"I know what you're saying, Lucifer. I can think of plenty of examples of harm done by our jilted qualities when they climb back up out of the Shadow realm and erupt in someone's life. But it's you who forces them back up?"

"Forces them? Hah! No, I may highly encourage them back up, to come out of hiding. But if they unleash havoc, well, that's what you humans get for trying to pretend they aren't part of your overall make-up. I love reading the news to see what Shadow indiscretions are popping up in various places. Every single day is full of people who have a Shadowling emerge from below and infiltrate their life. There's the charity CEO who gets caught embezzling funds; the pious man of God who abuses altar boys; the charismatic leader who reveals a massive inferiority complex, the famous actor who manipulates women to bed with his celebrity. Then there's my personal favorite: politicians who wrap themselves in the flag, pontificating about working for the 'good of the people' and then gladly sell their souls, their votes, to big money interests in exchange for favors. Want me to keep going? The list is endless. Human hypocrisy is hilarious!"

"How comforting to know we're such a source of amusement for you, Lucifer. I don't suppose you feel any remorse for all the havoc you wreak in people's lives?"

"Remorse?" A snort shot out his nose and his whole body jiggled with laughter. "Oh, that's funny. You're still judging me through your limited human value system."

I reflected on my own life. "Alright, so how can I recognize my Shadowlings?"

"It depends on how well you can observe yourself. To recognize a Shadowling, you have to pay close attention. Chances are you won't be able to spot it in yourself, but this is key. You'll see it in the way others bug you. Think of people you can't stand for one reason or another. Look closely. What is it about them that triggers you in some way? Is it something that makes you feel . . . humiliation? Disgust? Does it push your buttons or ignite unreasonable anger? Look for some kind of reactivity that's over the top. Spot that in yourself and you can bet you're projecting some Shadow quality of your own onto someone or something else. It takes serious self-awareness to acknowledge this, which is, thankfully, clearly not a human strong suit."

Whew! This was a lot to take in. I stood up and brushed the sand off my shorts, feeling the need to stick my feet in the ocean. Walking knee deep into the cool, foamy surf, I looked up just in time to marvel at a squadron of pelicans swooping by in V formation, gliding with expert precision just inches off the crest of the waves. That image triggered a sharp pain in my chest. Pelicans were my daughter's favorite shore birds. She would always stop and excitedly point them out. And just like 'that,' my heart felt drenched in sorrow. I kept my eyes on the gliding birds, as if to honor her and then whispered into the wind: "I'm so sorry Francesca. I miss you so much."

After a few minutes, I felt Lucifer's energy field and knew he was standing next to me. I turned, hands on my hips, as questions started rising up in me.

"So tell me, Champion of the Dark, how do you actually help these Shadow qualities escape from the Underworld of our psyche? What's your ploy to get them to come out of hiding?"

"It's simple but ingenious. My brilliant trick? I get you to unknowingly invite them up!"

"How do you do that?" I was waiting for Lucifer to answer when I distinctly heard a voice, my own voice, inside me say:

"I just whisper."

A grin spread across Lucifer's beefy face. "That's how I do it. It's so seamless, it's practically invisible. Your heart and mind can hear it, but your ears cannot. And do you know what's at the root of that whisper?"

"Give me a hint."

"Here's a clue. The guy who created Ziggy once said: 'The only time losing is more fun than winning is when you're fighting' . . . *what?*"

"Temptation?"

"Exactly, temptation is at the root of my whispers. The human being has a built-in weakness for it. You're suckers like mice to cheese on a trap. My language of temptation is an intoxicating brew, customized for each individual. The specific thing one is tempted by will change from person to person, but the core weakness exists in everyone, woven into the fabric of your very souls. All I have to do to tempt someone is to beckon their Shadowling of choice. The door down below opens, and it's you who lets it slither up that stairway. Amazingly, you don't even know you're doing it!"

"You seduce us, intentionally tempting us to invite in our own dark nature?"

"But Jack, that's the key! You just said it yourself, it's your own dark nature. People are so used to burying their Shadowlings that they forget the truth. Like it or not, you're just allowing in a part of your own self. You think that temptation's a bad thing, that it has no purpose, true?"

"I'd say more times than not, temptation is trouble. It encourages some kind of action that goes against the norm."

"The norm? And what might that be? Some unrealistic positive quality or value people try to desperately uphold? Through the art of temptation, I coax a person to entertain alternative choices, to take their foot off the brakes, be open to new, juicy options, pluck the low-hanging fruit, and expand their field of opportunities! And to you . . . that's trouble?"

I looked at Lucifer and shook my head. "You should be a used car salesman. Let me put it this way: temptation is trouble because it often makes one go against their moral principles. How does the saying go? 'It's easier to stay out, than to get out.'"

He broke into a grin. "Oh, ain't that the truth! But me . . . I'd put a different spin on it. How can you be good if you haven't had the chance to be bad? How can you make a moral decision if you don't know both sides? Temptation gives you permission to test the waters. And let's not forget, unlike opportunity, if you fail, temptation will always give you a second chance!"

That made me laugh. "Oh yeah, temptation's very generous. But this is enlightening. I can see how it's the calling card you use to encourage us to invite in our Shadowlings."

We started heading down the beach in the slow pace of those who have no particular destination. I found myself reflecting on all that we had discussed. There was still something gnawing in me that I wanted to ask him, but I couldn't quite put my finger on it. We walked a bit further, passing back by the man still deeply engrossed in reading. He seemed so at peace and I was moved by his contentment. I wondered what it was he was getting from his 'good book'? Something very deep was touching his soul. Suddenly, I realized what my question was.

"Earlier, you said that greed was not my particular weakness, but that I had others. Give me an example."

"Nah, let's not go there, Jack. My experience is that people love discussing the weaknesses of others, but they get all bristly when it's directed at their own self."

"Come on . . . I can take it. Tell me."

Lucifer stopped walking, crossed his arms and looked me up and down like an appraiser on *Antique Roadshow*. "Jack's weaknesses . . . whoa. Let me see, where do I begin?"

"Cut the crap and just pick one."

"Alright. Let's start with the simple and obvious. I can't help but snicker at the way you constantly push away your Pride."

"My Pride?"

"Yeah. You have so much to be proud of, and yet you bury it, pushing it underground. But take an honest look at yourself. Over the course of your adult life, you've absorbed a mountain of spiritual knowledge. You're a successful writer with a large and growing following. You should be allowing yourself to feel the exhilarating sense of pride that accompanies that. But no, not you! Instead, you try so hard to be humble. Aw, isn't that precious! Keep your head down, Jack, and put on the drab and dreary cloak of humility. Pitiful."

"You think I'm pitiful because I try to avoid being full of myself?"

"You've got it backwards, man. By trying to avoid being 'full of yourself,' what you're actually avoiding is claiming your personal power. You should be taking full credit for what you've accomplished, and boldly holding that space inside you that says, *Look at me! I'm special, dammit, and I know it!* Can you feel the confidence in that statement, Jack?"

"No, I hear arrogance and pretension."

Lucifer's voice took on an edge. "Who cares if that seems boastful to others? Screw them! They're probably just jealous! Jealousy's a good indication that you're doing things right. People are never jealous of losers. If you're not willing to own your own self-importance, why should anyone else give a rat's ass about who you are in this world? And if you're not somebody, then you're nobody. And what does that get you? Nothing."

"And so, the temptation you'd offer me would be what?"

"For you, my coaxing would be this: stop blocking your Pride. Just feel it. You'll love it! Your Pride wants in, Jack! Open the stairwell door and invite it up! Think of your Pride as a helium balloon designed to be inflated. It loves nothing more than to proudly rise high in the air for all to see. It's a beautiful sight."

"Look Lucifer, you don't have to sell me on the virtues of Pride. I get it because I know the voice of my Pride intimately. I understand what it's hungry for, what it craves. I don't encourage it because I don't need it like I used to."

"Oh, that's a good one. You actually believe you don't need it anymore, so you choose to ignore it? Look, just for the hell of it, why don't you humor me here, and let your Pride *in*. Just for a short visit. Then you can crawl back into your little humble world when we're finished."

I chewed on that one for a minute and decided, 'for the hell of it,' to take his bait. "Alright, for the sake of this discussion, why not?" I closed my eyes and sat in silence, getting settled within.

"Good. Now this is all I'm going to say: 'Just . . . let it . . . in.'"

I'm not sure how things unfolded next, but this is what I remember. As I sat there, a stillness opened up in my mind, and a quietness in my heart. I stayed in that place, relaxed and content. Then I heard my own voice, commenting on something excellent developing in my life related to the success of my blog. The voice was patting me on the back, saying, *Nicely done! Can you believe it? It's starting to really take off! You're getting well known!*

As I listened to myself speak in glowing terms, something was wafting up from below. Ever so slowly it spread out, like the wisp of smoke from a stick of incense. I felt warm, as if I were basking in the sun. It spoke to me of great reviews pouring in and how my writing was helping to generate more inquiry in exploring dimensions of consciousness.

The voice then pointed out how some attention was being given to me, the writer. To me! Was it the sound of doors of opportunity opening up? My mind was now hooked and my heart was following right along. A tingling excitement was starting to build. Just thinking about all this, I felt exhilarated, like a surfer who caught the perfect wave. I didn't want the voice to stop. Then another shimmering wave came cresting over. What was it? Gratification! It was a sense of indulging in satisfaction, feeling pleased with myself, as indeed I should be! I've worked hard and deserve it. It's so rewarding to realize that my writing was having an impact. *You did it, Jackson. Great job!*

I stayed right there in that moment, just kind of wallowing in the pleasure of that realization. I intensely felt my uniqueness elevating me to a new level. There was something extraordinary about actualizing my gift of expression, watching it come to fruition. The voice began whispering: *Fame is just around the corner, and with it maybe fortune following on her heels!*

Continuing to revel in the warm glow, my heart felt larger, swollen with Pride. My mind was crackling with thoughts about my work. *This ain't nothin' yet! There's so much more I can bring to the table!* I could feel the corners of my mouth starting to turn up into a smile. Damn, success was heady stuff!

Taking a deep breath and blinking my eyes open, I was staring into the face of Lucifer. He, too, was beaming with Pride! And when I looked at the up-turned corners of his mouth, I suddenly realized he was precisely mirroring my own expression back to me. His face was exactly what I looked like right now. He was the picture of a contented and self-satisfied winner. And yet . . . what? There was a smugness, too. Yes. Smug. I started to laugh.

Lucifer was all smiles and jovial now: "What's so funny? Let's hear it!"

"I just understood what's meant by the expression: 'He's a legend in his own mind.'"

He raised a bushy eyebrow: "Meaning what?"

"I mean, Pride, the kind you're selling, it's all just a story in one's own imagination."

"No, it's a big, beautiful self-realization."

"Wrong. It's a 'little-Self' realization. My little Self gets to feel bigger! More recognized. Grandiose!"

The grin that had spread across Lucifer's face was starting to fade.

"Why are you going all negative now? Stay where you were, damn it! You were lovin' it."

"Look, Lucifer . . . I get it. Pride does feel good. It can feel great, but mostly for my little Self. Pride's important to the little Jackson in me who needs shoring up, who's lacking in true confidence, who's, as you say, a sucker for flattery. This is the part of me who looks to the outside world to tell him the value of his own self-worth. Sure, it makes me feel like somebody special, but it's an inflated somebody. Pride is keeping me from seeing how insecure my little Self actually is."

"Are you forgetting how satisfied and empowered you just felt?"

"Empowered? No, Pride just gets in the way of Life. In my view, you need two qualities to function well in this world: to be awake and to be nimble. Pride swells me up. It inflates me just like that silly balloon analogy of yours. That balloon is empty, or more to the point, full of hot air. It makes me bloated, which then robs me of my nimbleness. And it's entirely self-absorbing, which then puts me into a state of 'hypnotic' sleep."

Lucifer was incredulous and didn't relent. "So are you advocating no Pride? You think being a nobody is some kind of advantage?"

"It's a question of moderation, Lucifer. It's, again, the law of diminishing returns that I spoke about before. Within a certain range, Pride is a terrific asset. Look at a mother beaming at her young child. How cool is that? Or the pride of craftsmanship when a worker takes a skill to its highest level. As for my writing, yeah, I can stand back and appreciate it if I've sculpted my words in such a way that I've actualized my personal best. Great! But this doesn't mean I have to open up the faucet and allow Pride to spill over the sink and flood my consciousness. Then it becomes something else entirely . . . like conceit or vanity."

"Oh sure, shut off the faucet, quick! How terrible that your consciousness should be infused with feeling proud. And so you think humility has more to offer?"

"Humility is what grows when I think about the steep limitations of Pride. It isn't that Pride is wrong, it's simply young and immature. It's full of itself, and full of what exactly? Superiority? Yup. Narcissism? Check. An insatiable need for praise? Definitely. An unquenchable thirst for recognition? You bet. A touchy tendency to be provoked and retaliate? Look out! And the most telling of all, let's not forget how easily bruised Pride can get, devastated by criticism. These are the traits that Pride's full of."

"Are you finished, Jack?"

"Not quite. I'll tell you another thing about Pride, the kind you're selling. It sucks the oxygen out of the room. When I'm full of myself, I'm filled up; there's no room for other parts of me to get a word in edgewise. My Pride isn't listening to anything other than applause."

Lucifer snorted. "Yeah, well, 'humility' can be a real joke, too, a Shadowling all its own."

"Sure, I know that. It's the way Pride can camouflage itself, wrapped in false humility. Ah, the hidden pride of the humble. How many of us have the outward act of humility down pat, yet are seething with Pride inside?"

That made Lucifer jiggle with amusement. "Yeah, you got that right, Jack. 'Pride perceives humility honorable, often borrowing her cloak.' I love that kind of self-deception! But let's get back to reality, your reality. Are you ignoring how lit up you were just a few minutes ago?"

"No I'm not. But my point, which is getting clearer to me by the minute, is this. If you're offering your brand of Pride, and you want me to tank up on it, you need to be communicating with the 'little Jackson' in me whose self-concept is unsteady and fragile. He needs your brand of Pride. But where I am today with my personal growth, my 'little Jackson' is not running the show anymore. His need to be coddled and inflated is fading away. I'm maturing, I guess. And that's an example of what I write about in my blog."

"You're claiming you're above it all?"

"Don't twist my words. What I said was that my little Self isn't running the show anymore."

"Oh, really? You're delusional, pal, if you believe your little Self has been retired. I suspect your Shadowling of Pride is still alive and quite healthy. Besides, the key point you're forgetting is that Pride lifts you up, elevates your whole inner world."

"Elevates? They say Pride comes before the Fall. In my view, elevation is just lofty arrogance. It's based on a story we tell ourselves, and the whole structure easily collapses since it has no real foundation. That's why Pride can take one helluva fall. And by the way, Lucifer, isn't that your story? The way I heard it, it was your insufferable, bloated Pride that brought you crashing down!"

Instantly, I knew I had crossed a line. Whatever I'd triggered, he was in no mood for. The atmosphere surrounding us suddenly turned glacial. I started shivering. Ever so slowly, Lucifer raised his head and stared at me, no, through me. For the first time, I was terrified of him.

In a voice dripping with icicles, he murmured: "That was a cheap shot, Jack." After a lengthy pause, he added, "Not that it's any of your business, but I would infinitely rather be the Master of my own Realm than part of an organized group. I'm not what you'd call a team player. Let's just say, I have authority issues."

That last line was laced with a razor's edge. Yikes! The energy rolling off Lucifer's body was now even more palpable. It felt like I was being hit with a frosty gale wind. I had touched a nerve. So, perhaps Lucifer, himself, has wounds. A tenuous stillness descended between us. I said absolutely nothing, barely moving, hardly breathing. After what seemed like a long time, I finally took a chance. I just had to know...

"So, is that what's in this Game for you, Lucifer? You get to call your own shots?"

"That's part of it, a big part of it. Master of my own Realm is no small thing. You have no possible conception of the vast range I have control over. I don't take orders anymore, I give them."

His last comment was oozing in Pride, but I thought the better of pointing it out to him. He now seemed to have shifted his mood, as the air temperature was gradually returning to normal.

So, do we have any food?" Lucifer queried, pushing my backpack towards me. "All this debating makes me hungry."

"I'm all out. You've already snarfed down everything I brought." I glanced at my watch. "Let's head back to the resort."

The *Mahana Kai* was about a half-hour trek. We followed along the water's edge. From a distance, under the shade of a stand of coconut palms, we could see a gathering of people tucked in towards the back of the beach. As we approached, it became evident that it was a wedding ceremony. Rows of white folding chairs, laid out neatly in the sand, were filled with guests. What a beautiful spot to exchange vows! I made sure that we stood way back and off to the side, so as not to be intrusive. The minister was going through the standard shtick:

"If anyone knows why these two should not be wed in holy matrimony, speak now or forever hold your peace."

Lucifer was staring intensely at a man standing to his left. I peered more closely, as this man's whole body began to twitch. Suddenly, in a frenzied burst, he raised his arm high and belted out: "I object!" Everyone froze, then swiveled in their chairs in unison, gawking in disbelief. Pointing with a shaky finger at the groom, he blurted loudly, "This guy is a felon, wanted in three states for the manufacture and sale of crystal meth!"

The groom's face went from shock, to recognition, to rage. "Stanley!" he roared, "I'll kill you!" With eyes popping and veins bulging, the groom leapt off the wedding platform and raced up the aisle in our direction.

Lucifer elbowed me, "Let's move on, shall we?" I was all for that and we disappeared back towards the surf line.

My heart was still thumping from that unexpected outburst. I could hear a fight breaking out once the groom had gotten his hands on Stanley, whose terrified voice was quivering: 'I'm sorry, Marty! It just came out! Ow! Ow!' I halted in mid-stride. Turning slowly around, I looked directly at Lucifer, who had an odd smirk on his face: "You caused that, didn't you?"

He shrugged. "I thought that boring little wedding needed something to spice it up." Looking back over his shoulder at the wild scene that had erupted, he muttered: "Looks like I succeeded!"

I was almost speechless, but spit out, "You . . . are . . . such . . . a . . . "

"Prick?" he suggested. "A *conscious* prick, if you don't mind. Do I have to walk you through it again? Hey, you have your fun, I have mine."

Whatever I was going to say next died in my throat. It was pointless. One look at his reptilian expression and I knew I might as well save my breath. As we approached the *Mahana Kai* beach front, a group of four locals were digging a pit in the sand, stacking firewood and lava rocks in preparation for the *luau* this evening. A thought of sweet Nalani popped into my mind. Her dancing would be part of the festivities and I felt a quiver of pleasure.

I glanced over at Lucifer who seemed deep in thought, or maybe he was just sulking. Although he had amused himself with his little wedding stunt, something else had taken over his mood. The way our conversation had ended up revolving around his Pride seemed to have impacted him. Well, he's the one who insisted on having that conversation, saying he wanted to show me a thing or two about my Shadow. But he simply had it all wrong with me about my Pride. I've worked hard on that particular aspect of myself and I just don't see it as a

Shadowling that I've shoved down the staircase of my psyche. So let him grumble and sulk. If we were going to continue our conversation, I needed to speak my truth. If he can't deal with it, then he could go find someone else's 'brain to pick.'

Trekking through loose beach sand is deceptively tiring. I was exhausted and needed to find a place to sit and take a load off. Just behind the beach as we entered the resort grounds was an area they called *The Greens,* a wide grassy space with benches and chaise lounges. It was a sweet place if you were looking for quiet. On my right, a string of lawn chairs wound around the edge of the area, where the grass butted up against a thick hedge.

A man in beach attire was lying on one of the chaises, a tablet device in his hands. As we walked behind his lounge chair, I happened to glance down, looking over his shoulder to see what he was studying so intently. My eyes locked onto the screen he was absorbed in. He was reading my blog! Wow, that gave me a jolt. The man sensed my staring, turned around and looked up. He did a double-take, subtly turning back to the blog and glancing at my picture on the page. Very new to the experience of notoriety, I was still unfamiliar with the experience of being recognized. Lucifer and I kept walking but I was thrilled! I heard the man call out: "Excuse me!" As I turned around, he rose up out his chair and headed towards us. As he neared, he politely said, "Sorry to interrupt. But aren't you Jackson Trent?"

I grinned and joshed: "Well, that depends. Do I owe you any money?" I held out my hand to shake his. He ignored it.

"I thought it was you," he exclaimed. "You know, I've been reading your blog this afternoon and I gotta tell you . . . your ideas suck!"

His unexpected blast landed like a punch to my gut. My mouth was frozen half-open, with nothing coming out of it. The man wasn't waiting for a response anyway, nor was he quite finished. Pointing at his tablet, he seethed, "My wife foisted this piece of nonsense onto me.

'It'll open you up,' she said. 'It'll take you deeper.' Well, who the hell says I wanna go deeper? Who are you to claim to know what might help me? I like my reality just the way it is. You seem to pride yourself on your own words of wisdom, yeah? Well, here's some for you. It's my life, so piss off!" Then with a barbed parting shot of 'Jerk' over his shoulder, he was gone.

It was the 'Jerk' that pushed me over the top, where I shifted from being shocked, bypassing astonished and landing with a hard thud in a place called stunned. I turned to Lucifer who was grinning from earlobe to hairy earlobe. The Cheshire Cat, was he, with a few canary feathers still fluttering to the ground. In a mocking voice, dripping with faux sympathy, he said, "Aw Jack, were you expecting him to say something else? A compliment, perhaps?" Then his smile vanished, and he glared at me: "Right now, what's it feel like?"

Finding it hard to talk, I wheezed out the words: "Honestly? I feel collapsed."

"Right! And what, exactly, is it in you that got deflated?"

I could taste it, like bile. It was my Pride, and it was wounded.

In a sarcastic babyish voice, he taunted me: "Could it be 'little Jackson' who you claim isn't running your show anymore? Ha! You could've fooled me!" He started vigorously cackling and snorting in the most annoying way.

I felt the harsh truth of it. Then my Inner Critic piled it on even more by playing back what I had said earlier to Lucifer: *And maybe most telling of all, let's not forget how easily bruised Pride can get, devastated by criticism.*

What a perfect setup this had been to see my own limitations. There I was, all primed to accept accolades from a fan. I hadn't seen the sucker-punch coming. And when it hit, *Bam*, the hidden underbelly of my hubris had revealed itself. I felt like a delicate peach, so easily bruised.

Lucifer kept up his jabs: "Hey Jack, next time you want to enlighten me on how you've outgrown some deeply rooted part of your nature, you'll pay attention to my skepticism. Lecture me? ME? Just who do think you're dealing with?"

I felt humiliated, but I had it coming. Pride, within my little Self, which I had been so sure was a thing of my past, was front and center, dominant in my current state, and I was now awash in shame. I sat there, stewing in it. Personal growth is an arena for such self-deception. You work on yourself, over time, expanding your inner boundaries and hopefully growing in some organic way. And when you get a foothold in some area of your inner world, it's so easy to miscalculate, to imagine you've outgrown old ways of behaving long before it's true. You may have trimmed the bush back, but the roots are still there.

As I contemplated all this, something in my consciousness shifted inside. I gradually smiled and started to laugh. Thankfully, a kinder perspective had rolled in, one that was more amused with myself than mortified. I could feel my shame morphing into a sense of humility. I understood that my little Jackson still had some growing up to do. Just then, Lucifer slapped me on the back, bringing me back to reality.

"Tell you what, Jack! Now it's my turn to suggest a place to go . . . assuming you're feeling brave. I've got a taxi coming in forty minutes. Meet me at the front entrance. I can guarantee you'll find where we're going mysteriously intriguing."

CHAPTER
6

Mama Kamea's Gift

The wound is the place where the Light enters you.

—Rumi

The narrow road leading away from the Mahana Kai was nothing but curves. There wasn't a straight line for fifty yards on this entire winding, coastal stretch. The taxi's suspension had that bouncy effect of a vehicle badly in need of shocks, especially with the hefty immensity of Lucifer sitting in the backseat. I was riding shotgun and starting to get a bit woozy from all the twists and turns, trying to keep my attention on the passing lush scenery. Every so often, there was a gap in the thick wall of green foliage and I'd be treated to a fleeting view of the cobalt blue ocean stretching out forever and the surf rolling onto some sandy beach far below.

My mind kept mulling over our conversation about Shadowlings. Aside from my Pride, what other characteristics of myself was I disowning, systematically pushing away from my awareness? At the same time, I was beginning to feel increasingly uneasy about exactly where this particular car ride was going to lead? Damn, me and my irrepressible adventuresome streak! Am I going to regret this? *Gulp.* Cranking my neck around to the back seat, and, with an edge in my voice, I asked: "So, are you going to tell me where we're going?"

Lucifer had his eyes closed, but responded: "Patience, Grasshopper. Relax. You're gonna like this."

"What makes you so sure?"

"What makes you so nervous?" he countered.

As I turned around in my seat, the uptick in traffic told me we were nearing some kind of village. As we drove into the main square, I was surprised at how thriving with life the town was. I'd expected something a little quieter at this time of year. We had the cabbie drop us off on a street corner. Lucifer glanced at his watch.

"We're a little early and I'm starving."

Quelle surprise! I took a quick look around, pointing out some promising food stalls along the edge of a park. A picnic table in the shade was the perfect spot to munch a sandwich and scoop mango shaved ice. This was also a great location to people watch, the crowd a mix of tourists and locals. It was easy to tell which was which. Many had the look and pace of those on familiar turf, going about their business. Others had the unmistakable wandering meander of vacationers, cameras slung around their necks and credit cards twitching in their pockets. Taking in the parade of people streaming by, Lucifer released a snort. I was now at a point with him where I could decipher the different tones to his snorting. The sound of this one said 'contemptuous.'

"What?" I queried.

He waved his arm, pointing vaguely at the throng. "Take a good look at all these people. Notice anything in particular?"

I scanned the crowd. "Well, I can tell by the lobster tone who forgot to slather on their SP-50. But I don't suppose that's what you mean."

Lucifer hunched forward, his eyes squinting as he peered more closely at the passersby. "Here we are in this alleged tropical paradise, surrounded by what most would agree is an environment that's interesting and full of what you'd call beauty, right?"

"Yeah. So?"

"Well check out how many people are walking around in a state of self-hypnosis. Look at 'em, staring down into their phones: texting, checking emails, sending off pictures, dialing numbers, watching their stocks. Smartphones, how's that for an oxymoron?"

He had a point. I've often noticed this phenomenon back on the streets of California, and everywhere else, for that matter. But it seemed particularly absurd here in the midst of this beautiful Hawaiian village. These people might just as well have been standing in the middle of a Walmart in Detroit for all the attention they were paying to their actual surroundings. They were totally oblivious. So many were shuffling along, heads down, deeply absorbed. I asked, "So, why do you disapprove? Why does that bother you?"

"Are you kidding? I love it! Look, trust me when I say I go back a long way. Part of my overall strategy with humanity has always been to try to nudge it in a particular direction."

"Oh? In what direction is that?"

Lucifer leaned back on the picnic table bench, resting his hands on his paunch. "I've always striven to direct human attention, as much as possible, so that they focus away from what's right in front of them."

"So you come up with ways to distract us, right?"

"Exactly. It's a key component of my Game. In every period of human history, my challenge has been to come up with ways to divert attention. Now, in the computer age, technology does all the work for me. I couldn't be more delighted as it allows me to focus on other things."

"Yeah, I know. I get sucked into that techie distraction, too. My cell phone is so seductive and habitual."

"Thankfully, you humans are incredibly child-like, easily manipulated. All it takes is some 'shiny object.' *Hey people! Lookie here! Stare into this TV. Stay glued to your damn phone!* Most people take something good and don't know when to quit. That's again the law of diminishing returns you're so fond of quoting. How ironic; a great tool like a smartphone makes people robotons. What's terrific about these gadgets from my perspective, is how they completely ensnare your attention, ensuring that your awareness is dulled. Just look at 'em. Zombies. Ain't it grand! And then there's the separation anxiety, too! Everyone feels so lost if they leave the house without that precious cell phone in their pocket."

I chuckled, recalling how true that was for me. "Alright, I agree that we deserve your ridicule on this one, but here's what I want to understand. Why do you need to distract us? And what are you pulling our attention away from? What's in it for you?"

Lucifer turned, lifted his sunglasses up just above his eyes and gave me a slow, sly grin. "Ah . . . another crucial part of my Game." He turned his gaze back to the throngs. "But let me tell you what I don't like about this evolving technology. It's this new collaboration factor. For the first time ever, and I do mean ever, people can, uh, what's the word, network anywhere and everywhere, instantly, and on a massive scale."

"So?"

"So, that disturbs me. There's such power in numbers. My strategy has always been to divide and conquer, which makes things manageable. This ability for huge groups to communicate instantly and globally is a new wildcard for me. Information and communication can expand so fast, I stand to lose control of things."

"True. Probably accurate. From a consciousness perspective, mankind may not have evolved very fast up to now, but the technology is zooming along. But you didn't answer my question: What are you pulling our attention away from?"

Before he could answer, Lucifer's movements began to slow down until he seemed to suddenly freeze, motionless. Then, his large head began rocking eerily and he grabbed the edge of the picnic table. His mid-section gave a sharp jolt and he let loose what could only be described as the belch from Hell. It was a bizarre, gurgling sound that I don't ever need to hear again. Then, sitting next to him, I got hit with a palpable wave of pure 'negativity' that emanated from his body. It swept over me like a bleak invisible force field and I felt suddenly awash in black, deeply oppressive feelings and thoughts. Lucifer placed his palms on the table to steady himself and then turned, starting to walk away.

"Hey! You didn't answer me."

I was talking to myself given that he was already plowing his way across the park. Things were taking a decidedly unsettling turn. I had no idea where we were, so I just followed behind his lumbering hulk, wanting to stay one-step removed from the dark, grim vibrations he was giving off. Lucifer had all the grace of a rodeo Brahma bull, marching his wide bulk right down the middle of the busy sidewalks, with no intention of negotiating space with anyone coming towards him. His body language conveyed: *Get the hell out of my way* and everyone instinctively did just that, giving him a wide berth. Walking behind him gave me a certain vantage point. Although I couldn't quite see over his massive shoulders, I was becoming witness to odd things happening on both his left and right side.

As he shuffled along, disruptions were unfolding, rippling out from him like waves of chaos. I had seen this phenomenon earlier today in more subtle ways, but now this type of occurrence had suddenly intensified. I saw a young skateboarder zipping down the sidewalk, expertly threading his way through the tourists. He was barreling right for

Lucifer and I could see that the kid was in no way planning on giving ground to this lumbering bear. Well, someone had to move aside and it wasn't Lucifer. Just before they collided, the lad's skateboard spun off the curb and he crashed into a light pole. He was unhurt but stunned. The boy, now on his butt in the street, gaped at us, astonished. Lucifer stopped, turned and leaned down: "Kid . . . sometimes you win, sometimes you learn."

Around the next corner, we came upon a street mime, complete with the painted white face, white gloves and a true gift for mimicking the various walking stride of the tourists passing by to the delight of an appreciative crowd. When the mime spotted the heavy, awkward stride of Lucifer approaching, his face lit up with glee as he nimbly slipped right alongside him, pantomiming Lucifer's *shuffle, shuffle . . . dip of the neck* to perfection. The crowd roared its approval. Lucifer, unamused, kept right on plodding along but swiveled his head and glared at the mime for a moment. Abruptly, this talented street performer stopped in his tracks, and then started slapping himself, with both hands! The crowd thought this was hilarious, and the only person looking dumbfounded and freaked out was the mime, who couldn't seem to stop smacking himself silly.

We then passed a kiosk where an elegant woman was looking in a mirror, trying on a pair of earrings. As we walked by, I heard the sound of a distinct crackling. The mirror had shattered leaving the woman with that wide-eyed, startled *I didn't do anything* look. As we rounded a corner, a cart heaped full of ripe fruit for sale toppled and let loose its load, sending papayas bouncing all over the sidewalk. Finally, to my utter relief, we began heading away from the shopping area. It didn't take long to lose the crowds completely. I, very tentatively, moved alongside Lucifer. He said nothing and walked with his head bowed, burping up that eerie bubbling noise. He looked like he had eaten bad food and was feeling progressively more poisoned.

At one point, I had to ask: "Are you aware of the craziness you were causing back there?" No answer. I peered closely at his profile and saw that his skin, never what you'd call a rosy complexion to begin with, had now turned a jaundiced shade of pale yellow. His eyes were hooded, giving him a dull, distant, menacing look. Finally he muttered, cryptically:

"Bad juju. It's reached the red zone. Gotta get to Mama . . . now."

What? Lucifer seemed to know where he wanted to go, so I just followed along. Within a few minutes we reached a cul-de-sac, where the edge of the village touched the hem of the jungle. Tucked away in the back was a bamboo structure, a large hut with a rusty tin roof. At the end of the entry path down the middle of the lush, green lawn, we walked up some steps and into the house. It was dark inside, lit only with the diffused sunlight streaming in through the open door behind us. A large ceiling fan was methodically stirring the humid air. It looked like a waiting room of sorts, with a few old couches that had seen far better days. A counter with no one behind it was against the far wall, next to a hallway whose entrance was draped with a colorful batik silk sheet. As my eyes began adjusting to the darkness, the sheet was swept aside and a large Hawaiian woman with snow-white hair and dressed in a flowing purple *muumuu,* swooped in. She stopped and leveled a steady gaze in Lucifer's direction.

"It's you," she said simply.

Burp . . . "Hello, Mama," Lucifer said, almost sweetly.

"This is your *MOTHER,"* I sputtered?

With that comment, both the woman and Lucifer let out a derisive laugh in unison.

"Please, let's not insult the lady. Mama Kamea, this here's Jack."

I smiled and put out my hand. Mama Kamea ignored it, serving me a withering look. Turning to Lucifer, she crossed her arms and said: "For you, of course, *Ho'opono Kapu,* a complete extraction . . . as usual. Quadruple my normal rate, with a 40% tip for the girls."

"That's fine," said Lucifer.

Then she slowly studied me from head to toe, up and down two or three times, finishing by staring in the area of my heart for a long moment. "And the same rate for your friend here, although he only initially requires the hot crystal cleanse."

"Done. Let's get on with it, shall we?" said Lucifer impatiently.

I piped in, "I'm not really his frien . . . "

She cut me off. "Take off your sandals and follow me."

As we headed down the hallway towards the back rooms, I was starting to really back-pedal on what I might be getting myself into here. I suddenly felt a surge of panic and had the strong urge to bolt. Lucifer's head whipped around and faced me, saying simply: "Don't."

Imposing and stoic, Mama Kamea was obviously a person of few words. Handing us each a large bath towel, we were both gestured into our own small changing room. As we reemerged, naked except for the towel wrapped around our waist, she turned and led us deeper into the house. This place was bigger than it looked from outside. Then we walked out the back door and stepped into the fresh, open air of an expansive backyard. Under the shade of a graceful, tented canopy, a few massage tables were set side-by-side about six feet apart. Beautiful soft Hawaiian music was in the air. Two native women, wrapped in silk sarongs, awaited us. Mama Kamea gestured to the two *wahines* to take it from here, saying quietly to the taller one: "Kahanu, I don't have to remind you about last time. Be careful and cautious. Call me when he's ready or if you have any problems."

She then caught the attention of the other girl and, pointing at me, said: "Pua. This one . . . just the gemstone cleanse."

Pua had me lie face down on the padded table. She whispered, "Just breathe deeply." Drops of warm oil were sprinkled on my back, followed by long, soothing massage strokes. My concerns were melting fast and I let go of my lingering fears. I've experienced a wide variety of bodywork over time, but this was clearly different. It was far more than just the kneading of aching muscles. Pua had a graceful flowing motion, using her forearms more than her hands and never breaking the continuity of her rhythmic movement. Her soothing touch was the essence of a deep healing energy. She concentrated primarily on the center of my back. Slowly, my mental chatter lost its moorings and I drifted off into a state of relaxation, losing sense of time or place. I heard Pua say: "I'm going to place warm gemstones on your back now."

"Huh? Okay, sure," was all I could utter. I mustered the effort to turn my head to watch the preparations. On a low table was an appliance that reminded me of a rice cooker. Lifting the lid and as steam escaped upward, she dipped into it with a slotted ladle, fishing out a number of crystals and gemstones of various sizes, shapes and hues and placed them carefully on a small tray. She touched each one, testing the temperature. Seeing me watching her, Pua lowered the tray in front of me to eye-level. I noticed each stone had its own symbol etched deeply into its surface.

With tender care, she began placing them strategically down my spine and on other areas of my middle back. As she did this, a pulsating hum emerged from deep inside her, in the most unusual tone. The effect of all this was at once mesmerizing, and counter-intuitive. It was as though the warmth from the gemstones was not sending heat down into my body, as one would expect with hot stones. Instead, like a magnet, they seemed to pull energy upward and out. As if reading my mind, Pua bent down and whispered: "You have much stress to release. *Hohonu* . . . very deep."

"If you only knew," I murmured.

"These stones are quite powerful, pulling tensions, *luna,* up and out. Cleansing *Uhane,* the Spirit. They give you *pono,* balance. *Apopo*, tomorrow, you feel much better!"

Pua's explanation was just what I needed to fully let go into her blessed healing hands. As I lay there, now deeply immersed, I had the distinct image of air bubbles of stress rising from the depths, slowly making their way up to the surface of a lake. After a while, I felt the gemstones being removed, one by one. Pua made a final pass of rhythmic massage to release the last of the stress that had risen to the surface. When she was finished, she said softly, "Just stay as you are. Please don't move. Rest."

I was startled by a sudden commotion over on Lucifer's table. He lay there, face down and stock still, but his masseuse, Kahanu, was wildly shaking her hands as if they were on fire.

Pua whispered to me, "Your friend . . . *very bad Juju!*"

"Look, we're not friends."

To that, she said nothing. "Mama Kamea will take this poison out of him. You are privileged to observe."

"Are you going to stay, too?"

"No. I can't bear to watch."

"Why not?"

Pua managed a smile, though her eyes were tearing up. "It hurts me. I fear that one of these times, this will kill her."

Then, wiping the oil off her hands with a soft towel, she said, "It's been my honor to work with you this afternoon. *Mahalo* and *aloha*."

The elder matriarch had by now reappeared in the back doorway of the hut and gazed out at us. Lucifer's masseuse, her hands still shaking, ran into the arms of the older woman. Mama Kamea took Kahanu's palms and pressed them to the cheeks of her rounded face. She then crossed them both over her heart, resting the palms on her pillowy bosom, her eyes closed. The two women stood like that for a long time. I noticed Pua, after taking her leave of me, bowed deeply, with true reverence, as she walked passed her mentor and into the house. Eventually, Mama Kamea released Kahanu's hands by kissing each one. The young masseuse turned one more time to glare at Lucifer, then vanished through the back door.

The old woman continued to study us from the porch, then stepped down into the yard. She proceeded to walk right past our tables to the edge of the property, turning to face the stunning emerald mountain in the distance. With her arms raised high in some kind of supplication, she chanted in a tongue I'd never heard before. I turned to Lucifer: "What language is that?"

"Ancient Polynesian," he mumbled.

I could feel her presence coming close to me, her *chi* was so strong. Turning my head, I followed the flowery pattern of her purple *muu-muu* all the way up until I was looking into her broad, flat face hovering above me. "So, now what?" I asked.

"Quiet. Turn over on your back."

I rolled over and Mama Kamea stared down at me, our eyes locking. Finally, she leaned forward and in a kind of hiss, whispered in my ear, "What are you doing with the likes of him?"

"I'm just . . . . We're just talking today."

"Don't be a fool."

"Don't worry about me. I think I know what I'm doing."

She pierced me with a look I won't forget. "You are a fool."

As she continued to keep her focus on my chest, I looked up and watched her eyes. Her harsh expression slowly vanished and her face softened, now seeming to shine with an ethereal sensitivity. The expression in Mama's eyes had changed from 'daggers' just moments before to a gaze like pure liquid compassion that poured down onto my heart area. As I sensed into my chest, I could feel how her loving energy was now holding my heart with the most exquisite tenderness. Her eyes gradually moved up to meet mine. In a soft whisper, she said, "You poor man. I'm so sorry for your loss."

Placing her palms side-by-side an inch above my chest, she held them there. Then something extraordinary began to take place. It was as though she had found that secret door in the center of my heart, unlocked it and gradually creaked it open. It felt like genteel hands reached in through this door and ever so slowly eased out of hiding my great, raw, terrible wound, bathing it in the most soothing, loving kindness. And in that most delicate of holdings, my wound relaxed, and in so doing, opened up, releasing waves and waves of my grief, my overwhelming sense of loss and guilt.

Way off in the distance, I could faintly hear the sound of my own unrelenting sobbing, and yet, right here in my heart, at the center of such emotion, was a state of utter relief, as all my pent-up, compacted anguish just came pouring out. Finally, when it was over, my 'inner landscape' was blanketed in the sweetest tranquility, the very essence of serenity. And that's how she left me, as a melted pool of profoundly deep *Peace.*

Mama Kamea moved over to Lucifer's table. I simply lay there, blissfully inert, but with my eyes observing. High on a shelf against the wall, she reached up and, carefully, with both hands, brought down an alabaster urn, lovely in its simplicity and open at the top. She set it down on a table next to where she was positioned. Kahanu now reappeared and handed Mama a cruet of cut glass filled with what looked like oil, the rich color of amber. She removed the stopper and poured the oil into the urn. A match was struck, lighting the oil on fire; the flames flickered just above the lip of the urn.

Mama stood at the head of the massage table, extending her arms straight out with her palms down over Lucifer's face-down body. She held them there, perfectly still. I heard her whisper, "Wash yourself... of yourself." It was then I witnessed the utterly surreal. Almost imperceptibly at first, and then with a gathering luminosity, her hands, from the tips of her fingers to her palms and then wrists, began to take on a glow as if they were being gradually lit up from within by a solar energy source. The light emanating from her hands was golden, like the mystical hue of a desert sunrise.

I've never been one of those people who can see auras, but I could see this. It seemed like she was wearing gloves made of pure sunlight. With a series of arm movements, she began making very specific signs in the air. A final look heavenward, her hands now ablaze with light, Mama Kamea placed all ten fingertips in the middle of Lucifer's back. Upon contact, her whole body jolted upwards, but she held her position. As if in a dream, I was now witness to the inexplicable. It appeared as though she pushed those golden fingers into his back, her hands disappearing up to the wrists. Then, with a twist, they were slowly extracted.

As they resurfaced, her hands were cupped and filled with a dark substance. Reaching out, she emptied this black 'matter' into the urn, the flames momentarily flaring up high in an explosive combustion. Back she'd go, easing her glowing hands in, pulling out this thick, dark substance and pouring it into the flaming urn. Although I could only see Mama Kamea's face in profile, it was dripping with sweat; her eyes focused only on the task at hand and yet filled with a deeply intense pain.

Finally, when apparently enough was enough, she placed her palms on the 'hole' in Lucifer's back she had been digging, as if to seal it back up. Standing stock-still in this position, the glow from her hands began to diminish, until the light went out altogether. Taking a few steps backwards from our tables, I heard her say in a hoarse whisper: "It is done." The urn still aflame, Mama Kamea carefully lifted it up, turned on her heels and disappeared into the house.

After a time, two young boys appeared and helped me peel myself off the table to sit up. They expertly wrapped me in a sheet of the softest material. It took both of them some serious effort to get Lucifer up into a sitting position. He seemed lifeless, with his eyes closed and his head bowed. The boys wrapped him in the same fashion. Then, like a grizzly coming out of hibernation, his eyes opened wide. He looked around, stretched, and, exclaiming with a beaming smile, "I feel great!" Wrapped like cocoons, we were helped to our feet by the young lads, who then led us back into the house.

As we shuffled down the hallway, we passed a room with the door ajar. Inside, I recognized the outline shape of Mama Kamea. She was kneeling at an altar that was ablaze with light from what looked like a hundred candles. Her head was bowed and she was sobbing, shaking with inconsolable grief. Her anguish touched my heart and I tried to stop, but the boys kept us moving, ushering us through another outside door that opened onto a wide deck on the far side of the house. Two comfortable chairs awaited. "Rest for a bit," is all one boy said.

If Lucifer felt great, I wasn't exactly sure what condition I was in, so altered was my state. My heart felt like an open window with a warm summer breeze wafting through it, perfectly tranquil within.

A pitcher of papaya juice had been left on a small table and Lucifer was downing it by the glassful. "Ahhhh." He was the picture of happy contentment. Despite my own sense of blissful release, I was disturbed by the image of Mama Kamea consumed in tears.

"Why was Mama so distraught?" I asked Lucifer.

"If you asked her, she'd say she was crying for the world."

"Meaning what?"

Shifting in his chair, he shrugged, "Look, I don't want to get into all that. Let's just say she and I have an arrangement. Mama Kamea has extraordinary talents. She's one of only three people on Earth I allow to work on me."

"Yeah, well, she didn't seem all too happy about working on you."

A sharp snort: "The truth is she despises me. Why? Because I am who I am. The only reason she agrees to perform *Ho'opono Kapu* on me is because she understands, if she refused, I'd only get worse!"

"She didn't seem to care much for me, either."

"That's because you were with me. The last time I came here, I brought along, shall we say, a new protégé. Today, she must have assumed you were my latest recruit."

"Huh. No wonder. So, what exactly is *bad juju*?"

"I said I don't want to get into all that! Anyway, it depends on whom you ask."

"I'm asking you. Tell me. I want to understand this."

Lucifer put his hands behind his head and looked skyward, contemplating: "All right, Jack, here's the short version. When I choose to be in human form, it comes at a huge price. Once you have access to the higher planes of existence like I do, you feel how slow and cumbersome the human experience is, in general, and the human body, in particular. It's like trading in a starship, capable of traveling faster than the speed of light, for an old Volvo."

I took offense to that. "Don't you find the human body to be an amazing creation, in and of itself?"

Lucifer let out a long sigh, slowly shaking his head. "Jack, at times you sound like such an idiot. You don't know what you don't know. Let me put it to you this way. For me, stepping into this so-called amazing body would be like you crawling into the shell of a tortoise. I do it because my work, at times, requires it. But it's difficult to function on the human plane, to say the least. It is what it is, and I have to live with it."

"What does that have to do with *bad juju*?

"I'm getting to that. First and foremost, know that *I* generate negativity in the world. That's my MO and, as I mentioned earlier, I'm damn proud of it. Negativity, in its purest sense, is every bit as valuable as positivity. Take a battery, for instance. Without the negative charge, what do you get? Nothing. I am that negative polarity. But here's the problem. The human is designed such that negative energy, instead of passing through, can get caught in the etheric energy body. Some call it your aura. And wherever it gets caught, it turns sticky. That's not good, because like anything else that's sticky and accumulates, it can transform into something worse, a kind of gooey tar. And the energy that oozes out of that tar pit of mine can have a really ultra-powerful negative vibe. That's *bad juju*."

"But Lucifer, why should it matter if you have *bad juju.* I would expect you to."

"It's too thick. It slows me down."

"So you come to Mama Kamea to get yourself, what . . . cleaned out?"

"Exactly. My energy field runs unfathomable amounts of negative current that passes through it. Over time, I end up getting filled up to my eyeballs with my own gooey tar. At some point, I need to empty out the accumulated *juju* so I can function. Mama Kamea is a master at that. As I said, she hates to help me, but understands that the world would be worse off for everyone if that kind of sticky matter builds up past a certain point in me. Things can get . . . shall we say . . . catastrophic."

Lucifer stopped and looked at me directly: "If you believe anything . . . believe this. I'm not someone you want feeling overly negative. Mama has seen what happens when I get ultra-saturated, and it ain't pretty. So, she steps up, does her part. And when she's finished, I'm good for a nice long while. Granted, it takes something out of the old gal, and I say 'old' but you wouldn't believe how young Mama actually is. She's not much older than the two other masseuses. She may look 'long in the tooth' but that's the physical beating she's willing to take for her kind of work."

"Do you care?"

"Nah, not really. There are two others on the planet that can do what she does. When Mama's gone, I always have my back-ups."

"Your appreciation is really inspirational," I murmured dryly. "Who else does she perform this *Ho'opono Kapu* ceremony on?"

"You wouldn't believe the cast of characters she works on! Drug lords, various dictators, billionaires who made their pile through nasty exploitations. The list is long and impressive. These are people who were never nominated to be in *Who's Who* but they're prominently featured in *What's That?* . . . Don't look so confused. That was a joke."

"And she does this for them for the same reason she works on you?"

"More or less, but on a much smaller scale. As I said, she does it for the good of the world, and she's right. Things would be a lot worse on this planet if it weren't for her and a few others. By the way, let me share a little secret with you."

Lucifer's head swiveled left and right, making sure we were speaking in total privacy.

"Unbeknownst to Mama, when she works on me, at the same time, I'm getting a download of all the other clients she handles. Their 'stuff' is still in her energy field in a way that she doesn't realize. So while she's removing my *bad juju*, I'm getting updated on how my influence is working in the world through some of my more prominent subjects."

"And how are things going out there, in the world?"

"In a word? *Smashingly!*"

One of the boys reappeared with our two stacks of clothes. He led us to the outside hot showers and stayed close by with extra towels. Once clean, dried and dressed, we were brought around the hut through the front door to the entry room where we had started. Pua was now seated behind the counter and grinned at me. She spent a few moments finalizing our bill, which gave me time to study her. She wasn't beautiful in the so-called classical sense, but she glowed with a kind of inner light. What a healer, and to be learning from the great Hawaiian shaman herself.

Pua set the bill on top of the counter and I picked it up. Glancing to the bottom line, I did a double-take and must have gasped, as she looked up: "Everything alright?" I smiled weakly, calculating in my head what my half was going to be. *Oh man, this is way, way out of my budget!*

"Oh, by the way," she said pleasantly, "I was handed a note by the young boy who helped you. Your friend said thank you so much for this birthday present and he'll meet you outside at the first street corner."

I whipped around to see an empty room. Staring now stupidly at the wall in front of me, the realization that I'd been 'had' yet again came crashing in. I felt cornered with no graceful way out of this. Handing her my credit card, I winced at the sound of the charge going through. Pulling myself together, I looked down into Pua's serene eyes, which seemed to help. My appreciation for her work today must have shown as she returned the gaze and said simply, *"He mea iki."* I turned to leave, stopped, and spun around.

"Pua, would you do me a favor?"

"Of course."

"I want to thank Mama Kamea for her gift, but I don't know how to say it to her."

Pua's expression was so lovely. "I do. I'll thank her for you."

I stepped out, squinting into the bright afternoon sunshine and walked through the grounds towards the street. A fire pit on the edge of the property had a large blaze being tended to. A strange time for a fire, I thought, here in the heat of the day. As I strode past, in the middle of the red-hot coals, I could perceive what looked like an alabaster urn.

Lucifer was on the street corner. He was just wrapping up another animated phone call with someone who must have cheered him up immensely. He ended his conversation with: "Just remember, pleasing everyone is impossible. But pissing everyone off is a piece of cake!"

He looked up to see me in a far less jovial mood, thinking about the bill I just paid. "What?" he said, with a touch of sheepishness. Then just before I launched in with an earful, he whipped his head around and said with an edge of steely defiance, "Tell me you can put a price on that. Just tell me you're actually considering complaining about this."

I hated how he could stop me in my tracks.

Entrapment

Nearly all men can stand adversity, but if you want to test a man's character, give him power.

—Abraham Lincoln

I looked at Lucifer in mild disbelief. "For chrissake, what is it with you and food? You're hungry again already?"

"Hey, if I have to crawl into this human physique for a while, the least I can do is indulge myself in what this body likes to do—and that's eat. And you guessed I was starving. . . how?"

"I thought your rumbling stomach was thunder in the distance. Alright, my traveling motto is always 'ask a local.'"

I stopped a native Hawaiian walking by. "S'cuse me, sir. Can you steer us to a nice café, some place quiet where the two of us can talk? A patio would be great, with an ocean view, even better."

The man eyed Lucifer's choice of clothes, chuckled to himself and then said: "Try *The Trident.* Go down this street. When you hit the beach boardwalk, take a left. About a block down."

The café was just what I had requested, with a spacious deck, close to the beach. It wasn't too crowded and I got the pick of the litter regarding the best open table. Before Lucifer could start his massive descent into a chair, I stopped him.

"This tab's on you, yes?"

"Absolutely. This one I take care of."

I stopped him again: "No funny business, right? Because my credit card is probably maxed out!"

He looked almost offended. "Chill out, Jackson. I said this one I take care of."

We took a seat and looked at the menus. At the very top of the page, above the afternoon specials, was the aphorism of the day. This one read:

The greatest challenge of life is discovering who you are.
The second greatest is being happy with what you find.

That made me smile. "I truly like that message. Discover who you really are and then relax within that unfolding."

Lucifer appeared incredulous. "Oh, come on! Happy with what you find? Happy? How could you be? The human being is such a muddled mess! For most people, 'who you are' is a train wreck of conflicts, grasping at wants, desires, needs and illusions."

"Lovely interpretation. But I guess there's no denying that we humans are full of contradictions. It's an interesting point that I try to address through my blog."

Lucifer set the menu down, shooting me a look midway between contempt and skepticism.

"Jack, you've such a long way to go. But we'll get into that later. Let's order."

I flagged down our waiter and we ordered drinks and entrées. We ate in relative quiet, which was fine by me. I was content to sit and silently appreciate the deep healing that Mama had opened up in my heart. Just as I was finishing an excellent meal of calamari, the blaring sound of a fire engine pierced the air. It was Lucifer's highly annoying cell. He reached down into his pockets and started pulling out a bunch of stuff as he fished around for his phone. By the time he found it, he had a small heap of things piled on the table.

"Will you turn that damn phone off?" I barked, vocalizing what everyone else on the deck was thinking by the angry scowls we were getting from all sides. Sizing up my mood, Lucifer looked down at the screen, rolled his eyes in response to whoever was trying to reach him, saying to me, "Okay. Give me a minute."

Lucifer muttered into the phone, "Make it quick." He listened for a bit, then added, "I'm gonna have to stop you right there. Listen to me, Numbnuts. I don't have the time . . . or the crayons, to explain it to you again. Oh, and if your phone doesn't ring, it's me." Click.

He looked across our table, exasperation written across his brow. "So many people want a piece of my time. And here I am offering you an entire day."

If I was supposed to feel grateful, I didn't bite. But now I was curious about all the stuff he had strewn on the table that had come out of his pockets. One thing caught my eye in particular, a metallic hoop of some kind.

"What's that?"

"This? Nothing . . . at least nothing you should concern yourself with. Don't touch it!"

Of course, now he had me really curious. "Come on, what is it?"

Lucifer pawed through the pile of assorted things and held up what looked like a bracelet. It was a snake that circled around itself and had its fangs sunk into its own tail, creating a loop. It was golden and intricately crafted. He held it up.

"This is an *Ouroboros,* one of the oldest mystical symbols in the world, the snake devouring its own tail. It has several meanings, depending on which ancient culture it came from: Greece, Egypt, China, Aztec, to name a few. To the alchemists of old, it represented the natural cycle of the Universe, creation out of destruction, life out of death. Others saw the *Ouroboros* as a symbol of the human condition, 'Man' caught in an endless loop, chasing his own tail. And then there's one of humanity's most perceptive thinkers, Carl Jung. He found it to have archetypical significance: the integration of opposites, light and shadow, creating Oneness."

"So, what does it mean to Lucifer?"

"To me? It means all of the above. The real question is, what does The Snake mean to a particular person? That all depends on the way they're perceiving the world."

"That sounds rather cryptic. Come on, let me see it for a minu . . . "

"I said DON'T TOUCH IT!"

Whoa! I pulled my hand back. . . and fast. Lucifer scooped up the pile, including the snake bracelet and stuffed it all back into his pockets. I signaled for the bill. "Let's go. I feel like walking some more."

The tab arrived in the typical little leatherette folder. I smiled broadly and, with an added flourish, pushed the bill across the table. "Yours, I believe."

Lucifer paused in his chair, as if to gather himself, and then, with no warning, let out a bellow that scared the bejesus out me and everyone else on the deck!

"Bloody hell! There's a cockroach on my plate!"

Everyone at every table froze. A man tending the bar inside came racing out.

"Look at this, will ya?" Lucifer's face was purple with rage. "A cockroach!" he shouted, in the direction of the most customers. Sure enough, under what remained of the Mahi Mahi on Lucifer's plate was a big, fat, black roach, antennas twitching. What made the bad scene even worse was, with all eyes on the plate in question, the roach decided to scurry down the table leg and run across the bare foot of the woman seated next to us. She screamed and jumped up out of her chair. Customers' cell phone cameras started clicking.

"Get me the manager!" Lucifer roared.

"I own the café, sir. I can't tell you how sorry . . . "

"Well, I can tell you! I'm calling the health department." Lucifer pulled out his phone.

"Please sir, that won't be necessary. Let me take care of your bill."

I watched in amazement as our tab disappeared.

"What else?" Lucifer snarled at the owner.

"What else? What else?" The nervous owner was now visibly perspiring. "Well . . . um . . . please be my personal guest at the bar. Would you care for a drink?"

At this point, I had seen enough and jumped in. "We're fine. Now, now, put your phone away, Uncle Luce." I patted the sleeve of the café owner. "We'll just be going."

With every eye in the place showering us with sympathy, we headed out. I refused to look in Lucifer's direction because I could picture his smug expression. All I wanted to do was put my head down and walk away, fast, anywhere. We headed down the main boardwalk onto the beach. After a while, puffing from the exertion, Lucifer was all for taking a load off. He pointed to an open cabana with a couple of lounges in it, close to the surf. We commandeered the chairs and got comfortable, at which point I finally looked in his direction. He crowed: "How'd you like the way I handled things? Effective, right?"

"I won't ask how you made that cockroach materialize. But yeah, effective, in a rather brutish way. You got what you wanted, I suppose. But let me tell you, you're way too gruff and crass with people."

"That was too gruff?"

"Yes, it was. You're being a total jerk, a conscious prick, as you put it. Well, I don't buy into your style, Lucifer. It leaves everyone seeing you as a crude scumbag."

"Really? I never noticed. I just know what I want and I get my way."

"Sure, at the expense of everyone else. You're doing the same with your *Dirty Laundry* advice column. These people write in, ask you a simple question to get your input and opinion, and your responses are laced with mean-spirited sarcasm and rude, back-handed jabs."

"Oh, piss off Jack! Tact is for people who aren't witty enough to be sarcastic. My advice is straightforward and honest. All I'm interested in is steering them in my direction."

"Oh, really? Let's take a look at a few."

"Fine." He pulled out the iPad from my backpack and booted it up. "Alright . . . this one came in yesterday. I'm actually quite proud of my pearls of wisdom to this lady."

Dear Lucifer,

My husband's out most nights, frequenting strip clubs with his male friends. He comes home three sheets to the wind with lipstick on his collar. We've been married twenty years, but I've just about had it! Do I toss him out or should I strive for more patience to keep the marriage?

Fed Up In Phoenix

I crossed my arms. "Okay, and your advice?"

"This one was so obvious." Lucifer cleared his throat.

Dear Fed Up,

Most wives are stuck with hubbies who just hang around the house. Familiarity breeds contempt! This nasty habit, in time, drives women to that exasperated place of: How can I miss you if you won't go away? You, on the other hand, have a man who seems to be alert to that relationship trap. He realizes that the secret to a successful marriage is that Absence makes the heart grow fonder. By going out philandering every night, it's his way of giving you space, allowing that tender yearning for each other to have a chance to bloom. The very fact that he's running around chasing young, single girls is his way of constantly reminding himself that, back at home, he has a truly mature, real woman waiting for him. Without all his infidelities, he'd have no contrast! You're being incredibly unreasonable. The good news is that it sounds like it's not too late to make it up to him. Next time he comes sneaking in at 6 a.m. stinking of gin and cheap perfume, at least have a good, hot breakfast waiting.

He looked up at my expression of disbelief and his massive shoulders lifted in a shrug. "What . . . I said something wrong?"

I buried my head in my palms. "This one doesn't even justify my response. You put new meaning to the term chauvinist. Your advice is absurd! "

Lucifer looked miffed. I actually believe he was expecting me to be impressed. "Alright, let's try another."

Dear Lucifer,

I'm a money manager by trade. I own and operate an investment firm for clients who want a nice, safe retirement portfolio. Very slowly, I've been yielding to the temptation of the Ponzi. You know the scam. Reel in new sucker investors with the promise of a higher-than-expected return and then pay those high dividends to the clients I already have to keep them happy and on the hook. The hoax is working all too well and I can't seem to stop my own greed from keeping this deceit from going ahead, full steam. Problem is, I'm being severely pestered by a nagging sense of shame for how I'm defrauding those who've put their trust (and retirement) into my hands. Can you help me stay the course here? And any suggestions on how not to get caught? I'm wavering.

Wobbling in Boston

"And your response was?"

"I'm getting there. Don't rush me." He looked at the iPad with an expression that was now far less cocky and read:

Dear Wobbling,

First of all, let's get something straight. This conversation never happened. Got it?

Look, I got to be honest. The vibe I get from you is that you're not cut out for this particular con game. To play the Ponzi, you have to be one cold-hearted sonuvabitch.

Wavering is not an option. If you have trouble making aging seniors cry, than pick another hoax to focus your conniving nature on.

Having said all that, should you decide to persevere, here's my advice, customized for you personally, so listen up.

To be good at this high-level hustle, you need two key characteristics: charm and a sense of mystery about you. The charm elicits a false sense of trust. Your mysteriousness creates a certain 'je ne sais quoi,' an enigmatic aura that the suckers will assume is the source of your 'Midas touch.' As they hand over their precious retirement cash, refuse it, at first. Tell them flatly: Don't want it, don't need it, I'm busy, go away. Make them beg you to take it. Then, as a big favor, flash that benevolent, charming smile of yours, scoop up their money, turn around and just feed it right into your pyramid scam.

And as to sweating about getting busted by the Feds? Are you kidding? Has there ever been an agency with more ineptitude, lack of experience and bureaucratic laziness?

Keep me posted. The Ponzi always intrigues me.

Yours, Lucifer

I closed my eyes, massaging my temples. "Did you send this already?"

"Yeah, why?"

"Why? Because I hear a man who's struggling with his conscience."

"Really . . . Well, what I heard was a guy asking for my advice on how to stay strong."

"Ah yes. You're encouraging him to invite up his Shadowlings of Greed and Deception."

"No. Those Shadowlings have already come up from the below and are now starting to run his life. He just needed a little encouragement to stay on target. And yeah, there's that annoying 'conscience' again . . . See how it gets in the way of what he wants?"

"What I see is how you feed his dark side."

"Precisely!"

"I think his conscience was trying desperately to break through and warn him."

"Maybe so, but too little too late! He's on the perfect track to have a colossal collapse!"

"What do you mean?"

Lucifer rubbed his palms together, his eyes lighting up. "He's playing the Ponzi scheme. At its core, it's a trap that always eventually snares the scam artist himself. Once you 'get in' there's no 'getting out.' It's a dead end and just a question of time till he's exposed. This guy is totally screwed!"

"And that's what he'll get for following your advice. Nice."

"No, that's what he gets for not recognizing the emergence of his Shadowlings, letting them ever so slowly take over and 'call the shots' in his life."

I mused to myself: *Well, maybe he has friends who can warn him and pull him out of it.*

Lucifer chortled heartily on that one. "Oh, he has friends alright. They're the ones who are currently keeping those convenient little 'blinders' on, turning a blind eye to him as they quietly profit from his ruse. But just wait till his fraudulent little game gets exposed. Those 'pals' of his will bail on him faster than rats escaping a sinking ship!"

"And what about all those seniors who are trusting him with their retirement savings?"

"What about them? Don't you get it yet? They're not my concern!"

This really infuriated me. It wasn't just the manipulative swaying of a man whose conscience was wobbling. It was the specter of all the retirees who'll be wiped out by this deception. I suddenly felt a blast of smoking hot rage. I got in his face: "You keep pointing out what a confused muddle we are as humans. Well let me tell you something. You're the one who's a frigging mess!"

"Oh?" He slowly put his tablet aside and sat very still. "How so?"

I was really feeling it now, anger surging through me like a hot lava flow: "The more I get to know you, the more I see how completely out of synch you are for this point in history. You're a terrible fit for the 21st century!"

"Well, that's a bold statement. But, I'm listening. Fire away, Hot Shot."

"For starters, just look at you! You have a face only a mother could love, if only you had one. And your sense of style? You have, far and away, the worst taste I've ever seen. Painful! And how about your walk? It's priceless! You shuffle along like a knuckle-dragging Neanderthal! And the way you gobble your food, I've seen slobbering dogs eat with better manners."

A big, ominous grin spread wide across Lucifer's countenance. "Oooh. Good one, Jack! Are you quite finished?"

He was throwing gas on my fire with his smugness. "No I'm not finished! Let's talk about your way with people. I'll grant that you're extremely powerful, no doubt way more than you're showing me. And you're smart as hell and crafty like a fox. But you seem to be totally limited by your own towering lack of grace."

He snickered in disgust. "Grace? And what might that be? Going around kissing everyone's feet?"

"No, being graceful simply keeps you from stepping on everyone's feet. If you want to reach out to others, you might consider learning some basic etiquette. You have the demeanor of a low-grade hick. You're brash, arrogant, rude and a bully. That's a huge turn-off, a point to which you're completely oblivious. We're living in a time where a certain considerate courtesy matters—and you don't fit in."

"What? I've been told I'm a perfect gentleman."

"You? Who told you that? One of your protégés?" I spat out my words. He had whipped me into such a froth!

"A gentleman starts with some sophistication, with a firm grasp of social graces, of which you have not an ounce! He has finesse, knowing when to speak and how to listen. He doesn't push his weight around. Does any of this sound remotely like you?"

"What, you don't like my personality?"

"Your personality is a joke! You need a major infusion of charm and refinement, some class and *panache.*"

Suddenly, I was done, the storm was easing. Enough said. I took a deep breath and, ignoring Lucifer to my left, stared off into the distant horizon. After a few long, silent minutes, the wide expanse of the Pacific Ocean began to settle me down and I felt that my anger had evaporated.

I turned to face him and was startled to see that Lucifer was gone. I wasn't surprised that he had taken off. I'd been rough on him. But damn it, he kept goading me! I felt relief, finally being free of him. I sat there for a while, taking in the ocean view and breathing in the salt air.

A lady passed by, letting her dog's sniffer decide where it wanted to leave its mark. A silver-haired man approached and gestured to the empty seat next to me, seeming to ask if it was taken. I signaled that it was available and turned my gaze back to the ocean.

"Can I offer you a mint, sir?" My new neighbor was holding out a small tin box.

As I reached across, I gave him a quick glance-over. I noticed his 'Aloha' shirt right away... very nice. I always take note of island shirts as it was what most men wear. There's such a wide range of them, everything from Lucifer's god-awful clashing patterns to handsome up-scale designs like this gentleman was wearing. I popped the mint into my mouth. "I like your shirt."

"Thank you." He looked down, brushing a leaf off his pressed cotton slacks. "Silk. Cool on the skin and looks great, to boot!" He had a pleasant smile, an engaging grin that puts you at ease right away. Tilting his head, he studied me. "Nice to get away for a slice of this paradise. I trust you're having a relaxing vacation?"

"I'm getting what I needed, although today has been . . . strange."

"How so?"

How to answer that? I took a closer look at the man. Deeply tanned, middle aged, with the lean, honed form of an aging athlete. An expensive watch and the leather sandals gave him the aura of confident success. He struck me as someone who wouldn't be thrown off easily by a startling revelation, yet why try to describe whom I've been spending my day with? Best to leave well enough alone.

"Just a series of bizarre events." I put out my hand. "Jackson," I said with a smile.

He took my hand with a firm handshake. Leaning in, he chirped brightly: "Hello, Jackson. Pleased to meet you . . . . The name's Lucifer."

It took a few seconds to register. As my eyes got big, I pulled back my hand . . . My mind felt like it was short-circuiting, as if the synapses were frying in my brain. Words weren't forthcoming. I jumped to my feet.

"Jackson, sit, sit. Please." This man turned to face me full on. In a smooth, articulate voice he cooed: "First, thank you for your honest appraisal of my dismal persona. I appreciate your excellent guidance regarding how utterly out of step I've been in my former, shall we say, incarnation. You're so right; that look was clearly for another time and a different place. This is exactly why I need to touch base with real people, like you, from time to time. I can be going along and not realize how much my exterior form might need modernization. Your suggestions were masterful! I already feel far more in tune with the times. By the way, you do prefer to be called Jackson, yes?"

Two attractive women walked past our bench, flirting appreciatively, their eyes on the handsome man sitting next to me. He gave them a wink and then, after a quick scan of their backsides, turned his attention back to me. I sat there, speechless, as a single thought kept rolling through my head: *What have I done?* With a sympathetic pat, Lucifer lightly put his hand on my arm. I recoiled.

"Don't touch me."

"Jackson, I know you must be rattled. I'm so full of surprises! You'll learn."

"It's really you," I mumbled stupidly.

"Indeed it is, my boy. It is, and yet . . . it isn't."

"Huh?"

"It's me all right, but my entire orientation has shifted. For example, *his* fixation with being a conscious prick? Oh please! How crude. There are much more elegant ways of going about creating my desired outcomes." A smile nothing short of dazzling illuminated his face.

"Same deceiving manipulator, just a more upscale delivery? Is that what you're saying?"

Lucifer threw back his head and laughed. "True enough. But isn't this exactly what you were suggesting I needed? Well, whatever form I'm in, my work never ends. I do hope you can relax. I think you'll now find my company much more engaging that my prior self."

"Relax? Are you kidding? I feel totally duped. Stepped right into your trap. Gave you everything you needed to know, and more! You just lifted it right out of me, didn't you? But I'm going to get the hell away from you, before I royally screw up something else!"

"Come on, I understand how you must be feeling. Okay, so I'm a little deceptive. But to be honest, Jackson, you're a great guy with a lot of experience, but not the fastest on the uptake."

"Thanks for that. I feel so much better."

"No, it's me who wants to thank *you.* By the way, what's wrong with your elbow?"

"What are you talking about?" I rubbed my right arm a few times.

"No, the left one. Does it hurt?"

I straightened out my left arm to look at it. "It feels perfectly fi . . . " In a blinding flash, Lucifer grabbed my outstretched left forearm and slipped something metallic onto my wrist. He gave it a squeeze and it tightened. Jerking my arm out of his grip, I stared down and gasped in alarm; a snake was now wrapped around my wrist! At first glance, I actually thought the snake had come alive, it looked so graphically realistic. Then, to my utter relief, I realized it was the snake bracelet I had seen during our meal.

"What the hell? What did you do? Take it off!"

Lucifer beamed: "What you now have on your wrist is the *Ouroboros* amulet. It dates all the way back to a kingdom of ancient India, at the foothills of the Himalayas. Look at me, Jackson, and listen carefully. This extraordinary talisman is the *Cuff of Kosala,* It gives you First Level powers on the *Zakiti* plane."

I looked at him in dazed incomprehension. The first thought that surfaced in my mind was that he was making me his prisoner.

"Look, all you need to know is that this opens you up to enormous potential. Just point your left arm directly at anything you choose, learn to command this Cuff, and watch what happens!"

I looked at the eyes of the snake. They were made of faceted gems and glowing like smoldering embers. "You can't do this to me. Take it off!"

"Here's the deal, Jackson. It's going to stay on you until I'm ready to leave. At the end of our visit today, when we're finished with our conversations, you can give it back, or keep it. It'll be your decision. While you're wearing it, you don't have to activate the potential in the amulet at all. It's entirely your choice! Free will, remember?" He chuckled in a sickeningly delightful lilt.

"Whatever it 'activates,' I'm not going to use it!"

"Sure, of course you're not. I've heard that before! But, hey, it's your call. Now, I'll just let you and the awesome *Cuff of Kosala* get acquainted. Listen to it. It may offer something important to you."

Barely breathing, I stared down at the Cuff. Half horrified, half mystified, I turned my wrist this way and that. I had to admit, it was a thing of exquisite artistry. I had no doubt it was from an ancient civilization. It had a slightly worn luster and I could see that it was made out of solid gold, with an iridescent burnished sheen, like *raku.* The snake's fangs were sunk deeply into its own tail as it wrapped around my wrist. I studied the scales etched into its loop. They were incredibly lifelike. It was heavy, as only solid gold can be, and yet, it literally hummed with energy. That potent vibration, oddly, removed its weight, giving the counter-intuitive impression that it was feather-light. My trembling wrist felt hot from the Cuff's oscillation. I tried twisting it off, but it was as if it were glued to my skin.

As I put my focus on its pulsation, the humming immediately intensified. Whoa! I suddenly sensed excitement being stimulated in some deep-seated part of myself. A tingling was emerging from the depths of my psyche. Something in me was being drawn to this force like a magnet. What was going on? I just sat there, transfixed, gazing at the snake, this *Ouroboros.* Unable to remove it, I let myself feel into it. What was the nature of this strong, throbbing vibration . . . its origin? Then, in a bolt of realization, it came to me. One word:

Power.

The force of Power has many faces. This particular face was in the form of an energy that clearly conveyed: *Power over, but over what?*

The Cuff seemed to answer me telepathically: *That's for you to find out! And oh,"* it added, *"don't waste my time. Use me or lose me."*

On that note, the excitement being aroused deep within me spiked! A surge of electricity rocketed up my spine, causing me to shiver uncontrollably. In a dazed state, I saw my left arm gradually lifting in front of my chest, bent at the elbow, the cuffed wrist pointing straight up towards the sky. Then, as if it had a will all its own, it began lowering, as my eyes scanned the immediate surroundings, looking for where to point. Something caught my eye. Ah, that will do!

Stop!! Jackson, you're playing with fire. You're out of your depths! It was my Wisdom Voice, knifing through my thoughts while it still had the chance.

"Come on. Give it a go! You can't be this close and not try it out. Just a little test run."

That was the soft, silky voice of Lucifer sitting next to me. He brought his face close to mine, gazing at me with those piercing, intense eyes.

"Now what was that quote you were so fond of? 'The greatest challenge of life is discovering who you are.' Well guess what, Jackson? You're about to find out just who you are!"

What's My Truth?

One does not become enlightened by imagining figures of light, but by making the darkness conscious.

—Carl Jung

It turned out to be good timing that my wisdom voice got through to me. *You're in over your head!* I dropped my arm and shook it to jar loose the spell. Damn . . . that was close. I had been inches away from taking this strange and exotic amulet for a test drive. I turned to Lucifer who was clearly masking his disappointment with a cunning smile.

"What's the problem, Jackson? It looks to me like your fear is showing. You might want to tuck that back in. You know, everything you ever wanted is on the other side of that fear."

I ignored his jab. Trying one more time to twist the amulet off my wrist, I turned in exasperation to face him. "I'm outta here. This conversation is over. If you want your precious Cuff back, you'd better retrieve it, right now."

Lucifer stifled a yawn as he stretched, his tan, lean arms reaching for the sky. My threat didn't exactly have him rattled. I upped the edge in my voice a notch. "You're not listening to me. I said I'm leaving!"

"Here's the thing, Jackson, I know you won't leave. I can't stop you, but you'll stop yourself."

"Do I look like I'm stopping myself?" I reached into my daypack and pulled out his iPad. "Here."

Ignoring the tablet, he gestured to the path. "Let's walk a bit and I'll tell you precisely why you won't leave."

He took a few steps and then turned, patiently waiting for me to join. I glowered at him as he stood there, calm, elegant and so utterly confident. It pissed me off to no end the way he seemed to understand exactly how to manipulate me. He knew how strong my streak of curiosity is.

"Alright. Two minutes is all you get." I glanced at my watch.

"Good. Now come on." His voice reminded me of how one speaks to a thoroughbred when you want to settle it down: soft, soothing, no rough edges. "There're two reasons, actually, why you can't refuse, why you'll agree to stay. The first is simple; you're a writer with a keen nose for the mysterious. You love nothing better than to investigate, to uncover information in unexpected places in order to gain new insight. It's your gift and we both know it's why you've stayed with me so far today, right?"

"So why should I bother to stay any longer?"

"If you leave now, you'll turn your back on the chance of a lifetime for some privileged information that, I guarantee you, will never come your way again. Answer me this. Would you be better off inquiring more deeply into what I'm really about? Or would it be smarter to walk away, remaining clueless for the rest of your life just because a stunning golden snake wrapped around your wrist has put you in a snit?"

I said nothing, but my expression conveyed: 'Screw you.'

"Are you better served taking full advantage of having a unique, inside look into Lucifer's Game or would you rather have a trivial chat with the cabbie on your way back to the resort about the weather? Admit it, Jackson, if you're being completely honest with yourself, there's no real argument here."

I tried not to show any visible reaction to his bait, but damn! Once again, I felt him reeling me in. "And the second reason is?"

"I'm offering to make things even more interesting for you. As a sign of my willingness to be revealing, ask me any question you want and I'll give a direct answer, or at least one that's within your human range of understanding. Any question you want . . . straight up."

I was dripping in skepticism. "A direct answer? I doubt it. In your previous persona, 'the lumbering bear,' every time I'd ask a specific question, you'd just cleverly dodge and weave."

Lucifer dipped his head slightly, in a deferring way. "My dear Jackson, can't you tell already that I'm completely different?"

I was not in the mood to agree with him, but I had to admit it was true. I was still adjusting to this new form he had morphed into. With his silver-haired locks, tailored clothes and athletic physique, he had transformed from a rough-hewn brute into a refined, debonair gentleman. Still, there was something in his new demeanor that was a little off. He was acting too sincere. His face would smile but his eyes did not. There was a subtle, but distinct, element of . . . what? Shiftiness. Yeah. He reminded me of one of those slick, elegant, world-class pickpockets whom you'd least expect to be slipping your wallet out of your suit coat at an airport while offering to help you find your way to the taxi stand.

And yet, I felt like screaming because it was true that I wanted to stay. I couldn't refuse! I'm so damn inquisitive by nature. But where was all this leading? I glanced down at my wrist and realized I was unwittingly caressing the Cuff with my right hand. Its pulsating reverberation clearly had an intoxicating quality. "Alright, but I'm pretty sure I'm going to regret this."

Turning his head in my direction as we walked along the path, Lucifer put on the most earnest expression, brimming with sincerity. "Good man, Jackson. So what's your burning question for me?"

"Alright. I asked this earlier today and you only gave me a partial answer. There are billions of people on the planet right now whom you could be paying a visit to. Why me?"

"Fair enough. There are two ways I can answer your question."

"Just get to it, will you?"

Lucifer pointed towards a bench nearby and we took a seat. "The first would be short and sweet . . . "

"And probably not the truth. And the second?"

"The second would be for you to go first. Give me some personal information. How do you, Jackson Trent, perceive the human experience? Just flesh it out for me a bit. If you were to take what you've learned over all the decades of your life and boil it down to its essential key points, what would they be? Once you do that, I can give you a complete answer to the question, why you, based on what you can understand. Deal?"

My perception of reality, metaphysically? I let my mind drift in reverse along the lanes of my memories. "Alright, I'll go first." I put my hands behind my head and stretched out my legs.

"So, I started out as a child. . . "

"Cute, but not that far back."

I sat up straight and got serious. "Okay, my first real exploration of the human experience started for me in my early twenties when my 'seeker' got sparked and came alive. Since then, I've been on a quest to find the way back to what I'll call my True Self. This has been the great challenge, following the thread within myself to discover my deeper nature, the Spirit within me."

"And you believe this spiritual exploration is your destiny?"

"Yes, I do, which is why I keep writing my blog, to help others where I can. This particular exploration has certainly been my *dharma.* I believe that every person is destined in some way."

"Ha! Destiny... If people are destined for anything, it's to find themselves playing my Game, which steers them in the direction I want them to go. But go on, Jackson . . . "

I continued. "Life, karma, or whatever you call it deals each of us a hand to play. And in my view, that hand can be played in myriad different ways . . . in various 'life games.' Some people are fated to play the noble game of raising a family; some are drawn to the arts or the sciences; many align with one religion or another; and quite a few get locked into the money game. There are others saddled by addictions. The list of life games is endless. But how well we play it is entirely our choice."

"And your choice, Jackson, was to become an explorer of sorts. Not one of the typical games, that's for sure."

"My calling to connect with my Spirit was sealed in my college years. For me, it was the game of waking up. Once I was introduced to the truth that our human consciousness has the capacity for a wide range of awareness, a light switch turned on in me, one of those powerful 'aha!' moments. My life's true pursuit had begun. I felt a clear, irrefutable message telling me: *If consciousness can be deepened, then, for chrissake, deepen it!*"

"And what has your exploration discovered about this deeper human awareness?"

"I found that my potential range of awareness was like an entire book and I'd only been sticking to the first chapter. I learned that the human experience is a question of *dimensions.* This term, dimensions, means different things in various spiritual teachings. In one particular matrix I spent years studying, dimensions refers to levels of consciousness or states that we can experience, specifically the 3rd, 4th and 5th dimensions. This is a map that comes from an ancient path of inner development that's still totally relevant today."

As I looked at Lucifer's face, it was suddenly taking on an expression that dogs get when they pick up the scent of something interesting: eyes sparkling, keenly alert.

"Intriguing, Jackson. And these dimensions or states of consciousness, can you describe them?"

"From the perspective of this particular Teaching, the 2nd dimension refers to the animal realm, so it's not our concern. Human awareness begins in the 3rd dimension, where there's a self-reflective 'I' that animals don't possess. This is our normal state of egoic consciousness, the level at which we're each aware of simply being ourselves . . . . It's the familiar 'me' that's aware of and tracks my life's history. The 4th dimension is when our awareness wakes up into the state of a mindful personal presence, when you become conscious of your own awareness in the moment. Then, with further inquiry and exploration, this state can really open and expand into the 5th dimension, Wholeness. This is the Unity state of Pure Oneness, where the personal presence willingly dissolves into the infinitely larger field of Universal Presence. Do you agree with all this?"

Lucifer strummed his fingers on the arm of the bench. "I'll let you know my opinion when you're finished. Keep going."

"So, what I came to understand is that True Nature, God, or whatever label one calls 'It,' has put human beings on planet Earth in the 'egoic' 3rd dimensional state of consciousness, that familiar place we all inhabit. It's up to each of us to take it from there. If we want to lift out of this 3rd dimension, to *wake up* as it were, it's possible but it doesn't just happen by itself. We have to find our way via 'working' on ourselves. On one hand, this egoic realm is a beautiful state. It's great to be human! I wouldn't want to trade it in for, say, being a rhino. But what I discovered, after years of exploration, is that, from a consciousness perspective, our normal 3rd dimension is a sleepy state."

"What do you mean by sleepy? Like all those people back in town with their attention sucked into their gadgets?"

"Yeah, but it's much more than that. The basic characteristic of the human 3rd dimension is that our consciousness is on a 'default setting,' where it's constantly distracted or absorbed. Our awareness gets ensnared, lost in whatever we happen to be doing. There's 'no one home' in the sense that we're not 'present' in that moment. That's not a judgment; it's just the way it is. A little honest self-observation reveals how true that is. The state of Presence or Being simply isn't a characteristic of our default setting. That state of awakened mindfulness inherent within Presence is the hallmark of the 4th dimension."

Lucifer's questions continued to probe. "And so how, in your view, do humans get there to this 4th dimension?"

"There's nowhere to get. Presence is everywhere, like oxygen. It's within us, always. I have . . . we all have, a higher Self that's in a constant state of unbroken, fluid awakeness. So, there's my familiar 'little me' and there's my True Self, both functioning at the same time! But we're usually disconnected from our higher Self. Why? Because we're each too identified with our 'little me.' We're stuck in the default setting. Our 3rd dimensional reality is so seductively compelling, so habitually familiar, that we get all caught up in that ensnared attention which cuts us off from stepping into, and experiencing, this Self as Presence. We get oblivious."

Lucifer snickered, as if enjoying his own private joke. "Oblivious . . . great description! But why not just stay put in this 3rd dimension? Why struggle?"

Now it was my turn to laugh. "Oh, I see. Don't wander off the reservation? Is that what you're suggesting?"

"Well, yeah. Why complicate reality?"

"You've got it backwards, Lucifer. It's when we enter the 4th dimension that reality simplifies. Nothing is as complicated as the convoluted entanglements of our 3rd dimensional egoic world. As human beings, we have options to evolve. The coolest thing is that, unlike other animals on Earth whose consciousness is 'locked in,' our awareness has the capacity to expand vertically. We can unhook from our default setting. Through our own choice, we can be more awake or more in waking sleep, up or down that scale. It's our choice."

"So your personal interest is to move up the scale, right?"

"Yeah, go vertical, shift my awareness higher. For me, I got interested in that study and spent years delving into it. I learned firsthand how difficult it is to stay fully 'in the present' for longer than a few moments at a time. But like a muscle that gets strengthened, eventually 'the work' becomes how to stay awake. Over decades of exploration, my quest has brought me to various schools of consciousness, with a variety of different teachers. And the bottom line of what I've learned is this: the gravitational pull of the 3rd Dimension, that 'waking sleep,' should never be underestimated. It's incredibly pervasive and presses down on us like a heavy, invisible weight. Just like in a dream, paradoxically, we can only know we've been asleep if we awaken!"

Lucifer, who had been very attentive, burst out into a hoot of laughter.

"What's so funny?"

"Oh, let's just say I appreciate your description of the paradox: *'You can only know you've been asleep once you awaken.'* Now you might understand why I chose to meet with you. I actually enjoy talking to someone who's 'on' to part of my Game. I've been so damn curious about how you've become successful at escaping my Web."

"Successful? Hardly. It's been a long inner journey of two steps forward, one step back . . . at best."

"But you have an insightful blog where you discuss what you've learned, and it's now gaining serious traction in the world, yes?"

"I created *Snap Out of It,* for the reason I described earlier, as a way to give something back. I write it as a metaphysical guidebook for others. In my mountain climbing days, a guidebook was crucial, written by someone who'd gone ahead and explored the routes. They could then report back and offer important advice that could save other alpinists so much time and trouble. That's the spirit I want to bring to my writing on 'inner climbing,' if you will, a map and a compass of the inner terrain that I've passed through for anyone who cares to use it."

"I find your breed so curious, Jackson. You're one of these individuals who refuses to buy into the default setting. What is it about this 3rd dimensional state that makes you want to escape it? Not interesting enough for you?"

"There's nothing wrong with the 3rd dimension, Lucifer. To be a person in our familiar reality with a relatively balanced ego is a terrific accomplishment for anyone. But in terms of my own potential evolution, my belief is that, when I am in my egoic state of consciousness, I'm only half-baked in a sense, half way to my True Self. So the message I've received from deep within me has always been keep exploring, keep inquiring! Metaphorically, take the elevator up a floor to the 4th dimension. 'Snap out of it' and step into my awakeness that's always calling to me in any given moment."

Lucifer was silent for a moment, his head bent in thought. Then suddenly, he blurted, "What if I tell you this 4th dimension is just a figment of your imagination?"

"Don't bullshit me, Lucifer. I'm getting more clear on what exactly your Game is and why someone like me, who can write about what I've discovered, is a threat to you. You know exactly what I'm talking about."

Lucifer's eyebrow arched. "So are you claiming humans are not awake or aware in the regular egoic reality?"

I turned to face him more directly. "What I'm saying is that it's a question of degrees. The simple, yet utterly profound state of Presence, with its clarity and palpable sense of awake aliveness, makes our normal state, with our constantly chattering mind and our chronic reactivity, seem like we're sleep walking. For most people, they either get it or they don't. They either have a taste for Presence or they're just not interested. Or, like so many, they simply haven't discovered it yet."

Lucifer was nervously scratching the back of his head, staring at me with an increased intensity that was making me very uneasy. I just stared right back. I was on solid ground here, as this was my Truth. Finally he seemed to relax.

He smiled thinly. "Okay, let's keep going. Tell me more about the difference between the 3rd and the 4th dimensions of consciousness, the egoic versus this so-called personal Presence."

"I will, but I'm doing all the talking here. When will we get around to you answering my question?"

"I'm getting there. But first, you continue on. I want to hear more about how you see the difference between the two dimensions."

I took a deep breath, exhaling slowly and allowed my thoughts to gather themselves around this core question of my life's quest.

"Okay, let me put it this way. If we look at the typical human experience, the familiar egoic 3rd dimension is a state of duality. Let me use myself as an example. There's me—and there's everything and everyone outside of me. I'm at the center. It's like we're all inside of our own movie. For each of us, the plot continually unfolds, with new dramas and comedies emerging as our life moves along. In my movie, of course, I am not only the star around whom the screenplay revolves, but also the producer and director. Different people in my life play various roles, depending on my relationship with each. But it's always the movie of my life being played out on the big screen in my mind."

"You got it, Jackson. That's exactly the way it is."

"Yes, but what's interesting is that every human being is having the same experience, starring in their own movie! It's hilarious when you think about it. Look at a hundred people walking down a street and you'll see a hundred different feature length films going on simultaneously, each one with its own unique storyline. This is simply how life in our normal human 3rd dimension operates."

"And what's wrong with that, Jackson? Each person is allowed to be a movie star! Dive deep into your movie, everyone! Very exciting! Everyone gets to be an Oscar winner!"

I shook my head. "Very exciting . . . until it's not. If we take an honest look at our own movie, give it a review, so to speak, we'd find that the screenplay has become boringly predictable, stale. Even the dramas, with their high-octane emotional charge, tend to be old, familiar terrain when examined on close inspection. What interests me is how to step out of the movie!"

Lucifer was incredulous. "What? Oh, come on! Why would you want to step out of your movie?"

"Because the movie, itself, is an illusion! It's created within the walls of my mind, which is lodged within that egoic 3rd dimensional view. I hate to break it to my deluded ego, but I'm not the center of the Universe, where everything revolves around me. When you peel back the layers, you see it's all a kind of self-absorbed dream. But if, even for a few brief moments, I can step out of my movie and into the immediate field of Presence, I can then experience the aliveness of Reality beyond my little ego shell. So hear me on this point, Lucifer, I want to get out of the movie business!"

"Okay Jackson . . . . So if you've stepped out of your movie and you're not your familiar self, who are you now?"

"That's depends on how easily I can let go of that old, musty database in my mind that tells me who I am, based on my life history. To what degree can I allow myself to relax into what is *now* . . . not what

I'm fantasizing my world to be? The 4th dimension is an experience of an awakened Personal Presence. It's still a state of duality, but now I'm mindfully awake. You simply have to taste the difference. Once I did it, and felt it, I realized how these are clearly two different dimensions of my own inner level of awareness. I can be in one or the other. The question becomes, which dimension do I prefer? It's my birthright as a human being to be able to choose."

"And what about the 5th dimension, Jackson? That's reaching pretty high for you humans, yes?"

I paused for a moment. "Frankly, aside from a few astounding yet brief moments of touching into that state, I admit that's a dimension that I've yet to penetrate. The 5th dimension is ridiculous to try to label, but the word 'Enlightened' may be the closest our language can come. It's the realm of Wholeness . . . what some call the 'Oneness of the Cosmic Realization.'"

This conversation had taken a turn that seemed to be impacting Lucifer in a strange way. He now appeared edgy, like he wanted to squash everything I had articulated.

"You're just asking for trouble, Jackson. All your talk about dimensions is full of contradictions."

"Okay . . . I'll grant you that attempting to wake up has plenty of contradictions."

Lucifer brightened. "Of course it does! Tell me which ones you see."

"Alright. For instance, the contradiction that I'm alive as a human being while my consciousness is asleep in a waking dream. Or that we have to make an effort to wake up, and yet opening the door to the field of Presence requires letting go of efforting! Or how the mind never stops thinking, and yet the true and deeper nature of the mind is quiet, open Spaciousness. Or the contradiction of how we covet our spiritual knowledge, as if know*ing* about Spirit is actually experiencing Spirit. How we crave the freedom of Realization and yet hold fast, and desperately protect, our little Self, who, out of fear of losing its grip, will always make sure to keep Realization at bay! Or how we're driven and pressured by time, and yet we're simultaneously immersed in Eternity. How's that for a contradiction? Or how our hearts are capable of radiance, beaming love like the Sun, and yet, because life can be harsh, we build a wall around ourselves to make sure we don't feel too much. Or how we seek the Truth, yet defend our lies. How we pray for guidance and then cherry-pick what we choose to hear from our Wisdom Voice. Or take the contradiction that I'm learning from you today, Lucifer: how we try to flutter our little angelic wings towards the Light and yet we're constantly sabotaged from below by our unconscious Shadowlings."

I expected a snarky response, but Lucifer just sat there with a wily grimace. Finally I broke the silence:

"Alright. I'm done. I gave you more than enough of what you asked for. Now it's your turn to talk. Tell me exactly why you chose me."

CHAPTER
9

Forcing My Hand

There is always truth in seduction. That's why it works.

—Zoe Archer

Lucifer slipped into stony silence, eyes hooded, body inert. Then, he abruptly stood up and directed me to follow him along the path. As we rounded a curve, we came upon a Hawaiian-style pub, a thatched roof over a large U-shaped bar in the open air. We pulled up a couple of tall stools in the far corner. Draft pints were set down in front of us and Lucifer served me with that smirk of his which was so hard to read. It made me wonder what was coming next?

I said warily: "I can see those pessimistic wheels turning."

Lucifer seemed to ponder that: "It's been said that the nice part of being a pessimist is that you're either constantly being proven right, or pleasantly surprised." He raised his beer stein in my direction: "To the glass . . . half empty!" He took a swig, then turned to me, his dark eyes drilling right in.

"So you want to know why you? To answer that you're going to have to stretch to see the world the way I do."

"Oh, I'm stretching. This may be the strangest yoga session I've ever taken."

He didn't laugh. "I've listened carefully to your map of the dimensions of human consciousness. Pretty good, Jackson, simple and clear. A fairly accurate picture. But your viewpoint is limited."

"By what?"

"By the fact that you can't understand things from my vantage point, which is on a higher level than yours. I have my own way of perceiving humanity, an entirely different, and shall I say, more systematic perspective. So I'm going to bring our two paradigms together, so you can see how they fit."

"How Lucifer categorizes us . . . this oughta be good."

"Pay attention and gauge for yourself. As you point out, there are basically three dimensions, or states of Awareness available for any human being to experience. I commend you for discovering that generally hidden fact. Most people don't have a clue. As far as I'm concerned, however, that begs the key question: 'Do I care which dimension humans find themselves experiencing?' Absolutely! More than you can ever imagine! Let me offer you a little peek into my reality. We're going to take a deeper dive into what *Lucifer's Game* is all about."

I found myself involuntarily shuddering, not sure where this was going to go. No turning back though; my curiosity was now at an all-time high.

"Let's start with the big picture from my perch." Lucifer stroked his chin, collecting his thoughts. "Okay, Jackson, similar to how you classify Awareness into three distinct dimensions, I break humanity down into three different categories that I simply call A, B and C. No need for complexity in my world."

"What do your categories refer to?"

"They refer to my degree of control. Category 'A' are basically those who perceive life from what you call the 3rd dimension of consciousness. I call these folks the *Sheeple*, the vast man-swarm of individuals who are basically living out their lives the best way they can. The key characteristic of Sheeple is that they just don't pay attention. Their awareness is so easily distracted that they require very little of my involvement. Sure, I do some tweaking from time to time, but, overall, my systems run beautifully on autopilot and are highly efficient to lead them down a particular path in life."

"Exactly what kind of path are you encouraging the Sheeple down?"

"I lead them into a virtual reality. In that world, they look but they don't actually see. Imagine thin layers of gauze curtains that keep them from being in contact with the real world. It creates a comfortable, if not fuzzy, fantasy of who they think they are. The bottom line is that the Sheeple are convinced that they are each their little Self."

"And so you force these Sheeple to stay deluded?"

"I don't force anything, Jackson. Sheeple are perfectly content living from, shall we say, the small view. They don't miss what they don't know. That particular way of experiencing their life is familiar, comfortable; it's 'home' to them. They never see those thin curtains in front of their eyes, let alone try to part them open. They don't question or inquire. I don't even have to work to get the Sheeple to push their 'rejected selves' down into their Shadow Realm. Within their own psyche, they not only do that for me, but they make damn sure that the Shadowlings they've renounced stay buried deep in my Underworld . . . until my temptation encourages them back up to the surface. My systems simply keep these rejects alive and well down there, ready and waiting for their chance to pop up again."

"But not all the so-called Sheeple are saps to your influence, right?"

"Sure, some struggle against temptation. But I love that, because the more they struggle, the deeper they go in playing my Game. They're caught in my sticky spider web and, what's so delightful, is that they don't even know it!"

"And this spider web of yours consists of what?"

"Think of it as a *Web of Illusion*."

"So, this Game of yours . . . it's essentially a subterfuge, right? You use deceit and trickery to hide something from us in order to achieve a goal. So what is your goal, Lucifer?"

"Very simply this. My goal is to keep the Sheeple in what you call that 'waking sleep.' Why? Primarily so they stay completely unaware of the true meaning of existence, developing the soul, awakening consciousness. They don't see the real Light as they just keep playing the game of hiding their Shadowlings and unconsciously releasing them back up again. They're like kids playing on that 'inner staircase.' But let me continue with my categories, and then you'll get it."

He paused a moment, his eyes dancing merrily. He was clearly now in his element. "As for Category B, we're talking about far fewer people, those whom I call *Aspirants.* These are individuals who, through their work on themselves, actually begin to escape from my Web. They're getting hip to my Game. If you start 'lifting the curtains,' so to speak, my carefully crafted illusion begins to fall apart."

"And how do these Aspirants manage to do this?"

"You mean, how do they snap out of it?" he asked, winking at me. "There are a number of ways they can lift the curtains, usually through various Teachings from those who have already made their way out."

"And you try to *stop* their escape of course, right?"

"Absolutely, every which way I can! Understand this, Jackson. I play to win. I want everyone to stay stuck on my Web, lost in the maze of my Game. So I've had to design a completely different strategy for these

Aspirants. It's a much greater challenge for me than with the Sheeple, but, believe me, I have my ways to reel these Aspirants back in."

"And your Category C? These are the ones who make their way off your Web?"

"Unfortunately, yes. Despite my best efforts, there are, indeed, a handful of individuals, the *Realized* souls, who manage to lift off and escape. Bastards! I hate to lose, Jackson, so these few souls receive my undivided attention. They may be currently out from under my thumb, out from my sphere of influence, but I will never cease attempting to suck them back in!"

"And these few . . . just what have they 'realized?'"

"They've realized, at their depths, who they actually are!" On that note, Lucifer stared at his beer glass, contemplating. Then: "But it's very rare, Jackson, very rare. There are only a few in Category C. For the most part, the human being is a species that suffers from amnesia. You've forgotten who you actually are."

"And I know you've had a hand in that, yeah? So, just who are we?"

"In a word, 'Creators.' The human being is a natural born Creator. When you're in touch with your true Power, you're capable of creating at will. In fact, long, long ago, Man the Creator experimented, and you managed to design your own 'operating system.' Like any good Creator, you, then, had to test it out, live through one's creation for a while. So, Man the Creator crawled into the skin of its creation. But then, unbelievably, you forgot who you were! *You got stuck as the creature you had created!* You neglected to return to your Source and got lost in your own house of mirrors. You took a huge fall and couldn't remember how to get back up! Now, stuck as the creature, you no longer create! You now believe that Life happens to you, which, then, makes you constantly feel like a victim of circumstance."

A picture of what he was describing was beginning to form in my mind. "So we, Mankind, took a fall, and you, Lucifer, stepped in to keep us lost and disconnected from our Source?"

Lucifer grinned: "You got it! That is my Game at the most fundamental level."

"But why? What's your great interest in keeping us asleep?"

Lucifer's stuck his face close to mine. "One word: the *Unconscious*... keeping the darkness hidden. That's what I stand for, my *raison d'etre!*"

"So that's why the Realized ones bother you so much?"

Lucifer rubbed his hands together with glee. "Bother me? Not at all. I love the challenge! The Sheeple bore me. The Aspirants, are beginning to become problematic, a pain in the ass. Ah . . . but the Realized are the ones who get my complete attention. At this high plane, I'm fully engaged. I adore the competition and the way my Game is played out at this level. Do you play chess, Jackson?"

"Yeah, I do."

"Well, imagine a kind of *Soul Chess,* if you will. The Dark versus the Light, competing for the loyalty of the Realized. Believe me when I say I'm a Grand Master."

Lucifer got up off his bar stool and launched into an imaginary conversation, mocking a Realized individual he pretended was standing next to him:

"Oh, so you're an Awakened One, huh? An Enlightened Teacher? You think you're completely free of your ego shell? Well now, let's see how you deal with adulation! Write your book . . . give your workshops, become a sought-after guru. And now, let's heap on the hero worship, all those starry-eyed Truth Seekers who throw themselves at your feet. Just how lacking in ego are you now, with all this intoxicating Power projected onto you?"

I burst out laughing at his performance. And yet, I saw that he was dead right. "I know what you mean. I've been around spiritual teachers like that. Years ago, I was involved in a particular metaphysical group. I loved the ancient knowledge I was soaking up, but the leader of this group became . . . well, suspect. Over time, he went from wonderfully ripe to horribly rotten."

Lucifer laughed derisively. "That's exactly the kind of human I'm talking about! Did you ever read *Halfway Up The Mountain?* As it cites, it's those who begin to enter the Enlightened state who are on the shakiest ground. Trust me. Despite their Awakening, it's amazing how prone they are to temptation. More than ever!" Lucifer's grinned with his own private thoughts. "Tell me about this teacher of yours."

I allowed my own sour memories from long ago to come to the surface. "Well, I once had this particular teacher who set himself up as someone who'd fully awakened. Indeed, I do believe he had awakened to a serious degree at one point in time, and it made him magnetic, which is what had attracted followers to him. But it was also what had put him, rather quickly, into a self-created position of all-powerful. His word was law. Who can handle being in that position of unchallenged power and not abuse it? Certainly not this guy... his soul slowly turned ugly. Unchecked indiscretions developed into what I'd call 'spiritually criminal' activity. In my view, his worst abuse was when he began taking the naïve, dewy-eyed new students, male and female, with their open and trusting nature, and exploited that devotion for his own pathetic, selfish ends."

"Jackson, I know exactly where you're going with that story. Just who do you think is responsible for disrupting the evolution of these Adepts? Am I good, or what? So, let me guess, in the case of your experience, it went something like this. First, anyone who challenged this Teacher was belittled and then, if they persisted, banished from the group, 'cut away from the herd,' right? He then justified his actions by saying things like, 'The lower cannot possibly comprehend the actions of the higher,' which, cleverly, gave him carte blanche to be as abusive as he pleased. How am I doing?"

I stared blankly at Lucifer; what he said was exactly the way it had unfolded. Over time, Power had spread through this teacher's soul like a corrupting disease and eroded away his conscience.

Lucifer's posture had subtly expanded and he was now the very picture of Pride. He crowed: "Ah, yes, I know the man well. A classic example of a Category C who crashes and burns. As the saying goes: 'The higher you climb, the steeper you fall.'" He put his index finger in the air and swiped it down. "Chalk that one up as a win for Lucifer!"

"You really enjoy bringing the special ones down, don't you?"

"Enjoy? I revel in it! Just because someone achieves a high degree of consciousness doesn't guarantee that they've also developed a corresponding high degree of enlightened morality. When one of them takes a tumble, it's 'drinks all around' in my world. How they fare against my very best temptations depends on one key element."

"Which is?"

"Their Shadowlings. As Jung put it: 'The brighter the Light, the stronger the Shadow.' This so-called teacher of yours is what you get when his Shadowlings were shoved down and denied, when he let his 'rejected selves' fester in the dark and never learned to deal with them."

He paused for effect. "And this brings me to you, Jackson."

Gulp. Here it is . . . why Lucifer was paying me this visit. Bring it on. "Okay, so what's your Game with me?"

He crossed his arms and took my measure. "So, here I am with you, Jackson Trent. There are times when someone is on the verge of breaking free from my Web. The usual systems that are in place have failed to stop their escape. That's when they show up on my radar. In some instances when this happens, I decide to make a personal 'house call.'"

A house call? So that's what this was. I looked down at my wrist and suddenly felt the snake bracelet tightening. "I really want this off."

Lucifer put his hand up. "Hold on, let me finish! All I'm doing today is assessing who you are and what special 'gift' I can offer to attract you to, shall we say, stay within the natural order of things."

"You mean, to keep me playing your Game? So what's your offer?"

"In your case, my gift to you is Power. Feel that *Ouroboros* on your wrist, Jackson. Look closely. *The Cuff of Kosala!* To say it has remarkable capacities and an interesting past is like saying a *Stradivarius* is just a violin or *Hamlet* is simply a play. It has an indescribably amazing history and is imbued with incredible properties. And this is my offer to you. Accept this Cuff and you can discover real Power. But, and this is a big but, it's only as powerful as the person who wields it wants it to be."

I turned my wrist left and right, studying the contours of the snake. "You're wrong about me. I don't want its Power. I have no intention, under any circumstance, to command this Cuff of yours!"

"Sure, so you say... But there's something about your relationship with Power that you're oblivious to, Jackson. Since we've been talking about the Shadow, let me tell you something that pertains to you. Not all the traits that are pushed down that internal 'spiral staircase' into the unconscious are unsavory rejects. There's also a side to it called the *Golden Shadow*—positive aspects of one's nature that have equally been shoved into the Underworld. These are parts of oneself that you'd assume would be on the embraced 'Light' side of their psyche. But for various reasons, for certain people, some of their greatest character assets have become unacceptable."

"Yeah, I know, like born leaders who push away their gifted talent for skillful command because they don't want to assume responsibility. Or self-assured, confident children who end up becoming meek when they're made to feel flawed and deficient by their parents. But what does this have to do with me?"

"You've done the same thing! You pushed your innate Power out of sight. And that precious *mojo* you say you lost? Where do you think it disappeared to? Down into your Golden Shadow. And that's the concealed, covert place in you that I'm zeroing in on, Jackson. Your personal Power is withering away down there. It needs its freedom, so, I'm here to help you invite it back up. You'll thank me later."

Lucifer went back to sipping his beer, studying me intensely over the rim of his stein. I sat there, mulling all this over. My Power... withering away down below? Yeah, I could feel it. Damn it, Lucifer may be on to me. While I mused, I found myself, once again, exploring the contours of the Cuff with my other hand. I began sliding my fingers back and forth along the intricate scales of the Snake. Like a cat that purrs when stroked, my fingertips could sense its humming vibration steadily getting stronger. I had to admit, I was feeling a building curiosity about what astonishing capacities were contained within it. Lucifer sensed the shift in me. He leaned in again.

"You know, Jackson, even after all the work you've done on yourself, all the knowledge you've garnered, you still have this gaping hole in your own development."

"Gaping hole?"

"I'm talking about where you've put your focus. Like so many others, you've only given lip service to your Shadow, in general, and your disowned Power, in particular. Sure, you have a theoretical understanding of your Shadow's existence, but you haven't explored your Underworld. You've basically systematically avoided it, turned a blind eye. Your focus has been in the other direction, chasing the Light. Maybe we can fix that."

On that note, he gave me a sly smile, slid off the bar stool and stood up to leave. The bartender came over and started to slip us our tab, but Lucifer caught his attention and just stared at him for a long moment. The bartender removed our empty steins and said: "It's on the house, gentlemen." I shook my head in disgust at Lucifer once again conniving the system and slipped the barkeep a tip.

As we got back onto the pathway, I was mulling over Lucifer's ominous comment about me, '*Maybe we can fix that.*' After a few minutes, we found ourselves walking past a small, modest church, constructed of black lava stone. A crucifix was affixed to the top of the steeple. I glanced at Lucifer as the church bell rang twice gently in the background.

"So, I'm curious, Lucifer. Don't churches make you uncomfortable?"

"Churches? Nah. I admit some ministers are actually attempting to guide their flock off of my Web. But more times than not, they're simply preaching fear, guilt and shame, which does me a huge favor. *Hello Shadowlings!* They fall like rain into my Underworld. And for every churchgoer who's actually connecting to, you know... *HIM,* there are many more just punching their Sunday 'God clock,' hedging their bets."

On that score, I didn't disagree. "What's the saying? Going to church doesn't make you a religious person any more than standing in a garage makes you a car."

We walked further through a beautiful setting of lush grounds and well-maintained, giant Royal palms. The roar of the ocean added a tropical music to the air. He proposed that we take a seat on a bench in the shade. When we were settled in, Lucifer pointed to the Pacific.

"Look out at that ocean, Jackson. Just imagine how unfathomably deep it is. Now, see that sailboat floating on top of the water? It's only in touch with the surface. That's exactly how the Sheeple experience their world, completely absorbed with the surface of their lives, with no curiosity, no awareness, no exploration of the mysterious vastness below, no interest in the untapped possibilities within themselves. Do you realize you've been Sheeple-like when it comes to your Power?"

"Look Lucifer, I've come to grips with Power and I don't need it."

"Really? Why don't you check in and ask your buried Power if it agrees. Your past experience with that teacher's exploitations clearly left a wound in you, didn't it?"

"A wound? Yeah, something got damaged. Let's call it a blow to trust. And yes, despite all the extraordinary spiritual guides I've been blessed to have had since then, the memory of that unsavory character unfortunately stands out."

"Well, I rest my case. You obviously have an issue with Power."

"I have an issue with its abuse."

"Exactly! In your world, nothing could be worse than the abuse of Power. Makes your blood boil, doesn't it, Jackson? So you've pushed it away, viewing it as repulsive. But, I'll ask you again. Just where do you imagine it got pushed away to?"

Yeah, I understood. It had gotten shoved down into my Underworld. "A few minutes ago, you said that maybe we could 'fix it.' What did you mean by that?"

"Look at me, Jackson. You're ripe to rediscover what you've buried. I'm making you an offer to play my Game at a much higher plane. I want to assist you in realigning with the Creator within you. That *Cuff of Kosala* on your wrist is the fastest track imaginable to rediscovering your true seat of Power."

"That sounds like you're giving me a way to get off of your Web. Why would you volunteer that?"

"No, not exactly. What I'm offering is a way to become incredibly powerful, as a Creator."

"I think I get it . . . wielding power over the other creatures, right?"

Lucifer gave a roguish grin. "Why would you want to escape when you can have everything you want? From my viewpoint, Jackson, you're at a very crucial juncture. You're a rock-solid Category 'B,' moving relentlessly towards the realm of 'C.'"

"So you've come to arrest my development?"

"Well . . . let's look at it from a different perspective. I've come to offer you an incredible opportunity. Your exploratory path has finally brought you squarely to a fork in the road. You can now choose one of two directions. Take the right hand path and, I'll grant you, it leads you in the general direction of Category 'C.' You may find yourself at some point entering the 5th dimension, that so-called 'Cosmic Realm.' But, doesn't that sound very vague and, if you think about it, downright terrifying? Losing one's familiar sense of self! For what? For whom? Who would you become? Why take that chance?"

Interesting. The oh-so crafty Lucifer was actually painting a picture of full-on 'Awakening' as a perilous, risky and alarming proposition. To the 'little me' within, he was right. He continued with his pitch.

"Ah! But imagine, Jackson, what can happen if you take the left-hand path? This would elevate you to a very special plateau within Category B. All kinds of incredible opportunities can open up, if only you let them! Look around you. You're living on a planet full of Sheeple! That already puts you head and shoulders above the sleepy masses. Why not take full advantage of your knowledge? How? Merge your growing sense of Presence with the inherent Power in the *Cuff of Kosala*, and the world is your oyster!"

As he spoke, I could feel some deep-seated instinctive part of myself quivering with excitement at what he was proposing. He wasn't finished:

"Do you really want to let your ego dissolve, and become some amorphous 'Cosmic' entity? Boring! Or do you wish to remain as the familiar man that you are, only now electrified and infused with real Power in the world over anything you want and anyone you choose? Is there really any choice?" He put his arm around my shoulder, pulling me towards him, like a trusted *compadre*. "Don't be a fool. Come my way. Become a real Player! Take the left-hand path."

Okay, now his agenda was coming into focus, and why he wanted me to understand his three Categories. Seduction, or more to the point . . . seduction using Power. Something akin to: *Here you go. It's all yours. Just don't leave my Web.*

I squirmed out of his grasp. Lucifer glanced at his watch. "Well, think about it, Jackson. It's entirely your call. No need to decide this moment . . . Oh, there's somewhere close by I want us to get to, but we have get a move on."

I followed Lucifer's lead as we made our way towards the beach, which was just over the little dune. The sun was sinking in the western sky, its reflection now creating a golden triangle on the surface of the ocean. It felt nice to be back at the beach again. As we walked through the sand, I was reflecting upon how different this 'gentlemanly' Lucifer was to be around in this version of himself. I felt as though I could *almost* let my guard down. But I was also pondering our conversation about Power. I knew Lucifer was drawing me into something but I wasn't sure what it was. I studied the *Ouroboros* on my wrist and I heard myself reiterate my position: *I have free will. He can't make me use this Cuff.*

As we neared the water's edge, I could see that there was a reef directly in front of us, a good place for snorkeling. I found my attention being drawn to someone who was knee-deep in the waves, staring out to sea. There was something odd about this woman's movements. She was pointing and waving her arms wildly. I looked out to where she was gesturing. Then, I saw a head bobbing in the water and knew instantly what had happened. Someone was caught in a riptide... a strong one! This swimmer was being carried and swept away on the rip current, a powerful underwater river created by certain wave patterns. Now the woman's screams were audible. "*My baby! My baby!!*"

I turned to Lucifer who was watching the drama with a keen eye and I yelled in his face:

"*Do something! DO SOMETHING, for chrissake!*"

Lucifer studied his fingernails for a moment.

"Jackson, I don't ever interfere in life or death situations."

"Come on, damn it! I know you can do something!"

"No Jackson, I can't. More to the point, I won't. But you... you could do something! You could create something. You know who that is out there? It's a young girl, about 10 years old. Hmmm... Isn't that the age that your daughter was? Oh, and if you're going to act, I'd do it soon. Take a look. She needs your help in the worst way!"

I felt the snap of his trap closing. He knew about my daughter and had never said so. Lucifer's expression was so smug, his manipulation unfolding perfectly. I gave him a murderous look, then turned back to the ocean to see how far the little swimmer had been swept away. Standing behind me, his breath on my neck, Lucifer advised:

"Remember, what activates the Snake is the strength of your intention. The trick is to envision exactly what you want to take place . . . exactly! Then, point your left arm where you want the Power directed. Push that clarified vision out of your mind, through your eyes and down your arm. Done correctly, as your intention passes through the *Cuff of Kosala*, it'll fire off your command. *Capiche?*"

The mother was frantically jumping through the waves. I raced to catch her, pulling her back to the safety of the beach. Spinning around to see where her daughter was, my heart sank as she now was being sucked out into the rough, roiling waters. Shielding my eyes from the sun, I began focusing on her little head, bobbing up and down. With intense concentration, my eyesight gradually became crystal clear, and from this ultra-lucid state, I generated a vision: *make the riptide change direction and flow back towards the beach.* Raising my left arm, I pointed it directly at her and poured my clarified intention into the Cuff: *Bring her back this way!*

At first, I thought my arm went numb, but, no . . . . It actually felt intensely dense, packed with an unfamiliar pulsation. Then, I sensed an enlivened, dynamic stimulation in my lower belly, followed by a massive rush of potent energy that shot up my spine and rocketed down my arm. As it passed through the Cuff at my wrist, this powerful dynamism seemed to ignite, exploding out my fingertips like a pistol shot. *Whoa! What was that?* I stood there, rooted in that position, arm outstretched, until the electrified energy finally subsided. As I watched the girl helplessly waving her arms and gasping for air, my heart ached for this youngster being carried off to where the wild surf was waiting to swallow her up.

Then, as if she was suddenly riding the back of a giant sea turtle, the girl began slowly knifing through the water in our direction. Sweeping to the left in a curling arc, the current brought her all the way back around, delivering her to the edge of the beach where we stood. As the girl touched the sandy bottom, her mother dove into the shallow water, scooping her up in her arms and just rocked and rocked in a tight embrace, smothering her child with an occasional explosion of kisses. The image of them together, entwined in such utter relief and joy, unexpectedly hit me like a blow. I had not been there for my daughter, no ecstatic hug for her. I stood there, swirling in a mix of bewildered happiness and a resurgence of my own grief. In a slow lope, Lucifer approached me.

"Amazing! Well done! Beyond my expectations! You know the story of 'The Sorcerer's Apprentice?' It's usually like that with most of my protégé's on their first attempt at commanding the Cuff. *Look out! Duck everyone!* But your intention was awesome. You really created that and look how the Snake responded! Even I'm impressed. So tell me . . . . How did it feel, Jackson, to do something so heroically noble, to use your Power to save a life?"

I said nothing, but inside I was dazzled, as if the genie had escaped the bottle. My whole body was tingling, a live wire. How did I feel?

Like someone taking their very first hit off a crack pipe!

CHAPTER 10

Freefall

Embrace the unexpected. The things we never saw coming often take us to the places we never imagined we could go.

—Unknown

SITTING ON THE WET SAND, I ALLOWED THE INCOMING surf to swirl around my legs. There was something soothing about the water lapping against my skin and it calmed me. I stared, wide-eyed, at the Snake on my wrist, trying to get a grip on what I had just done. Did that really happen, using this amulet to save that girl? I glanced away from the ocean in time to see the mother and her daughter, arm-in-arm, disappearing around the curve of the beach, happily heading home. Yes, that mysterious, mystical incident had taken place, alright. It was odd how an astounding experience could be simultaneously terrifying and exhilarating.

Strangely, this event lifted a big weight off my shoulders. It was as if a whole sack of guilt had been neutralized through this karmic event—that I had played a hand in this rescue. Feeling the surge of Power that had shot through my body into the *Cuff of Kosala,* and then watching it create what I had commanded it to do, was what had made it so exhilarating. But what had made it so terrifying?

Damn! I had just tapped into some kind of awesome energy source that could override the basic laws of nature! That young girl had been literally towed into shore by an unknown Force that was stronger than the sweeping clutches of a riptide, an ocean current so powerful that it's impossible to swim against. That encounter was so outside of my normal frame of reference that I had nothing to contrast it to, leaving my mind feeling blown. I sat there, rattled and mystified, staring vacantly out to sea. Wow. Power . . . what a heady brew that can be!

What Lucifer had described was now coming back to me: how we shove underground the parts of ourselves that we've rejected. It's one thing to push something away with your mind, moving it out of your field of awareness, pretending it doesn't exist. But it's quite another to actually experience the moment when this 'disowned self' rears up from below and breaks out into the open. Like a few minutes ago, when temptation and circumstance had overcome my resistance and I found myself taking a bite out of that rejected apple.

Although I could still feel my long-standing aversion to Power, and my attempt to push it back underground, there was an unmistakable thrilling excitement coming up from the Shadows, the 'piece of the apple' still tart in my mouth. Oh man . . . . What business did I have messing with a Force like this? None. And yet . . .

Lucifer cut into my thought stream. "Jackson, did it ever occur to you that you think too much? Just keep it simple! Look, you're overly fixated on rejecting Power because so many others have been abusive with it, right?"

"That's a big part of it, yeah. I don't want to become one of them."

"Okay, so here's your chance to show the world a different example . . . a benevolent one! Why not imagine directing this Power in the interest of good? It's yours to channel in whatever manner you choose. I really don't care what you do with it! My interest is not how you use it; it's just seeing that you do use it, one way or another."

"And that's because?"

"Because then, you'll come to love it . . . and in its own way, the Snake will come to love you. If you're disgusted with those who abuse Power, well, then, set an example of the proper usage of it. Show them how you are above reproach. Are you strong enough within yourself to make that kind of stand, that sort of claim? You judge corruptibility, but are you incorruptible?"

Good question, I thought quietly. The truth? I'm not really sure. How could I know how I'd respond?

"Talk is so cheap, Jackson. Hey, I get your resistance. It's understandable that you've a righteous indignation about how Power corrupts. It's true. It can. It does. But, look at it this way. In a world desperate for help, just imagine what you could actualize for the highest good of everyone! Or are you one of those who hides behind the limp excuse of 'I'm just not ready?' In my experience, there's being 'not ready' and then there's 'being ready, but needing a boost.' It's a simple question. Are you, Jackson Trent, corruptible or not?"

I closed my eyes, trying to let his question sink in, but he kept up the pressure. "Can you actually walk away from this test? No, it goes against your very nature. You love a challenge. All your metaphysical training has brought you to this very doorstep and you know it! What the hell were you 'working on yourself' for if not this very opportunity?"

There was something unnerving about the way Lucifer could frame his point with irrefutable logic, presenting it in such a way that, even when I'm itching to refuse, the answer 'no' is not an option. Damn it! What he just said about using the Power of the Cuff for the good of the world actually resonated within me. And now that he planted the seed, I could sense my resistance starting to weaken. But then, what makes me think that inviting Power into my life, and at this level, won't end up being a colossal mistake? I could hear my inner Wisdom Voice saying: *Jackson, one word . . . RUN!*

Lucifer just sat there, patiently biding his time, looking satisfied. That didn't bode well for me.

"You know Lucifer, when you look pleased, I get nervous."

"Me? Look pleased? Well, maybe it's because I've been following your train of thought. Yes, you took a 'bite out of the apple.' And you're right about something, Jackson: this is not a dress rehearsal . . . this is your life. As I always advise people: *Time is precious. Waste it wisely!* And I'll tell you something I normally don't reveal: with that Cuff, you've already shown the makings of an exceptional Creator. I mean that."

My 'little Jackson' and compliments—what a duo, those two! It made me start laughing, as I was suddenly aware of how quickly I was following the sweet aroma of temptation. Damn, he was good. Serve me up with a juicy proposition based on reasonable logic, put it in the form of a challenge and feed my vanity just enough. I turned to face Lucifer:

"My compliments on your stellar skill at baiting my hook. You've got this down to an art, don't you? Dangle the wrong bait and, like a finicky trout, we don't bite. Ah, but the right bait . . . "

Lucifer's face took on a glow. "My 'fishing technique' is successful because my strategy's simple. I just offer what each person unconsciously wants. You'd call that manipulative, but I call it being generous. Everybody has a weakness for something. For you, although you're, as yet, unaware of it . . . it's Power. For others, it might be unleashing their buried Revenge against someone who screwed them over, or their smoldering Hatred that goes with it. Or, maybe someone shy and reserved wants to finally let loose their repressed Aggression."

"And in so doing, you shepherd the Sheeple into sabotaging their lives! Releasing their Shadowlings is your life's work."

"My Game is never boring. But don't miss the forest for the trees. For you, Jackson, my aim isn't to sabotage. You're not Sheeple; you're unique to me. I have a different plan in mind for you. As I said, I'm inviting you to play the Game on a much higher level, the chance to become a Creator! You're not craving the usual power over others. I admit, that's a 'first,' a novel and intriguing approach I haven't seen before, but I'm perfectly okay with it! So then open up your exploration using the *Kosala Cuff* and create some outcomes that are benevolent in nature. Be heroic! There are only two types of people who would turn down this kind of offer—fools or cowards. Don't disappoint me and turn out to be one of those."

"Well, I think there's a third type: someone rational who has a strong self-preservation gene. Someone who says: 'I don't care how attractive the bait is. I'm in too deep and I'm outta here!'"

Lucifer's eyes softened and in a voice dripping with syrup, he said coyly: "But that's not you, is it Jackson?"

He was right about that. I've always been drawn to the edge of things. On the physical plane, that evolved into 'edgy' pursuits: mountain climbing, motorcycles, kayaking the ocean and wild rivers, to name a few. But, simultaneously, there's been a corresponding 'inner adventurer' inside me, a ridiculously curious investigator who's even more willing to explore, push the boundaries of my consciousness, take calculated risks within the internal landscape of my soul. This pathway taught me much, in both the inner and outer worlds: how to be nimble, how to scout terrain, the value of an excellent map, how to adjust to changing conditions, how to read people and spot bullshit, when to ask for help, how to really listen, how to get back up after being knocked down, how (or if) to cross bridges into unfamiliar environments that suddenly appear, how to muster courage or be afraid and yet hang in there.

"I think I'd put myself into the fool category, Lucifer. Not because I'm turning down your offer, but because I haven't yet. I'm at least willing to carry on with this conversation for a while, even though you've already repeatedly played me like a violin. What was it you said this morning about temptation, that we're suckers for it?"

"Ah temptation. Why does it work so well? One big reason is that humans are hardwired with a stimulus-response mechanism. So, of course, I use that to my advantage. I stimulate, or bait if you prefer, and you respond with a knee-jerk reactivity. That's the very nature of my Web. And here's the beautiful part: a person is either taking the bait or busy pushing it away. Either way, they're unwittingly immersed in playing my Game."

"So you make sure the unconscious stays in the dark, systematically releasing Shadowlings from below, inviting them up, inviting them in. 'Here you go, folks, your Shadowling of choice!'"

"Right! I'm the dungeon master with the ring of keys who acts counter-intuitively. I keep unlocking and swinging open your cell doors, encouraging whoever or whatever is in that prison cage, to come on out. 'You're free to go!' I'm just encouraging everyone to release forgotten parts of themselves that are dying for some fresh air."

"Only to wreak havoc in their life once you turn them loose."

Lucifer spread out his palms and shrugged. "That's not my problem! That's what people deserve for shoving vital parts of themselves into the Shadows. If, by having been rejected, these traits have turned into nasty creatures . . . well, *c'est la vie!*"

"Let me see if I've got this straight. I appeared on your radar because of my committed exploration of the 4th dimension of consciousness.

I've put a premium on waking up to the state of Presence. And the more Present I become, the more I lift off and out of your deceptive Web. Ah, but escaping is not something you're going to allow. So lucky me! You come visit to personally reel me back in with the greatest bait you can offer—Power. So why would I allow myself to be 'honey-trapped' in this way? Don't you think I see through what you're doing here? I get the sense that you want to me to stop writing, trying to help others through my blog. You hope I get all tangled up in using this Cuff. Get myself in way over my ability to control it so my worst nightmare unfolds and Power ultimately corrupts me. Right?"

"Look, that's what's so interesting for both of us, Jackson! There's always the chance that you might not be corruptible! Then what? This Cuff of Power I'm offering might be the very ticket that rockets you completely out of my Web! In fact, you could become a *problem* for me, but I'm willing to take that risk . . . I see you're still resistant. Why?"

"Because wielding this form of Power is screwing around with the natural order of things. Who am I to say what's a beneficial outcome anyway? What if my positive outcome in one area makes things worse for others in another?"

Lucifer bent over, stretching forward like a flexible yogi. Then he rose up abruptly. "Okay, fine. But I think you're ready for this. I'd tell you if you weren't."

He led us through a small park filled with people enjoying the fine late afternoon. Lucifer was quietly, but very attentively, watching, taking it all in through some filter of his own. I asked him:

"So, you must see Shadowlings everywhere you look?"

"Sure, I do. And you don't?"

"Not really, but then, I'm not looking for them, either."

"What's that John Lennon line? 'Living is easy with eyes closed.' Just look around you. The effect of Shadowlings infiltrating people's lives is everywhere."

"Show me."

Scanning the crowd, Lucifer stopped and pointed. "Okay, for starters . . . here's a simple example. Look at the outside deck of that pizza joint on the corner. See the man at the end table? The piece of pizza he's stuffing in his mouth, that's the sixth slice he's eaten. If he could hear his stomach right now, it's begging for him to stop. From a hunger standpoint, he had enough three slices ago. But he won't quit because his gluttony won't let him. That temptation for more is too strong an influence and he can't control it, so it drowns out all sense of balance and proportion, let alone the little voice inside him that's saying '*Stop!*' There's still half of an extra-large deep-dish pizza in front of him and he's going to plow his way right through all of it. Then, in about half an hour, when he finally, slowly, gets up to leave, he'll be subjected to a heavy Inner Critic attack of harsh self-loathing, as, just this morning, he swore that today would be different, given that he's diabetic. Classic self-sabotaging! Beautiful. See how it works?"

Yeah, I could see it, although I, frankly, would never have noticed that. I was about to respond when my head swiveled on its own accord as a hot, sexy woman sauntered by. Lucifer's snicker was directed at me.

"Ah, I see you just met the seductress! Scantily clad and oh-so revealing of her shapely figure. Notice her walk, that suggestive swish of the hips. See how she's subtly scanning the faces of the men, just like you, as they turn to 'drink her in'? Can you feel your own Lust coming up? That coy little smile she offers back to her appreciative and salivating audience has just a hint of 'possibilities' in it, making each man feel as though he had a sliver of a chance. This increases their rapt focus and the little vixen soaks it up like a sponge. This provocative woman is the very picture of utter confidence, right? Who would know that she's actually wracked with insecurity? She just can't get enough of attracting male attention. Seduction is her drug of choice; it's her addiction, but it stems from a desperate need to constantly feed her acute narcissism.

She has a huge 'hole in her soul' that she constantly tries to fill up with all this incoming male energy. It never really works, as that hole is essentially bottomless. Too bad for her, but it can't ever be filled."

Lucifer pivoted to the left. "Okay, how about some family dynamics? There!"

I turned to follow where he pointed. A family of three was crossing the street. The father was a military man, dressed in causal army fatigues. His gait was stiff and full of purpose, almost a kind of 'march' as he led the way across the intersection. The wife followed in his wake, shoulders stooped, a kind of meekness to her demeanor. Bringing up the rear, a teenage daughter lagged behind at a leisurely pace of her own, her long, blond wild hair streaked with bright purple and ear buds pumping music into her head. 'Dad' turned and gestured, in no uncertain terms, for her to hurry up, to which she slowed her pace noticeably.

Lucifer opined, "This family's an interesting mix. There you have the father, who clearly envisions himself as the 'commanding officer' of his family. As such, he issues orders and demands obedience. Those are the rules of his military profession and, consequently, those are the *same* rules he brings home and lays down for his wife and child. His wife has, long ago, capitulated her own personal will in order to 'toe the line' but is now lost in a kind of depressed martyr role, long-suffering and silently miserable. Her building rage towards her domineering mate is carefully and methodically shoved down into her Shadow where it's not going to cause trouble . . . not yet, but give it a few years! *Look out!*"

"The daughter . . . she's her Dad's worst nightmare, right?"

Lucifer gave me a 'thumbs up'. "Right! A born rebel. Where the father demands obedience, what he gets from her, instead, is massive resistance. In place of a snappy *Yes sir!* her response is more of an *Up yours!* Where Dad sees the world as 'straight and narrow,' this girl perceives her reality through a shifting kaleidoscope, a wide open surreal view, all of which is leading her into various teenage 'explorations' that would make her father go ballistic if he knew. So, the Lieutenant Colonel and his young rebel clash at every turn. The relaxed, fun-loving part of the father that could actually understand and connect with his daughter is buried deep, locked away in the underworld of his unconscious Shadow. He loathes and stamps out any hint of rebellion in the soldiers under his command. And the daughter? Buried in her Shadow is the 'obedient good girl,' so the two of them are always in conflict."

There was something very familiar about this particular family dynamic that gave me a sharp emotional sting. But there was also a counter perspective I had to shoot back to Lucifer:

"I get your point. But, you know what? You're missing something. We're surrounded by more than Shadowlings running the show. Do you ever notice or acknowledge the good and sweet side of human nature?"

Lucifer looked absolutely contemptuous. "Sweet side? It's not my interest. So, no, I don't notice it. Like what?"

Now it was my turn to scan the afternoon throng. It took no time at all for an image to jump out at me.

"That woman on the sidewalk pushing the wheel chair? You can tell that that's her child, as, even with the cerebral palsy contortions of her young son, there's a physical resemblance. Look at the mother's face. Yes, it's lined with worry that probably never ceases with her challenging role, but note the look of devoted determination, a compassionate caring born of the love she holds for her child who has been dealt such a tough hand. Do you see that?"

Lucifer just shrugged but I could tell he had taken it in.

"And over there, the bus stop on the corner? See that young couple helping the old man with the cane up the steps of the bus? Check it out. In one simple gesture, they're exhibiting a handful of great human qualities: kindness, patience, sensitivity, a gracious thoughtfulness, not to mention basic respect for an elder."

Lucifer gave me a blank look. "And you think these human virtues are more prevalent than the driving force of the Shadow?"

"What I think is that you're myopic, that you only focus on the negative and are hopelessly oblivious to anything else. It's your blind spot. You've buried away 'Lucifer the Light Bearer' of long ago, who could have seen the good in humanity."

He crossed his arms. "Wow... amazing. Is the world this full of charity and good intentions that I just don't notice?"

Well, maybe I was getting through to the Dark Lord. I was about to answer him when I felt a tug on my shirt. I looked down into the face of a little boy, maybe six or seven, with a head of curly brown hair and a frightened expression. "S'cuse me mister, but I'm lost!" The lad was on the verge of tears and I knelt down to be at eye level with him.

"Hey, don't worry, son. Are your parents here somewhere?"

He wiped his runny nose with his sleeve. "Yeah, they were right over there a minute ago."

I tousled his hair. "Okay. Tell you what. Would you like to sit up on my shoulders and we'll see if we can find them?" His little face broke into a grin and I hoisted him up. Before I could ask him what they looked like, I heard a cry from across the street: *"Brian!"* The boy squealed, waving with both hands. *"Mommy!"* I set him back down on the pavement as the parents raced across the traffic. The lad's father shook my hand enthusiastically and the mother gave me a sweet 'thank you' hug. We chatted pleasantly for a minute about our vacations and then they took their leave, the father giving the boy a stern warning about not wandering off.

Lucifer had said nothing throughout this little episode and I half expected him to acknowledge that maybe people *can* be kind to each other. Instead he simply said: "How's your wallet?"

"Huh?" I reached for my back pocket and got that sickening, cold jolt; it was empty!

"Brian, the little darling, stole it while you were chatting up the parents. They're working the crowd as a team. The kid's pretty good. You didn't feel a thing!"

"Shit!" I raced across the street, dodging cars and dashed down the sidewalk, just catching a glimpse of the trio rounding the far corner. When I caught up with them, pumped with an angry adrenaline, I grabbed the father by the shoulder, swung him around and gave him a look that I don't often reveal in my life. Through clenched teeth, I whispered: "Give it back!" We stared at each other for a long moment. His assessment of my mood seemed to register and he wisely didn't bother protesting his innocence. Quietly reaching into his wife's bag, he pulled out my wallet and handed it over. Then, in perfect unison, they turned and vanished into the crowd like ghosts. When I got back to Lucifer, I just looked at him and said evenly:

"You just always have to have the upper hand, don't you? I don't even want to know what Shadow qualities would bring parents to the point of turning their six year-old into a scamming thief! Is this the kind of thing that you get off on, seeing a whole family involved in a life of crime?"

"You keep getting it wrong, Jackson. You want to blame me for their nefarious actions? If that couple insists on being unaware of the Shadow side of themselves, then, sure, I'm delighted to help them along. Like I said, I open doors and, in their case, out comes their inner 'thief.'"

"I feel very sorry for that boy."

"Oh, he'll be fine." Lucifer snickered. "If nothing else, he can serve as a bad example to others!"

I reached for my pack. "Let's get out of here. I want to return to the *Mahana Kai.*"

We needed a cab to get back to the resort. Unfortunately, they were scarce in this town and there was a long line of tourists at the main taxi stand. Trudging to the end of the queue, I groaned: "We're going to be in this line for hours." Lucifer just kept on walking. When he got to the very front of the line, his legs suddenly buckled, and someone caught him as he fell. I ran up to see what was happening, as a small crowd was gathering around. Someone shouted: "Give him some air!" Lucifer's face was ghastly white and he clutched the front of his shirt in tremoring spasms.

In a wheezy croak he muttered: "My heart pills!"

A woman who had the skilled bearing of a doctor was taking control. "Where are they, sir? Tell me!"

"Back at the *(cough, cough)* hotel," is all he could muster.

The woman looked up at me. "Are you with him?" I slowly nodded. She and the man who was first in line lifted Lucifer up and eased him into the back seat of the arriving cab.

"Get him back to your hotel as fast as you can!"

With what appeared to be his last reserves of strength, Lucifer clasped the woman's hand in his. "You're too kind." he whispered. She blushed, giving his shoulders a last adjustment for comfort.

"Don't worry. You'll be okay," she smiled tenderly. I slid into the front seat and we were soon zipping along the road, heading for the resort. Lucifer sat up, straightening out the creases in his silk shirt, looking rather pleased with himself. I should have known.

"Different persona, same conscious prick, huh? You just have to manipulate."

"I won't deny it. It's kind of a sport for me."

Fortunately, our cabbie was the silent type because I didn't feel like talking any more. My mind kept returning to the memory of that family of the military man back in town. I could always tell when some kind of realization was knocking on my door, trying to work its way in.

There was a familiarity I had picked up about their family dynamic: the domineering father and the rebellious child. It churned up buried memories of my own upbringing. My father had also been a military man, an officer in Vietnam. After the war, he'd left the service, but all his ingrained training, discipline, and sense of duty he'd taken with him.

Being Catholic, he and my mother had a large brood of children. Within the chaos of a bunch of kids in a small house, my father's management style was to maintain order through a military mindset. Our home was thus regulated with laws and rules; above all, obedience was mandatory. The price for non-compliance was punishment.

I was the middle kid, lost in the pack. What made me eventually stand out, however, was my rebellious streak. My nature was a buzzing ball of kinetic energy, a wild child, who could run like the wind and, also like the wind, couldn't stay still for long. I probably was A.D.D., but it was back before there was any concept of that diagnosis in children. I was simply trouble, which continually put me squarely into the crosshairs of my father's disapproving anger. I didn't help matters with my tendency to challenge his authority regularly. His response was always heavy-handed, exerting all his power to break my wild nature and bring me into line. Unfortunately for both of us, what he hadn't counted on was that his little son had a warrior spirit too, just like him, only packaged in reverse as a rebel.

So, out of his increasing levels of discipline, a power struggle emerged between us. From mid-grade school all through my high school years, we fought bitterly. When I finally packed up and left for college, the battle was suddenly over. I was now out of his fiefdom. He'd done the very best he could in the only way he knew how, trying to straighten out what he considered to be 'defective' in me. He just had a very limited repertoire of parenting skills, a 'tool box' with only a hammer. It's an awful thing to be locked into an ongoing conflict as a youth, with power clashing against power; pitting yourself against a parent whom, in the heat of battle, you swear you hate and yet love so deeply at your core. Like many children from combative upbringings, my wounds were hidden, yet they had left deep inner scars.

This had been my introduction to Power. In battling my father, I had developed at least one form of it and yet it had exhausted me, leaving a bitter taste. Power to me meant conflict. I came out of my childhood with the conclusion that I didn't want 'power over' others, nor would I ever allow anyone to have power over me. So, I had shoved my Power, with it all its strength and vitality, down and away into my Shadow world, out of my sight, out of my range of choices in my life. I could now see how this early family struggle was one more reason that, to this day, I was indeed disowning my Power, why I had developed an inherent distrust of it. And no wonder . . .

Today's events were 'stirring the pot' inside me. Earlier, I had recalled the episode of my spiritual teacher who had turned so corrupt. Now memories from my childhood battlefield were also surfacing. All my buried stuff around Power was starting to emerge. I was getting flashes of how the loss of that vital force had adversely influenced my life, squeezing off my innate dynamism. I wondered how that had affected my relationships, in general, and Chloe, in particular? I needed to get centered. Closing my eyes, I relaxed and felt the breeze flowing through the window of the cab as we drove through the winding curves of the Hawaiian landscape, on our way back to the *Mahana Kai.* After a few minutes, a question popped into my head.

"So, Lucifer, from your perspective, what do you think about meditation?"

He scowled. "Hate it."

He didn't seem to want to elaborate, so I pressed the issue. "You hate it . . . why?"

"Because it works against me. Part of my secret sauce for keeping people in a sleepy state is how their mind ceaselessly cranks out thoughts, like a bad TV channel that spins out inane drivel. Meditation disrupts this mental chatter, and can actually allow the mind to quiet down! And just what do you think starts to happen then?"

"Well, when we meditate, the vibration of our energy field expands. The mind begins to settle. Not something you advocate, I assume?"

"You got that right. Breathing has to remain shallow. A tactic to holding people in my Web is keeping an undercurrent of a low-grade tension going. Generally, the five senses are constantly bombarded with incoming stimuli. In meditation, with the senses resting, the mind quieting down, and breathing going deep into the belly . . . stillness can materialize. That's troubling for me, because out of that stillness, a 'spaciousness' can open up. And what do you think that brings on?"

"I'd say that the nature of spaciousness is that it expands outwardly what we normally perceive as our 'boundaries.' And that's something you just can't tolerate, right?"

"Of course. Mental boundaries are the walls that hold everyone inside their ego shell. They keep Sheeple being . . . well . . . *Sheeple!* If the walls start to disappear in meditation, people can actually feel the expanded state of consciousness and that, damn it, is what enables them to start escaping my Web!"

"No wonder you hate meditation, but I wouldn't worry about it. I suspect many meditators don't actually increase their vibration much at all, let alone come anywhere near lifting off your Web."

Lucifer perked up. "Oh really? Why?"

"From my own struggles with meditation, I find the mind is so slippery, like a greased eel. Getting it to quiet down is way more challenging than it seems. I can look like I'm deep in meditation, but trying to stop thoughts is like trying to stop efforting. I end up thinking about trying not to think!"

Lucifer gave out a short laugh. "Well, that's exactly why I don't really concern myself about it too much. Most people just can't do it.

And besides, even if someone 'lifts off' in meditation, they usually drop right back down and return onto my Web, where they step back into their sleepy lives."

"And what about prayer, Lucifer? Now, *that* must really bother you having folks praying every time they feel the need to get some support."

He seemed to ponder that one for a long moment. Then: "Like meditation, it depends on their intention. There's the typical kind of prayer where somebody is just reading 'to the heavens' their laundry list of what they want. That doesn't budge their vibration needle very much. When I hear that kind of prayer going on, I like to jump in with my whisper: *Excuse me, but God is busy. May I help you?* But when it's prayer flowing through the heart, like when a person's praying for someone else's well-being, then I've got problems. That can generate such a powerful vibration that it catapults them right off my Web. I can't stand that! Fortunately, like meditators, this person rarely recognizes that internal expansion and quickly returns to where I want them when their annoying little prayer session is over."

"Well, I feel like meditating and if my vibration annoys you . . . as you say, deal with it!"

Lucifer said nothing but, whoa, speaking of strong vibrations! I could feel his displeasure behind me, like a volcanic mountain, beginning to rumble. I glanced over at our cab driver, wondering what he thought of this peculiar conversation, but his placid face gave nothing away. He was focused on the road. I glanced at the speedometer. His driving at 60 mph was way too fast for my comfort zone, given all the twists and turns, but he seemed capable enough.

Settling back into my meditation, my busy mind kept returning to the event on the beach with the young swimmer. I was still baffled how my intense wish to save her had become the Snake's command. I could still feel the awesome surge of power shooting through my wrist to bring her back to shore. *Shhhhhhh . . . Let it go. Breathe deep.*

It was the slamming on of brakes and the horrible sound of tires squealing that jolted my eyes wide open! On a sharp, hairpin curve, a bicyclist had appeared on our side of the road, taking up a good three feet of space in our lane. Meanwhile, a big, wide truck was lumbering towards us in the opposite direction, giving our cab no room to move to the left. It was the 'perfect storm' for an accident. It seemed that we had no choice but to crash into the bicyclist.

Seconds before impact, a turnout appeared on our right side, one of those panoramic view lookout stops. Our driver swerved to the right, missing the biker by an inch, as the taxi shot into the tiny gravel parking area. But as he banked hard left on the gritty rocks, it increased our sliding.

In a cloud of dust, the car skidded wildly, completely out of control. Just before smashing into a wooden guardrail on my side, I got a sickening glimpse of how high up on the edge of a towering cliff we were. The rail shattered into splinters as we plowed through it. Then . . . we were airborne! There may be no stranger feeling than a moment like that. I had a terrifying sensation of freefall as our car sailed straight out horizontally for a few seconds . . . and then dropped like a stone.

I could hear the driver crying out to his God in a language I didn't understand. Whipping my head around, I saw Lucifer in the backseat, an unperturbed grin on his face! He was pointing to something. His wrist. *The Cuff!* Without a moment's hesitation, I lifted up my left arm and as we plunged headlong towards the rocky boulders far below, a command gathered itself within me with tremendous force and power. With my arm aimed at the hood of our car, I cried out:

"SAVE US!" and braced for impact.

Then . . . my soul exploded open.

CHAPTER 11

The Long Descent...Upward

One new perception, one fresh thought,
one act of surrender, one change of heart, one leap of faith,
can change your life forever.

—Robert Holden

It takes a car less than five seconds to plunge a thousand feet. A blink of an eye! But in such a moment of utterly bewildering shock, strange things can happen. Time can expand exponentially, becoming elastic, breaking us out of our familiar space/time continuum. Seconds can unfurl and stretch. Consciousness, itself, can split wide open. Indeed, it's said that some people, within the span of a few heartbeats, see their entire life unwind before their eyes! Possible? Yes . . . after today, now I'm sure of it.

As our car whistled through the air in total freefall, my frenzied thoughts could barely keep up with my abject terror! It was all happening way too fast! As we rocketed downward, the nose of the car tilted to the right, plastering my face against the side window, giving my bulging eyes a view of the black lava rocks looming directly below. That was the exact moment when the absolute certainty of my impending death registered.

I . . . am going . . . to die!

The truth of that realization exploded an ungodly blast of fear and adrenaline through my entire body, my hair standing on end! Then something shifted, as if that explosion also blew the doors off of my consciousness. With just a sliver of time left in my life, everything suddenly slowed down, *waaay* down, until Time itself was obliterated!

In this new, extraordinary state, it wasn't the past memories of my life that appeared to me. It was the Present, that mysterious, illusive point of aliveness I've been exploring all my life. The Present burst open with such vivid intensity, and a camouflaged part of my deepest inner nature surged to the surface. I felt a powerful internal expansion open up, and then . . .

With eyes closed, my freaked-out, pounding heart was suddenly being held within the tender, loving embrace of a much larger Awareness. 'I' now felt wrapped in strong, gentle, protective arms. The immediate effect of this beautiful holding was a shift within my gut. That sickening feeling of dropping like a stone effortlessly morphed into a peaceful sensation of floating.

A shimmer of soothing calm rippled out, spreading across my inner world, creating, oddly, a sense of feeling totally settled, as if all was well. It wasn't as though I became oblivious to the fact that my life was about to end. No, it was this indefinable Awareness that swung open a portal inside me. And through this opening, Truth came flooding in. What first came to light was a profound sense of gratitude—for my life, for the loved ones in it, for the privilege of having been on Earth for a time. I so love being alive!

Following quickly on the heels of that gratefulness came a surge of regret—apologies never made, unfulfilled dreams, emotions I've suppressed, uttering 'I love you' not nearly enough. And out of this aching wave arose the greatest regret of all the time wasted along the way, not being Present. Why only at the end of life am I coming to fully realize that the present moment is all there really is? I had known this but how deeply had I been living that knowing? As I had passed through the decades of my life, all my incessant mental wanderings back into the past and forward into the future had had me sleepwalking through so much of the vital, electrifying Present.

With unflinching clarity, I saw how fear and procrastination have kept me lodged within the confined shell of my little Self. Yes, I had expanded my consciousness countless times, taking forays into the next dimension of Awareness, but always slip-sliding back, retreating within the habitual walls of my familiar egoic life. Time after time, I had lifted from the 3rd dimension into the 4th to bask in the state of Presence. But I would always succumb to that gravitational pull and drop back down. I never mustered quite enough nerve to stay out, to leave the shell behind and allow Presence to take the wheel of my life, once and for all anchoring me in my True Self . . . in Being.

In my last microseconds of life, finally owning this failing of mine triggered a powerful burst of courage in my chest. I felt suddenly *lion-hearted.* All fear instantly vanished, liquefied by the heat of my heart now on fire, my own awakening aliveness suddenly expanding out far beyond the boundaries of my body. In this lit up place, I could feel the palpable power of this larger field of Awareness, holding me with such strength and benevolence. It called to me:

Jackson . . . Let go. Come home.

I began to just surrender. And then, slicing through my mind like a sharp knife through butter:

"Jackson, come back! NOW!!"

It was the unmistakable voice of Lucifer, commanding, no demanding. I felt a magnetic force reeling me back from the brink. But my new Awareness was not to be denied. A whisper so soft and yet irresistibly welcoming was again caressing my heart:

Let go, Jackson . . . Come home. Come . . .

Yes . . . home! I relinquished my hold on my life and eased into a natural collapsing. I felt willing to abdicate my individuality as a physical Beingness and dive into the deeper Mystery. As I simply let go, I sensed myself sinking, then dissolving into the velvety stillness of pure Awareness. And then, through some enchanting magic, an extraordinary transformation took place: 'I' became the field of Awareness! Jackson, and all his personal history, were lovingly absorbed.

Who was I now?

This Awareness was free of any form or sense of individuality, with no centralized 'me.' Yet it was wholly infused with the bottomless, rock-solid Realization of 'I AM.' In the place of egoic walls tenaciously holding in my familiar identity, was an infinite boundlessness that expanded out omni-directionally. The essential quality of this field was a crystalline Awakeness, the very source of consciousness, pervading such deep peace and tranquility, yet crackling with the Power of Being, the shimmering aliveness of the Cosmos.

This immense Spaciousness had a paradoxical quality. It was, simultaneously, the very essence of a vast and still Emptiness, and yet every atom was bursting with Fullness, as it effortlessly held, in infinite expansion, all manifestation, allowing the Universe, and everything within it, unconditional freedom of expression. 'Timelessness' gently bloomed into an immeasurably deeper realm: Eternity! Eternity, where life never was . . . never will be . . . just IS.

And death? How could the Eternal die? This Cosmic Field was not just alive but was the heartbeat of the Universe itself! This conscious, pulsating Heart was radiant with unfathomable Love for all and everything. My spiritual quest had finally found its way back to the Great Spirit Itself . . . home.

Off in the far distance, there came the distinct sound of a car, whistling through the air, plummeting to Earth. Then . . .

Total Silence.

My eyes fluttered open and a blinding sunbeam caused them to squint. In that moment, the boundless infinite realm of the Universe instantaneously shrank and condensed all the way back down to the individual human soul known as Jackson Trent. Instinctively, my eyes started to adjust and focus.

Astonishingly, our car was now sitting safely within the parking lot of the roadside lookout, a few feet away from the shattered guard railing we had just plowed through! Our cab driver, hands frozen on the steering wheel, was shivering and babbling incoherently, his eyes glazed with the wild, distant look of a seriously traumatized man. Without warning, he bolted from the car and disappeared down the road towards the village. A protective instinct arose in me to chase after him and get him some help, but I couldn't move a muscle. Then, a voice from the back seat said:

"Leave him be. His experience and yours were very different."

I felt a sharp tap on my shoulder. My head swung slowly around and I peered into an unsmiling face. "You heard me calling you back, Jackson and you ignored me. Why?"

I said nothing. I could still hear with the most lucid inner clarity, but actual words were not forming for a reply, as if they required a cumbersome effort I just wasn't willing to make at this moment. My consciousness was completely absorbed in the experience of reintegrating back into my body. My soul had been blown wide open, and the pieces were taking their sweet time fitting back together again.

Lucifer studied my eyes, or more to the point, the look my eyes were revealing. He was not pleased. I could feel my lips shaped in a blissful grin, a reflection of what I had just experienced.

He snipped: "You find my question amusing? "

All I could mumble was: "What? What happened . . . with us . . . with the car?"

Lucifer paused. I could hear his fingers strumming on the back seat upholstery and it had an angry tone to it.

"You're a strange one to me, Jackson. I've empowered you with an ancient amulet of enormous capacities. I could tell you stories that would curl your hair of what *Kosala* has been commanded to do since antiquity. And despite experiencing a taste of that power with the young swimmer, it was obvious that you were still trying to resist using it. So, naturally, I turned things up a notch."

I could barely believe what I just heard. I mustered the words: "You call sending us off a cliff . . . turning it up a notch?"

"Look . . . This accident was supposed to be a simple 'set up,' dramatic perhaps, but designed to encourage you to get over your reluctance to command the Snake. Well, I succeeded. You did it, and with spectacular results! But then, unfortunately, you chose to take this experience far past what I had in mind."

I could sense I was fully back in my body by the anger rising in me. "I didn't take the experience anywhere, it took me! And look what you did to our cabbie. What is he, collateral damage to your ploy?"

"Don't fret the cab driver. Granted, he'll be rattled to his core for a while, but if you must know, he'll end up becoming a religious devotee of *Tangaroa*, the Polynesian god he was so fervently praying to on the way down. And besides, from now on he'll stop driving like a maniac on this twisting road."

"So it seems that my own petrified experience backfired on you, Lucifer. The terror of staring at my own death propelled me into . . . "

"Yeah, yeah , I know. I miscalculated. I simply wanted to force your hand to use the Cuff, not send you on a Cosmic journey, for chrissake! It sounds like you went on quite an adventure." He smiled wickedly. "Wanna do it again?"

My knees gave a reflexive jolt. "Very funny, but no. I wouldn't trade that astonishing experience in for a million dollars, nor do it again for two million! Now that I've experienced the true Light, my hope is that I can find my way back to Oneness under less harrowing circumstances."

"Well, there you go. The bottom line is, you got another taste of the Cuff, and here you are, all safe and sound. Nothing is really changed."

"Nothing is changed? Are you kidding? Everything's changed."

I sat there, staring out the car's window at the vast expanse of the sea. What do you say when your entire perception of reality has been blasted wide open? I knew that what I'd discovered about myself and the 5th dimension profoundly altered my worldview. Even the mystery of how the *Kosala Cuff* had saved us was trumped by having been launched into the miraculous Cosmic State. I'd never be the same again. And now, my reentry was a strange adjustment. I felt so small.

"Lucifer, I saw my Self in totality. I now know who I truly am, who we all are. No wonder Spirit has been calling me all these years! Thanks to your overplaying your hand, I inadvertently got a taste of that ineffable vastness, what I can only describe as a Wholeness. It's all . . . a Unity. How many times over the years have I heard Adepts say: *We are all One.* I always thought to myself, Yeah, sure. It sounded like such a lovely concept, but it made no sense to me. My experience, as a basically normal person had been just the opposite: We are all many individuals . . . a far cry from One.

But what I now understand is that it depends. Uncovering that Truth of a Cosmic Unified Field, discovering the Source Itself, is completely contingent upon the state of consciousness, the dimension, I'm experiencing. Oneness is a perfect description of the 5th Dimension, which makes precious little sense to my individualized egoic 3rd dimensional mindset. It just doesn't compute! It can't. How could it? Oneness can't be 'groked' intellectually, it can only be experienced. The drop willingly returns to the ocean . . ."

"Jackson, you're jabbering. You sound all baffled and confused. That's what you get for shifting into unknown inner territory."

Another surge of anger spiked through me. "Don't play me for a fool again, Lucifer. Cluelessness doesn't become you. You know precisely what I'm talking about. I tumbled into the realm that, for reasons of your own, you try so diligently to keep us away from. I heard your attempt to pull me back."

Lucifer went dead silent. Whoa, was he pissed! Although in this new form he had morphed into, his eyes were now the same color, his stare still felt like a power drill, boring into me. It made me quiver. Time to move . . .

"Let's get out of here. I've seen enough of this place. How are we getting back to the *Mahana Kai*? The cab driver ran off with the keys."

Lucifer served me with a patronizing expression. "Come on, Jackson! You've just survived certain death using the Snake. You could say that the rest of your life is, in a sense, a bonus. Why hold back from anything? Listen to me. The Kosala Cuff isn't just for harrowing moments and extraordinary events. You want a way back to the resort? Well, bloody hell, order it up!"

Sitting there in the front seat of that cab, staring at the cliff edge we had just sailed over, and instinctively squeezing my arms to make sure I was in one piece, I had no resistance left. I'd just been through something monumental and needed to chill out. Screw it. I'll use the damn Cuff! Closing my eyes and visualizing with a clarified, focused intention, I raised my left arm and pointed directly to the road behind us.

Bring me a ride back to the Mahana Kai.

I leaned backwards against the headrest, reflecting on all that had just taken place. What a mind-boggling day! Did I doze off? I was startled by the sound of a horn tooting. Blinking and sitting up straight, I looked out my window to the sight of an absurdly long, pearly white, stretch limo. The black-suited livery driver came around and opened my car door. "Mr. Trent?" he asked politely. I turned and gave Lucifer a wide-eyed look. He said simply:

"One thing about the Cuff; you'll discover that, unless ordered to the contrary, its default setting is full bore. If you wanted a simple ride back to the resort, you have to dial it down by telling the Snake so. Otherwise . . . " He tilted his head towards the limo.

Sliding into the back seat of the stretch, I was enveloped in unaccustomed luxury—supple leather banquettes and enough room for a party of twelve. My favorite music was sweetly filling the air. Lucifer reached for the bottle of *Cristal Brut 1970 Methuselah* champagne chilling in a silver ice bucket. He expertly popped the cork, filled two flutes and handed me one. I hesitated for a moment, and then just went with the flow. I was still in 'screw it!' mode. Rolling this heavenly elixir around on my tongue, I savored its exquisite taste. I've always enjoyed champagne but had no idea it could be this delectable. I knocked on the divider glass behind the driver. He lowered the window and looked at me in the rearview mirror. "Sir?"

"Could you please call the cab company and alert them that one of their taxis is stuck in that parking lot? And have them check on their driver."

"It's already been handled, Mr. Trent."

I slowly turned to face Lucifer with what must have been a stupid look on my face, if a dropped jaw looks stupid. He simply took another sip, raising an eyebrow that seemed to convey:

"What did I tell you? Full bore."

At that, Lucifer stretched out his legs, as if to accentuate the opulent roominess of this exceptional ride. I looked down at my left hand, studying the Cuff from both sides, now with less resistance.

"Tell me more about this Snake before I give it back to you."

This brought on a sly smile to Lucifer's face. I was finally showing interest. He refilled my flute and then explained:

"The history of the *Cuff of Kosala* is a spellbinding tale. The astounding dynamism contained within it blows away everything you thought was possible. I've even witnessed its capacity to alter the past, to redirect history! But, in order to activate what the amulet can unleash, the Commander has to master the flow of Power."

"How?"

"It's a series of steps, but in a specific order. First, visualize exactly what you want it to achieve, exactly; a clear, sharp, precise image. Then, holding that focused vision perfectly steady in the mind, command the Cuff from the source of one's true power; potency that can only emerge from the depths of one's 'belly center,' the *Hara.* That command, then, surges up the spine, passing through an opened Third Eye where it captures the visualized image. From there, it rockets down the arm and becomes tremendously amplified as it passes through the loop of the Snake."

"Yeah. That's exactly how it felt inside me."

"Listen to me. The fact that the Cuff not only works for you but already responds with full bore to your commands is somewhat unheard of. I'm telling you, you're a natural with it. Including this limo ride, you've now actualized the Snake on three occasions, and each time, it has, more or less, responded instantly and damn near perfectly to what you've commanded it to do! That business of saving the cab from smashing on the rocks was a spectacular achievement! A capacity on that level, so soon, is very rare and it's why I'm underscoring that you and this amulet are a perfect match. You're, shall we say, '*Kosala* material.'"

As he spoke, I, once again, felt the inflating 'fluttering up' of my vanity, that place in me that just loves hearing that I'm special. Always a red flag.

"If I've shown signs of being able to visualize well, it's because you put me in untenable positions which required nothing less!"

"Of course I did. That was the point! But tell me something. The Cuff fails to activate for most Westerners who test it, as they can't access their *Hara*. You were able to. How so?"

Ah, the Hara . . . "I learned about the belly center from Eastern traditions. *Hara, Kath, Dan Tien,* it goes by many different names. I've been in touch with that hidden organ of *sensing* for decades. *Hara* balances me. My little Self thinks that my 'center of gravity' is in my head, but my Presence knows that *Hara* is my true balancing point. It grounds me to the Earth and it supports my heart and my mind above it. In the East, one's *Hara* is cultivated from an early age, yet here in the West, that dynamic source of inner sensing and true balance is virtually undiscovered."

"Ha, the Western world. It doesn't miss what it's oblivious to. I like to keep it that way!"

"But here's something I don't understand, Lucifer. You've made it abundantly clear that your primary interest is to keep humans 'asleep.' Developing the power inherent in the Third Eye is exactly what many spiritual paths encourage. Why would you support that development if you're opposed to spiritual work?"

"Because Power is Power. It can be directed towards the 'Light' if you will or used by elements of the Shadow. Power can propel you into deeper dimensions of the human/spirit connection or turn you into a Creator, all-powerful in this current reality."

"Ah, I see. The true spiritual path leads to: 'Be in the world but not of it.' What you're offering is to 'Be in the world and control it.'"

"And why not? Why not have things your way: how you want it, where and when you want it? This Snake allows you to have 'one foot in the Underworld,' as it were. And don't forget, my globally-concerned citizen, you can turn this gift into doing great work for humanity! Who are you to turn away from that kind of opportunity? The planet needs you, Jackson!"

"Okay, give me another straight answer. I'd imagine that this particular path you're offering is littered with 'wrecks,' people who have used this *Ouroboros* amulet only to unleash their own destruction. True?"

Another long pause, and then: "Let me put it this way. Success is not guaranteed."

"You're not answering my question. Give me a percentage? How many lives end up getting ruined by being tempted and toying with this Power?"

"About 75%."

My eyes got huge. "Are you kidding? Three out of four of those who've tried out this Cuff of yours have had their lives blown up? Give me some names!"

"Names? Oh, come on. What's the point? So what if some individuals end up going off the rails?"

"Some names, Lucifer."

He stared out the window at the scenery, deep in thought. Then:

"Okay, here are a few of the more famous . . . er . . . infamous characters who, I'm afraid, went a bit off the deep end. Ever hear of Tomas De Torquemada? No? Spain, back in the 15th century. He started out as a genteel, pious young priest. His Power was buried deep in his Shadow until he took on the Cuff. Ended up being the Chief Inquisitor of the Spanish Inquisition, torturing thousands. Now, that guy had an imagination on how to extract the truth out of supposed heretics! Then there's Robespierre, the leader of the French Revolution. He'd been working hard for freedom for his oppressed countrymen, and then he tried on the Snake. Before long, he got carried away, guillotining all his friends in the public square. Even I'll admit, that wasn't pretty."

Lucifer saw the look of growing apprehension on my face. "Okay, that's enough. Let's not dwell on the failures of those too weak to handle the power inherent in this *Kosala Ouroboros*. Instead, let's concentrate on your upside possibilities, Jackson! Remember 25% become true Creators; one-out-of-four! The question remains, do you have what it takes?"

On that manipulative note, I just let it drop.

The bell captain, having seen our limo, pushed aside a few of the bellhops under his command and made a beeline for my door. With an exaggerated sense of deference, he cooed: "Good evening, sir! No luggage, so I assume you're here for the luau?"

The *luau!* With everything that I'd been through this afternoon, I had forgotten about the evening's event. "I'm a guest here. What time does the *luau* start? And the *hula* dancing, is that after the feast?"

"The *luau* begins in an hour, around sunset on our private beach. The *hula* presentation commences after the feast, sir."

I found it mildly annoying that I felt obligated to offer the bell captain a sizable tip, as if I had to live up to our ostentatious arrival. I needed to clean up and change. More than anything, I wanted to be alone for awhile. It was my turn to get some answers out of Lucifer and I needed to collect myself. I turned to him: "There's a string of hammocks on the left side of our beach. Half hour? We can pick up the conversation then. You still owe me some answers."

"Fine. I'll be there. In the meantime, hand me my iPad. I need to check in on my advice blog."

"You're still going to keep up *Dirty Laundry?* I thought that was the other Lucifer?"

"Well, my perspective may be quite different from his, but the need for advice is obviously still there. I *have* decided to change the name. I'm calling it: *Terms of Endarkenment.* What do you think?"

An 'eye roll' is a very hard thing to suppress. For myself, I was still feeling clearly altered from the afternoon's profound experiences. I wasn't sure which event had the greatest impact . . . an astounding deliverance from certain death or having been graced with a taste of the Infinite. Strange how the two are interconnected. By being absolutely certain that my life was over, I'd been catapulted into a dimension within myself where life is Eternal! I've never felt more alive than the moments before I thought I was going to die.

The Cuff. The Snake. I gazed down at my wrist and started to entertain the question: Is it possible I could be the 1 out of 4 who could control it? Or would I end up destroying myself, a casualty of my own hubris?

CHAPTER

12

Cutting a Deal

To share your weakness is to make yourself vulnerable; to make yourself vulnerable is to show your strength.

—Chriss Jami

STROLLING BACK TO MY COTTAGE THROUGH THE VERDANT grounds of the resort, I found myself moving at a much slower pace. It was clear that something fundamental had shifted within me.

I washed and changed into evening attire. Before heading out, I stretched out on the bed. Leaning back against the headboard, wanting to quietly take stock of my feelings, I closed my eyes and scanned my inner terrain. I was almost reintegrated back into my accustomed 'sense of self.' Yet, there was a fresh recognition that this self of mine, this Jackson, in this body was being held by a pure, unwavering, loving, Light-filled Presence that the entire Universe is basking in. I was getting flashes into how everything . . . all manifestation, is just arising, moment-to-moment within the timeless unfolding of Eternity. It was both strange, yet exciting, to feel individualized and boundless, finite and infinite, at the same time. I was immersed in an enchanting conundrum.

And my heart? I felt into it. Despite everything else that had unfolded this afternoon, the state of peace that Mama Kamea had left me with remained. That secret door in my heart she had unlocked was now left wide open, swinging on its hinges. Very tenderly, I allowed memories of my darling Francesca to emerge. Oh, I could so clearly feel the difference! As my daughter's image appeared in my Mind's Eye, there was the familiar immediate sense of loss. But the biting grief, with its accompanying baggage of guilt, of a sad emptiness, was now absent. It had been replaced with something else, a kind of container that seemed to be able to effortlessly hold my love for her ever so gently. That awful acidic taste of angst was supplanted with a sweet and joyful remembering. I felt the tears flow, but as they ran down my cheeks, they passed through the contours of a warm, benevolent grin. I stayed in this beautiful heart-space until I realized it was time to leave.

Meandering my way back to the beachfront, I was now eager to continue my conversation with Lucifer. This sense of feeling 'cracked open' was expansive and yet a bit discombobulating. I needed information. It was my turn to probe him with some pertinent questions that had emerged from my touching into the Cosmic realm.

The beach directly in front of the resort was a beehive of activity in preparation for the *luau*. I walked passed the *Imu* pit that held the roasting pig buried under a heaping inferno of red-hot lava rocks. Off to the left were the hammocks and Lucifer standing close by. He, too, had changed clothes and was the picture of the impeccably dressed gentleman, casually 'island chic.' He was chatting with an exceptionally attractive tourist, whose rapt attention and body language conveyed her infatuation. With his head leaning in close to her ear, she burst into an effervescent laugh. Seeing me approach, Lucifer introduced me to the woman, Sophia, who gave me a dismissive 'how-do-you-do' and immediately locked her gaze back onto him.

I was clearly a third wheel.

"I'll come back later."

"No, no, we were just having a little fun." He gently took her hand and gave it a soft kiss. "We'll pick this up later, ma cherie, oui?" She swooned and her eyes said, "*Mais oui!*" As Sophia reluctantly walked away, he stood there taking in her lovely sashay. She peered back over her shoulder, and Lucifer gave her a suggestive wink. The thought crossed my mind: *Should I warn her?*

Stretching out on a hammock, Lucifer put his hands behind his head and boasted:

"How did Twain put it? Go to Heaven for the climate and Hell for the company!" He cracked a smile. "Some people will believe anything, especially if it's cooed softly in their ear."

I plopped into the adjacent hammock, my annoyance rising. "Everything is a manipulation for you."

"And your point would be?"

"My point? I guess it's summed up by a different passage that comes to mind: "Beware of the heartless who make yours beat quickly. They're just using your heart, because theirs won't start."

Slowly turning his head, he stared at me. I changed the subject. "So, how's the advice column going?"

"Oh yeah. Human life . . . endless issues. The queries keep pouring in." He flipped open his tablet. "Listen to this guy."

Dear Lucifer,

I'm a lonely bachelor and I've finally decided to try out online dating. I'm not having much luck, as I seem to possess a knack for turning women off. I've no idea what I'm doing wrong! I've been really honest in filling out my profile with clever quips that describe me accurately, and, yet, put me in a favorable light. For example, I said: 'I like long romantic walks to the refrigerator.' That way, I hint at my passionate sexiness and, at the same time, show that I can feed myself. To attract nature lovers, I wrote: 'I'm the outdoorsy type. I like to get drunk on the back porch.' Or to show that I'm realistic, I say: 'I'm counting on your standards being far lower than mine.' I finally got a woman who agreed to a date. She replied: 'I'll meet you, providing it's in a well-lit, very public location.' That sounded positive, I think. Well, after only ten minutes of awkward conversation, she got up and left, saying: 'Let me put it this way. You incomplete me.'

What am I missing here? Can you help?

Lonely in Louisiana

"I feel for this guy, Lucifer. He's like a million other clueless, lonesome men out there. So what advice did you give him?"

"I simply focused in on his most glaring mistake, not knowing the key to winning the relationship game.

Dear Lonely,

I saw your problem right away when I read the word 'honest.' You obviously are lacking in the one, single talent that is absolutely necessary for successful online dating, how to lie. Let's start with your profile. You need to dig up some photos taken years prior, way back '60 pounds lighter and a head of hair' ago! Whatever you look like now, trust me, you looked better then!

Now, let's say you actually do get to meet in-person. When you see that immediate look of disbelief and shock on her face as she's staring at a guy who looks like the older, fatter father of the man she's expecting to meet . . . start flattering! You've got to be nimble as you only have about 30 seconds (or less, depending) to patch up your phony picture ruse.

Pick out something about her and start lying fast! For example, you might quickly try a reverse tactic: 'Oh hello, Miss. You must be the lovely daughter of the woman I'm waiting to meet.' You know, that kind of b.s.

Chin up, 'Lonely.' I'm here to tell you that you're not a hapless loser. You're actually a fine and remarkable catch for some lucky woman out there!

That was a lie. See how it works?
Yours, Lucifer

Lucifer looked up at me, awaiting my reaction. "Well?"

I gave him a big smile. "Now, that advice was excellent. You nailed it. Beautifully done!"

Lucifer beamed with pride. "It was?"

"That was a lie. So, how does that feel?"

I leaned back and took in the dramatic skyline. The sun was sinking fast, soon to drop, sizzling, into the awaiting sea. Far out on the horizon, large puffy clouds were already starting to turn a salmon pink around the edges. This had all the makings to be an outrageous Hawaiian sunset, arguably one of the greatest natural shows on Earth. I mused:

"Look at this gloriously ethereal sunset. It's a perfect reminder to me about the paradox of two realities operating simultaneously."

"How so?"

"Well, what's the essence of a sunset? It marks the passage of time, right? The end of the day. And yet this expansive, wide open sky puts me back in touch with the eternal, boundless Timelessness I experienced this afternoon. I still feel I'm in two worlds at once . . . and continuing to enjoy them both."

"Well, Jackson, that's because you 'passed through the looking glass,' so to speak. I remember, eons ago, hanging around the temples in ancient Greece. Plato and his fellow philosophers understood those two worlds you're experiencing perfectly. 'Time,' in your Earthly human existence, they called *Chronos*, which they depicted as *Father Time*, a bearded old man, trudging along the 'horizontal path' of Time, with an hourglass in one hand and a scythe in the other. The hourglass is a reminder that your time is limited and, one day, the sand will run out. And when that happens, his scythe is ready to mow you down like a weed."

I shivered. "Nice image."

"But the Greeks also understood that, simultaneously, in a higher dimension, in a more clarified Awareness, there is no such thing as time, there's actually only Eternity. Now, for a human, there's a special point where horizontal time intersects with Eternity, which they called *Kairos,* a magical passageway that, under certain extraordinary conditions, one can suddenly step out of *Chronos Time* and open into the Eternal."

"I think that's what happened to me as we plunged off the cliff."

"Right, a *Kairos* moment presented itself and you shot right through that portal into Eternity. Did you sense what was different about that state, Jackson?"

I closed my eyes and remembered. "Yeah, there was absolutely no fear of death."

"Exactly. That scythe of *Chronos*, 'Father Time,' usually generates in humans an ongoing, unconscious terror of the sand running out of the hourglass, of death. That specific fear is so powerful that it drives everything in one's life. There's a constant subtle anxiety that shows up as worry of what the future may, or may not, hold. So what does Man do? As long as a human is driven by fears, he will naturally shove anything that scares him down that spiral staircase within and right into the Underworld . . . my Shadow realm. So, happily, everything comes my way. Most everyone is forever playing into my Game."

Okay, that was my opening. Now was the time to pin Lucifer down on just what he's up to with humanity . . . and why?

"Alright Lucifer, it's my turn for questions." I sat up in the hammock to face him squarely. "What's your angle? Why are you so committed to keeping the human being small, keeping us from discovering 'the vastness' of who we really are?"

"My angle? Hmmm. To answer that, let me start by asking *you* something. When you entered into this Cosmic Illumination today, what do you remember when you looked at the human experience?"

I thought back . . . "I saw how Oneness, Wholeness is the great backdrop completely hidden behind our world of Duality. I saw how the very nature of our dual perspective turns this Oneness and breaks it out into Many. This Duality naturally splits everything into halves; 'me' and 'other.' And so, out of that split unfolds life as we know it, as we experience it. Up has its down, in has its out, hot its cold, on its off, wet its dry, good its bad, and so on."

"And Light has its Shadow."

"Yes, I understand, Light has its Shadow, and that natural opposing interplay creates the split between the two."

Lucifer rubbed his palms together. "Yes, the split between the two. And that's precisely where I come in. My complete focal point is on one half of that split. As I described earlier, the Shadow World is my realm. I breathe it, enliven it and defend it with all my Powers."

"But why are you so committed to keeping us small?"

"You're off the mark! My main focus isn't to keep you small. Do I tempt and distract? Hell yes, but you keep yourselves small. Remember, my focus is keeping the Shadow World alive and well. It's not my fault that the human tendency is to take their Darkness and, via denial, bury it alive, rather than deal with it consciously."

"And this sleepy reality you create for us?"

"Ha! You think I'm creating that? Hardly. Get this straight, I don't create anything. I'm not an Originator, I'm a Facilitator. There's a world of difference there. I didn't create this foggy state of consciousness the human race finds itself in and I don't originate action to force the hand of Man. I'm a Sheeple-herder; I simply guide you along. I facilitate the direction your precious ego always seems to want to go. Is the candle to blame that the moth flies into its flame?"

"But you said it yourself earlier today. You're all about keeping our attention ensnared."

"Look Jackson, follow what I said closely. You put yourselves into a trance in the first place! You give me far too much credit. It's Man that insists on keeping his head in a dream world. I simply feed, guide and facilitate that tendency with all my craftiness and skill. Now *that*,

I'll take full and well-earned credit for. And I don't create that massive, heavy gravitational pull of this sleepy 3rd Dimension you've identified, but I sure as hell use it to my advantage."

"The Bad Shepherd."

"Exactly! But let's put a different spin on it: The Shadow Shepherd."

"You do fight against any attempt we make at expanding our awareness, yes?"

"Of course! My strategy is to drive things in the opposite direction. The *Un*-conscious! Contraction . . . not expansion! You talk about waking up. Well, not on my watch, pal! I'm wholly and completely anti-Presence! Why? From my point of view, Presence brings Light. Generally, Light is not in my best interest. Awakening souls are troublesome; they just create far more work for me. If someone starts to open their eyes, lift up out of their sleepy fogbank and begins to see a fresh Reality, what happens? They stop being Sheeple! Instead of herding sheep, I'm now herding cats! Which translates into way more work for me. So you see, it's a management issue."

"And your Web of Illusion? That's not your invention?"

"My invention? Hell no! I just manage that Web, but again, you humans create it! The Web is nothing but the stickiness of your human delusions. Ancient Hindu texts understood this long ago. They identified five illusions that are the source of perpetuating human suffering: One, people don't recognize who they really are. Two, they cling to that which is fleeting which doesn't actually exist. Three, they run away, petrified of intangibles that also don't exist. Four, they identify with their false little Self, which is a figment of their imagination. And *lastly*, identified with their little Self, they're naturally terrified of death."

"And how do these delusions feed into the Shadow?"

"As long as Man is convinced that those five illusions are true, then what does he do with his Shadow side, this large slice of his psyche? His little false Self can't handle the darkness and drives it down and away.

And *voilà*! What we get is clear-cut separation, the Light and the Dark. And as I said, I stand for the Dark!"

"But, what I experienced from the Cosmic state made me realize that our evolution is to eventually arrive at Wholeness, not separation."

"I'm not denying anything you experienced. Does this dimension of Oneness exist? Of course! Does it concern me? Only peripherally and I don't support it. It's not my focus of interest! I'm completely wrapped up in my half of that split of opposing energies. For creation to exist, it must have oppositional forces. Well, I'm simply busy holding up my end of the deal. Believe me, there are key players on the side of the Light, the 'conscious' direction if you will, that equal or exceed my Power and so we clash, we do battle. It's another aspect of my Game, played out at the highest level of existence, one you can't even fathom. It's the tug-of-war between the two Great Impulses, Separation and Unity. But without me, without my Dark, without my unconscious Shadow World, there would be no Light. You cannot have Light without a Shadow! Do you get that? That's not an inconsequential statement!"

"Then what is your relationship to Wholeness?"

"Ah, great question, Jackson. You want the 'big picture, huh?'" Swinging his hammock from side to side, Lucifer slipped his palms behind his head and seemed to be gazing at the swaying trees above us. Then, after quite a long silence:

"I'm going to offer you an extremely valuable piece of information here, a piece that, fortunately, eludes many, if not most, on the so-called spiritual path. Just what do you think is the best route to get to the 5th dimension of Wholeness? Not just a taste like you received today, but I mean the direction that can get you there so you can stay there?"

I was suddenly holding my breath. What secret piece of information was this? And what was it going to cost me? "The best route? Yes, tell me."

"I will, and it's the last direction most individuals would ever want to take, which is why it's so well hidden! You get to true Wholeness only by passing through my Underworld, not avoiding it! The awakening of the unconscious is the passageway to Oneness. Chase after the spiritual Light, while ignoring your Shadow side, and you're just dangerously fooling yourself, as you'll never get to Wholeness. At best, it gets you to, let's call it *Halfness*." He burst into a fit of laughter, amused by his own imagery.

"And take note of this, Jackson. As I said earlier, the brighter the Light, the stronger the Shadow. Woe be to those developing souls who only operate from a place of this Halfness, who've focused strictly on the Light and haven't uncovered and integrated their Shadowlings. When they least expect it, they'll get consumed from below." Lucifer smiled thinly. "You can bank on it."

I could tell by the utter confidence of that smile that he wasn't bluffing. 'Consumed from below' is how he had put it. A high price to pay for turning a blind eye to what we don't want to acknowledge. Okay, so what to do with this somewhat frightening truth?

I asked, "So, Lucifer how does one successfully enter and pass through your Dark World, without getting lost, trapped or all turned around? How do you get to the other side, to unfold into Wholeness? Help me out here."

"Help you out? I'm trying to recruit you, dude . . . not the other way around! You want to put me out of a job?"

"Oh, knock it off. We both know that your position is secure. Just tell me, if I need to pass through your Shadow World, what do I need to know?"

Lucifer sat there with a bemused expression. "Alright, Jackson, I'll make you an offer. I'll give you the guidelines on how to work within my Shadow World, but on one condition."

"Which is?"

"You must command the *Cuff of Kosala* three more times tonight. Any command you want. I don't care! Just *use* it. Deal?"

"Why do feel I like I'm being lured into something? And why three times?"

"It's simple . . . The Snake demands to be put to work. Each time you command it, the Cuff grows more familiar with you. Three times in one evening will allow it to adjust and tweak itself to your unique specifications. And frankly, Jackson, I enjoy the challenge. If you take the advice that I'll offer, and you end up balancing your Dark side with your Light, then, as far as I'm concerned, you might just escape from my Web and have earned your way back to Wholeness. Not that I won't try to reel you back in at some future point in time."

"But, should I happen to get stuck, or trapped or seduced by my own Shadowlings, then you win. Something like that?"

"Yeah, something like that. But here's a fact. Anyone can wake up to the Light. That's easy. But can you wake up in your Darkness? Ah, that's the question. Well, first and foremost, you need to see clearly, just what's 'down there' and take a good look at all those unsavory Shadowlings that you swear aren't you. Are you sure you're up for playing this out?"

"I have no idea, but I am curious?"

"Is that a 'yes' and do we have a deal about using the Cuff?"

I said nothing, but slowly nodded.

"Good. Now, let's just take a look into what you've rejected and have hidden away down there, shall we?" Lucifer's eyes seemed to 'unfocus' as he scanned me with his gaze.

"Hmmmm. Alright, we've already met your Vanity, your issue with Power and that elusive Pride, but I see plenty of others. How about Spitefulness, followed on the heels by Arrogance, which is carefully masking Insecurity and Doubt. Do these sound vaguely familiar?"

I swallowed hard. "Vaguely, I guess."

"Well, good then; let me keep digging. Ah ha! I see Lust simmering away with Jealousy perched on its shoulder. And behind it? Revenge! I see your Rage is carefully bottled up, along with Hatred and Hostility. Why, there's Unbridled Ambition that tends to partner with Deception and Dominance. Looks like Denial is busy keeping a lid on your Envy, Recklessness and a nasty Vindictive streak."

"Okay, okay, that's enough." I was starting to get reactive; pissed off at the way he was skewering me.

"Really... enough? But, Jackson, we haven't even gotten to your Savior and your Charmer? And what about your Victim and Bully, the Martyr, the Thief and the Glutton? Your Narcissist and Manipulator could chat with each other all day about your Justifier and Perfectionist, with Fear being the bedrock for all of them! I can keep going, if you like."

I emphatically waved my arms to get him to stop!

"Well, all of those Shadowlings, and more, are down there, hovering around in your basement, my boy. Do you see why no one wants to venture into my domain, why it's not a popular destination spot to explore? It ain't pretty to your precious self-image! It takes massive courage just to get glimpses of one's Shadowlings. But do you have any idea how much energy it takes you to keep such powerful character traits Underground? Say, Jackson,you look a little pale. How are you feeling? Or, a better question is, are you feeling them, or are they too well smothered by your own self-deception?"

"For the most part, I don't recognize those awful traits in myself."

A snicker escaped his lips. "Ah, of course you don't. But let me ask you this. Do you see these same distasteful aspects in other people?"

"Oh yeah. I see most of those all around me."

"And do these specific traits really bother you?"

"Are you kidding? Definitely. They 'push my buttons' big time."

"How?"

I thought about that for a moment. "Well, to name a few, I can't stand how some people thrive on revenge, or get eaten up by jealousy or have a vindictive streak, or are insensitive. I have no patience with manipulators, or hateful people and I have a short fuse with spiteful types and those who hide behind justifying their appalling behavior. Most of all, as we've discussed, I go crazy when I see Power being abused."

"Oh, so you're free of jealousy, are you? Well, let's see about that. Think back to your freshman year in college. What was your cute little girlfriend's name?"

"Rebecca."

"Right. As your high school sweetheart, she joins you at the same college only to discover that, lo and behold, you weren't the only guy in the world. And then one night you walked in on the two of them, didn't you? Surprise! Caught her in a . . . er . . . compromising position. Broke your heart, didn't she? Shattered might be more like it, yes? And seeing Rebecca around campus, now arm-in-arm with her new beau, just ate you alive with jealousy, didn't it? So what did you do? She wounded you so deeply that, ever since, you've carefully chosen to be with women who would never, ever make you jealous again. On closer inspection here, it isn't that you're not the jealous type, you've simply been systematically hiding that characteristic away! Well guess what's still down there, intact, in your Shadow? Can you feel it?"

Whoa. It had been almost 20 years since I dredged up my memory of Rebecca, and damn . . . I could still feel the hurt! But am I still susceptible to that ugly jealous streak? I didn't think so.

"Oh, and you say you can't tolerate insensitive people? Well how about today in town? There was that ragged panhandler with the big sheepdog, remember? He made you angry and you muttered under your breath something like, How can he be responsible for a dog when he can't even take care of himself? It ticked you off, right? You were completely unaware of the very acute fact that this man had nothing to eat since yesterday and he was starving. You couldn't relate, given that you had just feasted on the resort's huge brunch buffet table. Now tell me, who's the insensitive one?"

I heard myself groan, blushing with shame. I'd been exposed.

"Shall I go on?"

"No, I'm getting the picture, Lucifer."

"Good, because every one of those Shadowling*s* is a real part of you. Now, what does that realization make you want to do?"

I felt into the question. "I guess I want to get rid of them, bury them even deeper."

"Exactly! That's everyone's impulse . . . that is, if they ever see clearly enough within themselves to even recognize them. And yet, to get to Wholeness, that's precisely what not to do. Now . . . here's the secret I promised you. You can't fight it out on the same level as the problem! The solution is found on a higher plane. It's impossible to root out something that's a part of yourself. And get this, if Shadowlings feel that you're coming after them like a witch-hunt, they'll simply vanish for a while, till the coast is clear."

"Alright. So what's your suggestion?"

"Remember my analogy of the stairway?"

"Yeah. You said to imagine we have spiral staircase in our psyche that leads all the way down to our Shadow underworld."

"And?" He was clearly prompting me to think it through.

"And . . . and our unwanted characteristics get banished down those stairs. You also said that, given the opportunity, these Shadowlings will sneak back up that stairway and jump into our lives to raise all kinds of disruptive hell."

"Right! And remember, Jackson, all that takes place unconsciously. Typically, a person isn't aware of their 'staircase' at all. Now, here's a whole different approach to consider. Imagine consciously, with full awareness, (and if you're smart, with the aid of a knowledgeable guide), descending that spiral staircase, all the way into the dark Shadow realm to discover just who's down there. Then, explore around, check it out! One at a time, see if you can find a Shadowling within yourself and acknowledge that it exists. Give it permission to show itself. Come on out. Step out of the Shadow. Ah, there you are! Then feel it, fully, whatever it is, without judgment. From there, with practice, you can learn to just embrace it, as part of yourself, as one of your own. That opens up a whole different relationship with your Shadow than if you just keep shoving it deeper and deeper down those stairs."

"But what if I don't want, say, my unconscious Spitefulness or Revenge or Greed to be brought up to the light of day? I don't wish to give them any energy at all."

"See, that's the huge fallacy, a person's biggest mistake. It's by keeping those rejects down in the darkness that you empower them with *energy*. Then, they just might explode unexpectedly, blindsiding you. Understand something crucial. Embracing your Shadow selves doesn't mean letting them run loose in your life. No. It's more like you clearly but firmly tell them:

'Hey! I now see you, I feel you, I recognize that you're a part of me and I embrace you as such. But get this . . . . You're also not in charge here to run roughshod whenever you want, so don't lash out and sabotage me. But I 'hold you' as one of my own selves, as a part of who I am.'

Get it? In time, if you're skillful, you can make a strong, powerful ally out of a formerly rejected, angry enemy. You start balancing out. You, Jackson, already know how to hold the 'Light.' You're great at that. Now get skilled at holding your 'Dark.' You can then stand in the middle ground between the two, awake to both sides. The Light and the Dark can now collaborate together, healing the separation. Then . . . you might just be able to slip through the gap between the two, well on your way to Wholeness."

"By passing through the Shadow World."

"Yes. In fact, here's a tip. When you are at the top of that stairway, looking down into the Shadow Underworld far below, if you look more carefully, at the very bottom, in the middle of the darkness, you might see a pinpoint of Light. That, my man, is the portal *through* the Shadow that opens up on the other side . . . into the realm of true Wholeness. Well, I think that's enough information for today. Any questions?"

I sat there stunned at the simple, yet profound, roadmap I'd just been given. But now I was perplexed.

"There's still one question that comes to my mind right now. You just offered me a clear way through, and possibly out of, your Underworld. Doesn't revealing that concern you at all?"

Lucifer apparently found this incredibly amusing.

"Concern me? Uh . . . no! I realize that all this information sounds great. But looking at a map is far different than actually walking the terrain. Are you capable of stepping into your Shadow World without losing your way on that most slippery of slopes? You're either very sure of yourself, or incredibly naïve. I'm not going to make it easy. And keep something else in mind, Jackson. Yes, you just had an incredible Cosmic expansion this afternoon. But remember the spiritual 'rubber band' axiom: After any huge expansion comes a huge contraction. So . . . just warning you. Beware."

Off to our right, a young Hawaiian man in a traditional native sarong stood on a platform and blew a distinctive note through a large conch shell, the hollow sound echoing across the beach. It was a sonorous invitation to come and be seated. I was suddenly cognizant of the amazing blend of delicious aromas wafting across the breeze. An authentic *luau!* Now it was me who was suddenly starving . . . and this event was bound to be fun!

CHAPTER 13

To Win Can Be a Loss

It is a revenge the devil sometimes takes upon the virtuous, that he entraps them by the force of the very passion they have suppressed and think themselves superior to.

—George Santayana

WHAT I SO LOVED ABOUT THE MAHANA KAI WAS THE understated elegance of the place. This resort seemed to understand that in Polynesia, it's the natural world where the true magic lies. On their lovely grounds, they made no attempt to guild the lily with flashy fountains, fake stone South Sea idol carvings, or the like. They focused on exquisite landscaping, and then, stepped back out of the way to let Hawaiian nature unfold its beauty and grace.

The resort's approach to the *luau* feast adhered to that same elegant principle. On most of the islands, when it comes to *luaus*, the big hotel chains typically stage an over-priced, glitzy extravaganza, designed for the flocks of tourists. The production comes complete with piles of over-cooked food and lackluster entertainment performed by local *hula* dancers who seem barely able to hide their contempt for the visiting *haoles*. Added to that is the stereotypical, annoying local MC, unfortunately armed with a microphone, attempting to be clever.

Not so at the *Mahana Kai*. This resort captured the true essence of this ancient tradition: a gathering of close family and friends, feasting together in the open air and celebrating life. Yes, of course, the resort's *luau* was put together for us guests, but they managed to create an atmosphere where you felt invited to be part of a traditional native gathering. It was a relaxed, joyful event where the spirit of *aloha* permeated the fragrant air. With the stunning sunset now fading and darkness inching its way in, the grounds were alit with *tiki* torches, strategically positioned. They cast a romantic glow throughout the *luau* setting on the beach.

I took a seat at a round table that held eight diners. Lucifer slipped into the chair to my left. I had a *Haupia* in hand, the delicious rum drink that Nalani had turned me on to this morning. The truth was I felt rattled. The last conversation with Lucifer wasn't sitting well with me and I was trying to let the drink smooth out my agitation. In his inimitable way, he had rubbed my face into what he claimed were *my* Shadow characteristics. I still didn't buy it, as too many of those unsavory aspects just didn't fit me. I mean, come on! Revenge? I have a lot of weaknesses, but that was one that didn't resonate at all with who I took myself to be.

On top of that, I was now annoyed by the deal he had lured me into agreeing to. I had foolishly put my word on the line to actualize the Snake Cuff, not once, but three times this evening, for chrissake! Once again, my irrepressible curiosity had gotten me into the deep end of the pool. And what was that cryptic remark of his about a contraction following on the heels of an expansion? I didn't need to hear that. I had most definitely experienced an incredible expansion this afternoon. Why would I have to be subjected to a possible contraction, and if so, in what way would it show itself?

I was flustered, alright. The more I thought about it, the more I was pissed at him . . . and myself. What was I doing with this . . . this . . . Creature of the Dark? I could feel myself getting revved up, an inner voice starting to fire off barbed internal commentary. *Why'd you have to swear to that agreement? He's a sociopathic manipulator. Can't you see the Snake's trouble? Idiot!*

I must have been mumbling out loud. Standing up with his empty glass in hand, Lucifer reached for mine. "I'm heading for the bar. Can I get your Inner Critic a drink?"

"Sure," I said, only catching his jab after he had walked off.

Alright . . . enough. Being raked over the coals by my own inner judge was not how I wanted to enjoy this festivity. Now, left to myself at the table, my gaze scanned the crowd. Ladies, dressed in casually elegant evening attire, were everywhere, gracing the festivity with their loveliness. As I sat there, taking it all in, I couldn't help but marvel at the beauty of the feminine. Here was such a wide range of women of various ages, body types, different skin tones, and ethnicities, all unique expressions of the extraordinary and mysterious Goddess. On one hand, it was refreshing to feel the return of my innate attraction to women again after so long a drought and yet, suddenly, I felt so lonely. The image of Nalani appeared in my mind. What a beautiful person. And I had refused her invitation to share this evening? What's the matter with me?

"Good question. I've been asking myself the same thing."

I wheeled around to find Lucifer had returned and was again sitting on my left. He handed me a fresh drink. I resisted it at first, but it just looked too delicious. What the hell . . . Lucifer lifted his glass to clink mine. "*Okole maluna*, Jackson. Hey, it's a party! Loosen up!"

"Alright, but stop with the mind reading! It's irritating and invasive."

"Sorry, that I can't do. Reading the minds of people is always going on within me. There's no better way to get a quick update on what's taking place in someone's life." A sly expression emerged on his face. "It's also a never-ending source of amusement for me. I wish you could hear the inner dialogue chattering away inside all these people. Like that guy over there, who's trying hard to impress your gorgeous waitress friend."

"What? Where?" My head whipped around.

"Over there, by the last table."

There she was, looking even more lovely. Nalani's long black hair was adorned with a single wreath of small yellow orchids. She had changed into another colorful silk sarong. Wrapped around her pleasing frame, it subtly accentuated her curves.

Lucifer leaned in and pointed: "Now, you see that man she's talking to? What she hears is his best attempt at being engaging and witty. What I hear are his inner thoughts and, whoa! Now, there's a guy with a vivid imagination about what he'd like to do with her. Whew, what a wolf!"

"Oh, piss off! Stop rubbing it in just because I screwed up."

"Well, I suspect it must hurt knowing that it could have been *you* basking in her delightful company." Taking a step back, Lucifer looked me over. "Ooooh, I do believe your hibernating panther is emerging from his cave!"

It was true. My heart felt so unburdened. Mama's healing was now spreading out, touching other places within me. Energies that had been blocked were beginning to stir. I couldn't take my eyes off of Nalani! I could feel the emergence of an instinctive male energy force working its way up to the surface, my passion beginning to circulate.

"That's it, m'boy! Let that panther roar. *Jackson-the-Numb* is returning to the land of the living. Maybe it's not too late to reconnect with the lovely dancer, eh? Although, you may have to take a number and get in line. Check out all the men hovering around her, waiting their turn to make their move. Yes, she's delightful, that one!"

This resurgence of my male potency was so surprising and yet I welcomed it! I'd been shut down for too long. Taking a sip of my *Haupia,* it made me cough. "Whoa! Is this the same drink?"

"I asked them to make it a double to help you chill out. Drink up!"

Our table was filling up. I looked around it, studying the faces of a pleasant cross-section of people. Everyone was friendly, with that relaxed 'on vacation' vibe. A big, jovial, barrel of a man commandeered a seat to our left, with, who I assumed was his wife, next to him. Turning to Lucifer, he naturally stuck out his huge hand:

"Mitch Slanderson," he offered.

"Well, hello Mitch, my name's Lucifer."

Mitch's hand, which had been enthusiastically pumping Lucifer's, froze in mid-air. Then, cautiously: "Come again?"

Lucifer threw his head back and laughed. "Yeah, I always get that reaction. You see, my parents were strict Fundamentalists. They thought it'd be a good idea to stick me with that name so I'd never forget who I needed to watch out for. Counter-intuitive strategy, wouldn't you say?"

Understandably, it seemed to take a moment for that piece of information to thread its way through Mitch's big skull. Then, he burst into a hearty chuckle, slapping Lucifer on the back.

"Lucifer. Ha! Must have sounded like a good idea to your parents at the time! So did it work?"

"You bet it did. Nobody watches out for Lucifer like me!"

"So whaddaya do, Luce?"

"Well, Mitch, I'm a shepherd."

Mitch froze yet again. This was the second piece of information in a row from this odd neighbor of his that he couldn't quite get a handle on.

"A shepherd as in . . . *sheep?"*

"Oh yeah, as in sheep. And you?"

"Hedge funds in NYC."

Lucifer brightened noticeably. "Oooh! So you were knee-deep in the big meltdown of '08?"

Mitch's face darkened and he gave a quick, awkward glance around the table, his voice noticeably lower. "It was . . . complicated."

Lucifer cocked his head with a quizzical look. "Complicated? I beg to differ."

Mitch slowly leaned back in his chair, taking on an imposing posture. "No offense, but what does a shepherd know about it?"

Lucifer rubbed his chin theatrically. "Well, correct me if I'm wrong but the financial crisis was triggered by a complex interplay of policies that encouraged home ownership, providing easier access to loans for sub-prime borrowers, overvaluation of bundled sub-prime mortgages based on the theory that housing prices would continue to escalate, questionable trading practices on behalf of both buyers and sellers, and compensation structures that prioritized short-term deal flow over long-term value creation. A recipe for disaster, in retrospect, wouldn't you agree? All this created a lack of adequate capital holdings from banks and insurance companies to back the financial commitments they were making. The whole thing was a 'house of cards' which collapsed onto itself. How am I doin' Mitch?"

His neighbor said nothing but I saw where the term slack-jawed comes from. Lucifer continued on with his needling. "And how did you make out, Mitch, in that fiasco, if you don't mind my asking?"

His mood beginning to sour and clearly uncomfortable with the direction of the conversation, Mitch seemed, nonetheless, strangely mesmerized by his wide-eyed, engaging neighbor.

"I made out okay."

"Come on, don't be modest!" Lucifer was staring just above the crown of Mitch's head. "You must have raked in, oh, 18 million and change, yeah?"

With a clunk, Mitch set his glass down and strummed his fingers on the table. There was a long pause, and then: "You sound pretty damn sophisticated for a farmer."

"Hey, with a name like mine, you gotta be a little sharper. So, tell me, as a master of the Hedge, what's your secret?"

Mitch took another quick look around, and then in a whisper: "No big secret. Very simple, the whole trick is getting out early. The smart money knows when to bail."

Lucifer's eyes sparkled. "Good thinking! Wait for the regular folks to finally muster their courage to jump into the market with their hard-earned life savings. And when these suckers arrive, that's your signal to bail out. Beautiful! You're a champion, Mitch!"

Lucifer's sarcasm didn't seem to register at all. Instead, Mitch's expression narrowed with caution as he leaned in and whispered: "Yeah? I wish my wife, here, thought so. Aside from my business associates, most people think I'm a merciless douche bag for the way that all came crashing down."

"Well, I assure you, I'm not most people." Lucifer turned and gave me a quick wink. He was having fun, but I was getting the feeling that his surgical skewering was for my edification.

Lucifer returned his focus. "Hey, when there are fortunes to be amassed, what's a little name calling, right? What do you care about people slinging words in your direction like avaricious, guzzling, gluttonous, grasping, insatiable, miserly, gormandizing, ravenous, selfish, devouring, gobbling, stingy, voracious or piggish? Sticks and stones to you, Mitch?"

The big man's face was now going from a sunburned ruddy to a creeping scarlet, with blood-red blotches spreading out, especially around his neck. I could sense that the fuse of a powder keg had been lit. I instinctively leaned backwards. Unabashed, Lucifer kept up his taunting jabs:

"At the peak of your raking it in, was there ever a moment when you said to yourself: *Mitch, this pile's enough?* Or was it just a bottomless pit of profit to you?"

Snorting like a bull, Mitch slammed his fist down, making everything and everyone at the table jump! He roared: "My attitude's you can never have enough. Too much isn't part of my vocabulary! Beside . . . . " He gave a sidelong glance at his wife. "The best things in life are expensive!"

His outburst had everyone at our table locked into a stunned silence. Mitch's wife whispered something desperate and pleading into his car. I poked Lucifer: "Knock it off. He's about to blow. I get it, okay?"

Lucifer put his hand on Mitch's burly forearm. "Hey, relax, pal. I'm just playing 'Devil's Advocate' with you. I'm very good at that! And you're just being true to your nature. Trust me when I say I understand all about exploiting opportunities."

Lucifer leaned in closer, lowering his voice conspiratorially. "Listen, how would you like a smokin' hot tip on a high-tech product in development that's gonna explode on the global market in two years? Interested?"

Mitch was now clearly befuddled. He had been steamrolling down the greased pathway of a developing fury. There was only *one* thing that could stop that momentum. His big head now tilting quizzically, he nodded like an eager ten year-old. "You bet, I'm interested!"

"Okay, pay attention. I'm only gonna say this once. The company is Pervertron Technologies. It's being backed by some Vulture Capital friends of mine with super deep pockets."

"Pervertron? Never heard of them."

Lucifer's grin spread wide. "Oh . . . but you will!"

"What's their product?"

Lucifer looked left and right and then whispered in an undertone: "They're called *Oogle Glasses.* They look exactly like regular shades except for their newly patented micro-camera in the upper left corner."

Mitch was vigorously trying to grasp the concept. "What does the camera do?"

Lucifer raised an eyebrow. "*Oogle Glasses* see through clothes!"

Mitch's eyes flew open wide as his seasoned marketing mind immediately got it.

"You mean . . . ? "

"That's exactly what I mean!"

Slowly eyeing the lovely women walking by with an emerging leering gaze, Mitch's head suddenly snapped around. "But, that can't be legal!"

"Don't you worry about that. Pervertron already has top law firms lined up to defend it. And if all else fails?" He gave a cagey wink. "Well, at the end of the day, the Supreme Court knows what to do."

Mitch was suddenly beside himself with excitement. "Here's my card, Luce. Promise me we can talk later!"

"Sure, Mitch. I may have a short, one-page doc for you to quickly sign and then you're in!"

The tension now completely evaporated, a palpable collective sigh of relief spread around the table. As Mitch and his wife excused themselves, Lucifer looked over to me. "Well?"

"Okay, I got your little lesson. I could clearly see the way this guy was in the grip of his Shadowlings."

"Very good! Which ones?"

"Well, obviously Greed and Corruption."

"That's it? Just two?"

"What did I miss?"

"Remember, Jackson, the ego typically tends to mix and match a number of Shadow qualities. You're right about the first two, but didn't you notice Denial . . . he takes no responsibility for the damage done, or Arrogance, as his amassed fortune makes him feel superior and condescending? What about his Gluttony, as his view that having enough is just for suckers? And all the while, he's under an umbrella of his

Justifier, which shields and insulates him from any attempts from his conscience to bother him, thus having it all carefully explained away within his own mind and heart. Impressive!"

"Okay, but explain this to me. This morning, you were all in favor of his kind of greed oozing out of Wall Street. 'Olympians,' you called them. So why were you mocking him like that, making him look foolish?"

"Why not? I just enjoy messing with people of all stripes. Ever watch a cat toying with a mouse?"

"So even though Mitch is your kinda guy, bullying his way through life, you still screw with him?"

Lucifer's eyes flashed like headlights. "What makes Mitch 'my kinda guy' is because he's so unconscious. I'm all in favor of his worldview. He's a first rate hedonistic glutton, bulldozing his way to get what he wants, a real prick. But, you're right, all that repartee I had with him was simply a lesson for you."

Well, Lucifer, you did surprise me by offering Mitch such a juicy investment tip. Maybe you actually do have a kinder side."

He looked at me, shook his head and chuckled. "Mitch is going to lose his ass on that deal. *Oogle Glasses* will create a global firestorm of protests. They'll eventually be banned worldwide and Pervetron will be shut down—and sued for millions, too! Mitch and his cronies will lose a fortune in what'll become a pile of totally worthless stock."

"Why would you? Oh, I get it. You're going to make him pay by tempting his greed."

Lucifer beamed. "Finally, you're starting to understand the nuances, Jackson. That's what I do. It's how I roll on the 'Sheeple level'. And take note of my efficiency. I tempt Mitch's greed and he'll fan out and tempt all his greedy pals. He, unwittingly, does my work for me."

On that note, I pushed my chair back. Most everyone at our table was heading for the buffet line. Now famished and feeling dizzy from the *Haupias* coursing through my bloodstream, I was getting a bit looped. The *luau* buffet was an impressive spread. The sacrificial pig, the *Pua'a*, had been hoisted up and out of its carefully crafted inferno and was now offered as succulently roasted *Kalua* pork. For those preferring something from the sea, *Lomi Lomi* salmon was presented, grilled to perfection, with tomatoes and caramelized onion. As a sushi lover, the marinated raw *Ahi Poki* caught my eye. Platters of yams, plantains, distinctively purple sweet potatoes and many more choices were elegantly laid out along the serving tables.

After serving myself, I was heading back to my table when I jolted and nearly dropped my plate! There was Nalani, alone, sipping a drink, scanning the scene as if she was searching for someone. Was she looking for me? I tried to make eye contact. Dropping my dinner plate on our table with a clank, I headed straight towards her. My hasty move didn't escape Lucifer's attention and I heard him release that throaty growl as I bolted past.

My pulse was racing. Okay, slow down! Taking a deep breath, I paused, gathered myself and then calmly walked up to her. "Nalani! So great to see you again!"

Her head turned in my direction, but my friendly grin was met with an indifferent neutrality. "Oh, hello."

Her unexpected coolness threw me off but I was fully committed now. "I wanted to thank you for our talk this morning."

"Thank me? Why?"

"Well, sometimes a sympathetic ear is the perfect tonic. I was very grateful to have had a chance to share with you all that's happened to me this year."

Nalani said nothing but, unlike this morning, this silence felt tense. Something had changed in her. I scrambled for something to say. "I appreciated you confiding in me with what happened to your husband."

Did you ever wish you could snatch your words out of the air and stuff them back into your mouth? The split second I mentioned Kekoa, I understood my blunder. Her arched unsmiling eyes revealed much. That sharing with me earlier today of her devastating loss had unfolded within an ultra-tender space, which our intimate conversation had opened up. It had been a fragile and delicate exchange where we both had felt safe, deciding to trust each other with our deepest vulnerabilities. For me to be now using Kekoa's death as a conversation starter was all wrong. I felt like a fool. Nalani sensed my struggle and bailed me out, her expression softening.

"Well, Jackson, you do look different. Something's changed. Your whole demeanor seems, I don't know . . . lit up."

I'll bet! I could barely contain this rush of energy, as Eros was most definitely making its return. At the same time, I had drunk quite a bit of rum and was also hungry, making me lightheaded and a little giddy.

"Well, something's happening, Nalani. I seem to be coming back to life."

"I'm glad for you, Jackson."

Nalani began glancing around the crowd, her body language signaling eminent departure. Quick. *Think!* An inner voice back in the peanut gallery of my mind shouted out: *Say something entertaining!* I blurted: "I can read your mind, you know."

Giving me a dubious look with a hint of amusement, she quipped: "Oh really. Okay, let's hear it?"

I tried to mimic the expression of confident assessment I'd seen on Lucifer's face when he had been reading me. "You were just thinking: Better late than never, Jackson, to take me up on my offer to have dinner together. Am I right?"

Nalani took a step back in mock amazement. "Wow, that's incredible! I was thinking something . . . just not that." She reached out and lightly touched my shoulder. "The thing is, I've already made dinner plans with a hotel guest I just met."

Rats! My picture of how this evening was going to unfold started collapsing onto itself, like a condemned building. She continued, softly: "Listen, I didn't mean to put you on the spot with my invitation this morning." She paused. "There's something you should know about me. I've a history of taking on 'wounded birds' like you. I can't seem to help it."

"Wait, you don't understand! That's not me."

"Let me finish, Jackson, please. When I meet a man who's emotionally injured, it triggers something in me. My first impulse is to nurture him. With my husband, it was the same story. When I met him, he was a wreck, so gifted physically, yet crippled emotionally. His last relationship was like a shattered window and he was still bleeding from trying to pick up the broken shards. I swooped in and eventually nursed him back to wellness, but at a cost to me. I've vowed to stay clear of men with broken wings."

"But Nalani, I've turned the corner. Have you ever heard the expression 'New beginnings are often disguised as painful endings?'"

She put her hands on her hips, her head tilted to the left, as if taking my measure. Then: "You're a strong and decent man, Jackson. I get that. It touches me that you miss your daughter so much. And I understand how you suffer the loss of your marriage. But you need more time. Don't rush it." She kissed me on the cheek, putting a palm directly on my quickening heart. "You've been going through Hell. My suggestion? Don't stay there. Keep going." Then, with a wink, she turned to head back into the crowd.

I stood there, feeling helplessly inept. I heard a croak come out of my mouth: "I look forward to seeing you dance tonight."

She didn't hear me as she bumped into a man who had stepped directly into her path. He apparently had been watching us, waiting for her. He must be her date. Bastard! I winced as his opening line of wit made her laugh while she lightly took his arm. Shit! I took a hard look at my competition. He had the style of one of those professional lady-killers; you know... the Smooth Dog. Aside from being distinguished, well dressed, tanned and good looking... okay very good looking, he had absolutely nothing going for himself! I turned away in frustration and headed for the bar.

"Give me a glass of Rejection on the Rocks."

The bartender understood. "Got it. Here's just what you need," sliding me a fresh drink.

Back at the dinner table, Lucifer gave me a sidelong glance and shook his head, turning in my direction: '*I can read your mind*' was the best you could come up with?"

"I panicked, okay? I thought she'd laugh with me, not at me."

"Well, so you screwed up. Get back in there and try a different approach!"

"Too late. Nalani not only blew me off, but she's with some other guy she just met."

I looked up and things went from bad to worse. Being seated at a table in direct line of my vision were the two of them. "Oh great, now I have to watch them." I groaned, took another swig of my drink and looked away.

In a taunting tone, Lucifer piped in: "They sure do appear to be having fun."

Turning back, I found myself looking directly at the Smooth Dog. He seemed to sense my stare as he turned his head in my direction. Our eyes locked. I saw the recognition in his expression that silently said: "Oh... it's *you*." A thin, menacing smile pursed his lips, as he slipped his arm around Nalani. Now chatting cheek-to-cheek, he occasionally glanced my way, twisting the knife in deeper. What a creep, this guy! I took heart in noticing that Nalani didn't seem comfortable being so enveloped by this man as she was making subtle moves to back him off.

"Ooooh, he's suave and slippery, that one," Lucifer taunted. "There's a word that describes that man: Scoundrel."

"Nobody uses that word anymore." Nonetheless, I got his implication. I said nothing, but thought to myself: *Scoundrel, huh? I thought so*. Now, on top of everything else, I was feeling protective of her!

With night having fallen, the *tiki* torches were now the *luau's* sole source of illumination. The atmosphere the flames created was dramatic, casting a flickering golden hue over the festivities. My edginess was increasing. Even the soft roar of the waves in the background, which usually acted like a tonic, did nothing to calm the growing agitation. I stood up, feeling the need to stretch, to disconnect from the visual of Nalani in the clutches of this nefarious guy. I didn't even *know* this woman, and yet, I was now falling into the grips of a feeling so compelling.

Lucifer handed me his glass. "How about getting me another drink?" He slid my empty glass over to me, too. I headed for the bar and asked for both drinks to be refreshed. While I waited, someone approached the bar, standing next to me. I glanced over and received a shock. It was him, the Smooth Dog! Right about then he realized he was standing next to me. Uncomfortable doesn't begin to describe the prickly vibe that surfaced between us. Clearly, we were adversaries. He broke the deafening silence:

"Well, there he is . . . Mr. Second Fiddle. Too bad, my man. Nobody likes to lose."

I looked at him and heard myself say: "Nothing personal, but you look like I need another drink."

The Dog had the smugness of the one with the upper hand. He snickered, "What's wrong, buddy? Can't attract a woman? Shall I ask her to find a spare girlfriend she can loan you?"

Before I could answer, the voice within me reappeared: *Muzzle it! Walk away*. If looks could kill, he'd be a dead man, but I picked up my two drinks, spun on my heels and stepped away.

He apparently wasn't finished with me, though. "Aw, don't hate me because I'm handsome; hate me because your dream girl thinks I am. Tell you what. I'll let you know how good she was, when I'm done with her!"

I hesitated then turned back around and said with a controlled fury: "Hard to believe that out of 10 million sperm cells, you were the fastest."

When I got back to the table, my hands were shaking as I set the drinks down. Lucifer gave me the once-over.

"Whoa, what happened to mild-mannered Jackson?"

"I ran into him."

"Yeah, I know. He walked past our table a few minutes ago and left you a message. He said, 'Tell that guy, 'I'll bet losing feels worse than winning feels good.' How's that for a slap in the face?"

That bastard!

"Yeah, this man is thoroughly enjoying tormenting you. It's delightfully fun for him. He controls what you want, which makes him feel powerful. And you can't deal with it, which only plays into his hands. He seems to think you're weak."

"Weak? He doesn't know the first thing about me."

"Well, maybe so, but he's sized you up as a pushover, one of those guys who's too nice to stand up for himself. Nice, to this character, means weak. 'I'll bet losing feels worse than winning feels good.' Are you actually going to let him get away with that? A jackass like him needs to be taught a lesson!"

I knew Lucifer was purposefully fanning the flames of my building rage—but it was working. I was captivated by the allure of this beautiful woman, and yet, there was this despicable guy at her side, skillfully antagonizing me. And my ill-advised drinking was clouding my thoughts. I could hear my words starting to slur.

Lucifer poked me with his finger. "Stop wallowing in self-pity and take action. One little word: *vengeance!*" He pointed to my wrist. *The Snake!* In my rum-infused haze, I suddenly felt a bolt of command, the tide turning in my favor. Hell yes! I could feel the shape of a crooked smile inching across my face. Revenge!

Oh, when the gears of 'payback' start turning! As I played with the Cuff on my wrist, thoughts of reprisal were hatching in some devious incubator deep inside me. Just how should I mess with this cretin? I looked across at their table and glowered at him. I could hear the knives sharpening in my mind.

Lucifer clinked my drink with his. "It's been said, 'For certain offenses there is only retribution.' Desperate measures for desperate times, Jackson! What's your plan for this obnoxious playboy?"

The truth was, there was a crisscrossing of contradictions going on within me. I could hear the voice of my Wiser Self, attempting to cool me down. At the same time, that prudent perspective was being shoved aside by the swirling, raging currents of ... yes ... *retribution.*

There was a taste for it, a justification gathering itself and taking shape in my mind. And here was Lucifer, stirring up the winds of my gathering storm.

I took a final look across the way, waiting for this jerk to give me one more . . . *just one more insulting gesture.* Come on, I dare you! It didn't take long. After catching my stare, he pulled Nalani's mane back in a slow erotic gesture and kissed her neck. Then he raised his glass in a mock toast to me, complete with that malicious sneer. Something in me went off. Boom! And with that eruption came a flash of insight. *I got it! Mr. Smooth . . . you wanna toast? Well, here's a toast you'll never forget.*

Closing my eyes, I visualized precisely what I wished to see take place. I let the cauldron of my angst and building frustration just boil over and pour through me. Pointing my arm directly at The Dog, I commanded the Cuff. I felt that now-familiar sense of awesome power surging through me, rocketing out through my fingertips. I just sat there, eyes closed, allowing the intense vibration of that energy to finally settle. *Whew.*

When my eyelids fluttered open, I sat quietly, patiently waiting. Then something began to develop! The Dog slowly got to his feet and loudly clanged his wine glass with a spoon. It took him a full minute to get the attention of the entire gathering. Nalani was looking up at him with a quizzical expression. A hush finally came over the entire *luau*, everyone peering at him expectantly. He had a strange look in his eye as he held up his glass and launched into a surprise toast: "Thank you, one and all. I have a few important things to share. You be the judge, but I think you'll find that what I have to say is well worth the interruption." He paused for a long moment, his brow visibly furrowed. And then:

"You know, I believe we'd all agree that the *Mahana Kai* attracts a special kind of clientele." There was a soft murmur of friendly agreement. "Indeed, if morons could fly, this place would be an airport!" A collective gasp erupted throughout the gathering.

"I'd like to offer a personal toast to the woman I'm dining with tonight. Nalani. I simply want to say . . . I just love the sound you make when you finally shut your trap."

The entire crowd went dead silent.

"I also adore what you've done with your hair. How do you get it to come out of your nostrils like that?"

Another collective gasp. Nalani's eyes were huge. Her head turned left and right as she looked to others, as if to confirm that this was actually happening.

The Dog plunged on. "You know, Nalani, you're going to make some rich guy a great first wife.

Oh . . . In case you folks didn't know, Nalani works here at the *Mahana Kai.* When I think of all the people I respect the most, she will be right there . . . serving them drinks."

Lucifer, his forehead on the table, was convulsed in laughter." Oh Jackson, you're gifted!"

The Dog was now soaked with sweat. His eyes were wild with desperation, as he seemed to be frantically struggling to stop, yet his lips kept flapping.

"This evening, I was introduced to a few of Nalani's siblings. Her family tree must be a cactus, because everyone on it is a prick!"

That did it! Nalani stood up and slapped The Dog, hard. Quivering in shock and with her hand covering her mouth in horror, she burst into tears, turned away and ran from the table. Two security guards had already been summoned from the resort's main building. They each took a firm grip of his shoulders. As they dragged him off, The Dog was heard shouting: "Nalani, if I've hurt your feelings, truly, from the bottom of my heart, *I don't give a damn!"* Then he was gone.

A profound silence hung in the air like a pall. Finally, as if a switch was suddenly turned on, everyone in the crowd started talking at once. It became a madhouse of excited chatter at every table. Nalani, who had been weeping behind a palm tree, was immediately surrounded by friends and loved ones. She seemed resilient enough, as they were all now laughing heartily together; she most of all at the nutcase who had been her date.

Lucifer got up to leave our table. Glancing at his watch, he seemed to have somewhere to go. As he walked past, patting me on the shoulder, he was beaming with the expression of a proud uncle. I sat there for a long while, basking in the glow of smug self-satisfaction. So many excellent things had just gone down! I had vanquished a despicable foe in a humiliating way. Destroying an enemy who has it coming is exhilarating! There's an instinctive, visceral pleasure in the experience of vindication. I looked down at the Cuff. . . and grinned. What a weapon!

I now felt the urge to walk around. As I stood up, I had to grab the edge of the table. Whoa! Steady there, Jackson! I centered my inebriated balance and, threading my way through the gathering, headed for the beach, just out of range of the *luau* torches. I dropped down onto the sand. The euphoria of my success over my adversary was fading fast, evaporating in the warm wind coming off the ocean. Something else was slowly replacing it, and it was far less upbeat. Then, out of the shadows of the distant trees came Lucifer with Sophia draped on his arm. Her elegant coif was disheveled and her dress could have used a bit of straightening. Seeing me sitting there, he gave her a dismissive slap on the rump and she headed off back into the crowd.

Taking a seat next to me, he crowed, "Enjoying the moment? There's no substitute for victory!"

I gave no response and kept my eyes on the white foam of the waves sweeping in from the inky darkness of the sea. I was feeling weird. At the height of my explosive strike at my foe, I'd felt full of powerful energies that all merged together into a laser of intensity. Now, all of that passion had drained away, leaving in its wake a disagreeable residue.

Lucifer poked me in the shoulder. "You don't look like a man who just won the gold medal in Retribution."

I absently toyed with a seashell. "It's just that this victory is beginning to feel hollow."

"Come on, Jackson. The guy got his just desserts. Stupid should hurt."

"Maybe, but I'm more interested in what came up for me in all that. Characteristics I don't normally associate with who I am."

"Ah, so you noticed! An experience like what you had tends to go in one of two directions. Either the Shadowlings explode up out the depths, have their moment in the sun, and then quickly recede away, as if they never existed or while it's still fresh in your mind, you have an opportunity to recognize those energies and see them as an integral part of you."

"I admit I lost it back there. Nalani makes me weak in the knees. When she showed no interest in me and fueled my disappointment by dining with that idiot, it sent me into a tailspin of . . . "

"Of Shadowlings. Interested in taking a look?"

"Damn, this is sobering. Take a look at what?"

"Jackson, while it's all fresh, let's analyze it. It all started out with your feeling the emergence of Lust. Right? As you let your panther come alive, you found yourself lusting over this native girl. Well, when it turned out that it wasn't mutual, what came up for you? Rejection, which wounded your Pride, triggering your Victim. Then, to add to your distress, as you correctly perceived yourself, you then became consumed with Jealousy and so, of course, Envy reared its ugly little head, yes? That's six Shadowlings right there! Want to challenge any of this?"

"No, I'll cop to those. Now I'm starting to recall others. He was goading me, damn it! Well that raised my hackles. I felt real Malice, and it was stirred up by . . . *(gulp)*. . . Hatred. I really did feel hate."

"That's right. Then you had your little face-to-face encounter at the bar. You got to see up close what kind of guy this was. He filled you with loathsome Contempt and harsh Judgment, not to mention a boiling Anger, given the cutting insults he spat at you. Now your stew was really cooking! A whole host of Shadowlings were simmering together, one enhancing the power of the next.

Ah, and with his last provocation, 'kissing her neck,' your Anger exploded into full-on Rage. It didn't take much for the soup to start to boil over. And that's when you attacked! And with what? Hostile Aggression! You were seething with Spitefulness and let loose a plan using Vindictiveness and Manipulation which was not just totally Insensitive but laced with Ruthlessness and Cruelty."

I groaned at the sound of the last two. Cruel and ruthless? Yeah.

"So then what happened? As per your directive, he launched into his shockingly dark comedic toast. What were you experiencing as you watched his self-destructive meltdown? Here's a hint: the expression on your face was wreathed in it. You were the picture of someone in the throes of wicked, pitiless Revenge. Ah, Revenge, the kingpin! 'A dish best served cold.' Indeed!

And after his utter humiliation, you were overflowing with Arrogance, with yet another dash of Pride for having witnessed your enemy humiliated. Any sense of Conscience was kept at bay by Self-Righteous Justification. 'He so had it coming.'"

I rested my head on my knee, absently drawing circles in the sand with a stick. I muttered: "Okay . . . enough."

"Alright, I'll stop there."

I felt nauseated. The walls of Justification that had kept me from experiencing the repercussions of my actions had just come tumbling down. I was now filled with yet another unsavory emotion, Shame. But this was not the shame inflicted on me by my Inner Critic. This was of a higher order, shame coming from my Conscience. Suddenly, my head snapped up as a realization struck home. I arose quickly, brushed the sand off my pants and bolted towards the resort grounds.

Lucifer turned in surprise. "Hey, where're ya going?" And then, in his sarcastic style: "*Something I said?*"

I walked as fast as I could, just short of breaking into a trot, taking a shortcut through the property that I knew of. Within a few minutes, now breathing hard, I'd made my way to the entrance of the resort. I shook the sleeve of a bellhop:

"Excuse me. I'm looking for a man in a black, silk shirt with a palm tree design. He's about 5' 9" and . . . "

The bellhop pointed to a bench off to the right. "Oh . . . that guy. He's waiting for a cab."

Sitting alone, under the light of a single overhead bulb, sat The Dog. His head was buried in his hands and he was weeping. I quietly took the seat next to him. He glanced up with a look of embarrassment to be caught like this. Then his bloodshot eyes opened wide with recognition. All I said was: "Hey," extending my hand. He stared at it for a long moment.

"Come to gloat?"

"No, I've come to apologize." I kept my hand extended until he finally, very slowly, took it.

"Apologize? You? For what? I'm the one who made a complete, freaking ass out of myself. I don't know what in hell came over me! It was like a nightmare that I couldn't wake up from."

A wave of fresh, agonizing memory seemed to sweep through his mind and his head dropped back into his hands with a groan.

"Please let me just say that I'm so sorry. I can't really explain. What's your name?"

He sat up, pulling himself together. "Milton. You?"

"Jackson." We sat there together in silence; me, wondering what to say next and Milton no doubt questioning why I was sitting here with him. For the sake of levity, I took a stab at humor:

"So Milton, have you ever considered a career in stand up?"

His head whipped around and he gave me such a look that I tensed, expecting him to take a swing at me. Instead, after an interminably long pause, he burst out laughing, which got me going, too. Then, we couldn't stop and we were both doubled-over together. My comment wasn't remotely that funny, but it opened up a much needed release valve. Milton finally took a few deep breaths and leaned back against the bench.

"The thing is, I'm such a competitive bastard. Came from a family of six, all boys, and guess who was the youngest? We competed for everything. And me, being the runt, I had to try twice as hard. So that tendency is just burned into me. I've never known how to win gracefully. Still, I don't understand why tonight I'd . . . "

I put my hand on his shoulder and said it again: "I'm really sorry. I wish I could tell you why."

Just then the cab arrived. Milton stood up and opened the back door. We shook hands again. He looked me in the eye and said simply: "She's a fox. Good luck, man!" Then he was gone.

As his cab moved off down the driveway, I remembered something Lucifer had said: 'The Snake has consequences.' I had wickedly disgraced that man. And on the heels of that recognition came yet another: 'With every expansion comes a contraction.' As I stood there on the sidewalk, watching the taillights of Milton's cab disappear around the bend in the road, I felt humbled. I saw how that 'rubber band' concept had been actualized with me. I had, indeed, contracted, snapped backwards from the awesome experience of Oneness today. My little Self had reemerged, reasserting itself with a powerful vengeance. And in a moment of clarity, I realized what was happening. Expansion of consciousness scares my 'little me' and triggers reactivity. So, it pulls back hard and retreats behind the oh-so familiar walls of my ego shell, defending its turf.

A wave of new arrivals was pulling into the resort entrance. I glanced at my watch: 7:55. I meandered back in the direction of the *luau*. The famous *Mahana Kai hula* presentation was about to begin.

CHAPTER
14

Curiouser and Curiouser

I know who I was when I got up this morning, but I think I must have been changed several times since then."

—Through the Looking Glass

Back at the luau, I noticed the lighting had changed. Most of the tiki torches illuminating the dining area had been extinguished. What was now aglow was the stage, a raised wooden platform, maybe 40 x 30, with a set of stairs going up the right side. I slipped back into my seat at the dining table. Lucifer was now engrossed in an animated discussion with a new neighbor, a priest, no less! I heard a snippet of Lucifer's last remark: "Listen padre, you're not someone who's going to want to hear my advice on religion. Can I interest you in a sarcastic comment, instead?" For myself, I just wanted to sit back and get comfortable, feeling the anticipation starting to build within me of seeing Nalani's performance.

A group of musicians with guitars, ukuleles, drums and some instruments I didn't recognize quietly took their position on the far right side of the stage. A hush emerged from the crowd. Then, off in the distance, two lit torches could be seen racing towards us, zigzagging between the palm trees and moving fast. They threaded their way through the darkness like a couple of flickering fireflies.

To the sound of a building drumbeat, two men, with their torches now held high, sprightly bounded up the stairs onto the stage. The *Fire Dancers* had arrived. They were dressed in the native garb of a short *pareo* sarong with grass leg cuffs. They were bare-chested and barefoot, with a wreath of shiny leaves around the crown of their heads. The dancers, athletic and nimble, began engaging each other with their torches, spinning and weaving like a couple of expert samurai warriors locked in combat. Then they lit the other side of each torch so that both ends were aflame. Taking a position on the two front corners of the stage, and to the continuing beat of the drums, they proceeded to twirl the torches in perfect synchronization and at such a speed that each gave the illusion of a unbroken circle of fire. They flung the blazing fire sticks high in the air, catching them expertly, spinning them behind their back and above their heads, and over, under, around and through their legs at a dazzling speed. With the dramatic effect of the whirling flames against the backdrop of the dark night, it was a stunning display of confident power, grace and fluid motion.

Wow. This was an *exciting* opening for the evening's performance and the crowd responded enthusiastically. In the midst of feeling so thoroughly entertained, I was hit unexpectedly with another piercing wave of sadness as an image of my sweet daughter, Francesca, emerged in my mind. Like me, she had loved fire and would have been thrilled with this elemental display.

Next to take the stage was a group of six beautiful female dancers. These *wahines* wore exotic headdresses of vibrant feathers, grass skirts and fresh *leis* draped around their necks. Each of the women was exceptionally lovely. Four of them had lithe, petite figures, while two were of the pear-shaped body type, representative of many native Hawaiian women. The *hula* they danced was to a very rapid beat. The main movement was their hips rotating so fast that their grass skirts were a blur. They were equal to the Fire Dancers in terms of amazing body control, their head and shoulders held perfectly still while their bodies shimmied below.

At one point, six male *kanaka* dancers joined in. They, too, were dressed in the same simplicity of the Fire Dancers. Their masculine *hula* was grounded, strong and potent but with smooth actions and no rough edges. The two groups, the *wahines* and *kanakas,* alternated in a kind of seamless, organic choreography. It was a balanced expression of native *yin* and *yang* energies, merging together in a kind of ecstatic celebration.

Finishing their set, and to a rousing ovation, all the dancers slipped off the stage and the music went silent. A stillness descended, the only sound remaining was the soft rustling of the palm tree fronds above us. Then, very quietly, the band starting singing to the sweetest of melodies. I don't understand Hawaiian, but this tune had to be a love song, filled with a genteel, heartfelt tenderness.

A spotlight, hidden far above in a coconut palm, shot down a single beam. There, at the base of the stage steps, in a pool of soft light, stood Nalani. As she slowly ascended the stairs, her image reminded me of a swan lifting up off of a lake. She was dressed in pure white, a short sarong with a small top. A purple *lei* of delicate blossoms around her neck matched the *lei po'o* encircling her head. Her bronze skin and jet-black hair glowing in the torchlight created a stunning contrast to the ivory cast of her clothing. She was a visual feast.

It was obvious that Nalani was someone special, like the *prima* ballerina in classical ballet, the truly gifted one. She moved to the music with graceful ease. It was as if the dancer and song became one expression of exquisite flow. Her hips rotating with the smoothest fluidity, Nalani's extended arms glided through the air, riding on the wings of the music. Her expressive hands were telling the stories of waves and sunlight, of rain and of Madam Pele, the volcanic Goddess of Fire.

There was something else that gave her a special radiance. Nalani exhibited no narcissism, not a whiff of the vanity that so often is evident by the *prima* dancer of any form. It was as if she was not performing for a crowd of people, but simply from a deep place within herself, the *hula* Goddess offering up her gift of dance to the island gods. The band led her into a variety of different variations of assorted tempos and speeds, one dance more mesmerizing than the previous. When it was finally over, I just sat there, too dazed and dazzled to partake in the standing ovation.

Lucifer seemed to take note of my enthralled expression and elbowed me back to reality.

"Hey Romeo . . . Romeo! You should see your face! A hopeless romantic, completely fixated on one woman. There she is . . . your Juliet!"

Nalani and two of the *wahine* dancers coasted past our table. I contemplated his remark: My Juliet. Oh yeah. Most definitely.

Sporting a leering expression, Lucifer eyeballed me. "You're smitten alright. I assume you're not going to pass up the opportunity to reacquaint yourself with this beauty." He pulled his chair closer. "Listen to me. She may have shut the door on you, but you have the wherewithal to unlock it, right there on your wrist. Need I remind you that you swore you'd activate the Snake three times tonight and I'm holding you to it. You've used it once, beautifully, with two more to go. What better way than to direct it towards what you want most? Just look at her!"

I got up and walked through the mingling crowd, needing to think. I wanted, in the worst way, to have the chance to reconnect with this very special woman and yet I was so torn. I hadn't yet come to terms within my own conscience regarding the use of the *Cuff of Kosala* just for my own selfish purposes, my own edification. Saving a life was one thing, manipulating reality to serve *me* was something else altogether. What gave me the right to have such power over others?

On the other hand . . . why not? Am I hamstringing myself with some outgrown morality that keeps me back from indulging in full-on enjoyment? How will I know if I don't act?

But all this mental back and forth was only window dressing to the most basic fact. Everything boiled down to what Lucifer had said earlier: "Why activate the Snake? Because you can!" It was as simple as that. Oh, temptation was creeping in on me ever closer, slinking up that spiral staircase from the darkness below. The scale was tipping. Then in a burst of lucidity, an inspiration hit me. I knew exactly what I had to do. I took a few deep breaths to settle myself. This was going to test my courage to the max.

Nalani was standing across the way, politely receiving accolades. Closing my eyes and clearing my mind, I conjured up her image and pointed towards her. I pictured, with crystalline focus, the vision I wished, no, commanded to have unfold. Holding that picture steady within my Mind's Eye, I tuned in to my *Hara,* feeling the power of the command rising, firing up my spine, capturing that clear image and rocketing, once again, out my outstretched arm. My body shivered with intensity. This time I stayed fully in touch with the experience of this intense flow of pure dynamism until it had completely passed through and out. The die was cast.

And now . . . the great challenge. I turned and made straight for our dinner table. Lucifer's chair was empty, but I spotted him off to the side, leaning against a stone wall. I walked up to him, feeling strong and focused.

"I've made some decisions. I promised you I'd activate the Cuff three times this evening. Well, the second attempt was just directed towards Nalani. I couldn't pass up the chance to reconnect with her. I had to do it. If not, I'd spend the rest of my life regretting that I didn't try to see what's there."

Lucifer's face took on an etheric glow. "Excellent! That's the spirit. Now you're getting into the swing of it. Each time you initiate the Cuff, it gets a little easier, no? It wants you to take control. It likes being ordered to deliver exactly what you want. Now you're starting to play *my* Game at the level I'm offering. Power over anything you want!"

I matched his grin with my own. "Exactly. So, in that same spirit, I'm also clear on how I want to activate the Snake for the third time tonight."

"Great! What's your plan? Dial up another limo ride around the island for you and your 'Juliet?'"

"No."

"What then?"

"I'm going to command it to have you disappear."

The glass Lucifer was raising to his mouth froze in mid-air. His lip quivered. "You can't be serious."

"I'm dead serious. Yes, with this amazing *Ouroboros*, I can get what I want. You said it. And what I want is for you to *go away.*"

"After all I've done for you? Why?"

"Because I'm so far out of my depths. Because I'm foolishly trying to hold my own with the master of manipulation. Because I can feel a whole new form of temptation creeping in and getting a foothold in my soul. You're shrewd and devious and I'm freaked out by the direction this is progressively taking me."

"You're still afraid of Power, aren't you?"

"Screw you! I told you I want to step out of my movie, remember? The Power you're offering is incredibly appealing. But in essence, it's basically controlling my movie, which still has me firmly stuck on your Web. I want out of your Game, not deeper into it."

"My Game is offering you the chance to be a master of the world you know. Come on, Jackson, don't be a fool by underestimating the value of this proposal."

"Your offer? That's my point! What's behind this proposal of yours? Look me in the eye and tell me it's not some form of deviousness! You made it clear that you've shown up in order to keep me from lifting off from the sleepy 3rd dimension. I got on your radar for that very reason. And what do you do? You try to tempt me with an incredibly powerful amulet that can override the basic laws of nature. Alluring? Unbelievably but it's too much. Why? Because I know myself. I know who within me is strong and where I'm weak. The part of me that would 'go for your deal' is not the guy within myself that I want in charge of that kind of Power in my life. He can't be trusted with it."

I looked down, turning my wrist from side to side. "I've used this Cuff four times now and the last two were, clearly, abuses of this Power. I had no right to humiliate that man publicly like that. As you've shown me, what made me do it was a whole collection of Shadowlings that emerged. You were masterful in egging me on tonight, plying me with drinks, goading my panther, fanning the brushfire of my Envy, my Jealousy and much more. I ended up exploding, releasing buried rejected aspects I didn't even know I had within me."

"And you consider this a bad thing?"

"I consider it both good and bad. This experience brought to the surface my 'dark side' energies that, up till now, I haven't been willing to own as part of me. Okay, now I'm not so blind to what's been, for me, unconscious. Granted, it gives me more understanding of myself. If I can, I'll be sure to include all of those Shadowlings into my revised, more accurate and realistic self-image. And yeah, I can feel how that acceptance already makes me far more balanced within myself, as I can stop denying what I don't want to see."

"And the bad side is?"

"The bad side is that I saw how my little Self can be manipulated. I've seen how it can be easily talked into using the Snake for its own purposes. That alarms me, Lucifer. I also uncovered that my greatest fear is around Power and its abuse. Well, look at me! I've abused my Power twice already."

"But you had no problem abusing it to attract in Nalani tonight. That's a double standard, Mr. Moral High Ground."

"You're right, and I fully agree. That's exactly my dilemma. With Nalani, again I question what gives me the right to impact her life. Is the attempt to turn her in my direction yet another abuse of this Power? Yeah, clearly, but I've gone ahead anyway. I just can't pass up the chance to be with her. That's the bargain I'm making with my own conscience. We'll see soon enough if the Cuff even works with her."

"Oh, I suspect the Snake will have performed just fine. Wait and see. But Jackson, step back a minute. You're shooting from hip, blowing off an offer that billions of others would jump at!"

"I'm not a fool, Lucifer. I realize full well what's being dangled here. But the bottom line is that this magical Snake is designed to keep me locked into a dimension that my Spirit wants to transcend. You don't seem to get it. My deepest interest is to snap out of the fogbank of your Web and to wake up! I'm not going to allow your juicy temptation to distract me away from developing my connection with my deeper nature. As of right now, I'm done with this amulet of Power. And my conversation with you is OVER!"

In a slow, ominous movement, Lucifer stepped forward from the stone wall where he had been leaning. There was something chilling about the sudden shift in his character. The elegant gentleman was draining away fast. His body language now took on an aggressive stance, face stretched taut and glowering. His finger jabbed my shoulder.

"Now you listen up, you sanctimonious ingrate! You repeatedly asked: 'Why me?' Okay, here's the deeper truth. Part of why I chose to drop into your life today is because you've been in a debilitated condition; your heart broken through your loss and, thus, emotionally vulnerable. I specifically look for vulnerable humans, especially if they're from Category B. Vulnerability tends to translate into weakened, which usually makes a person more pliable to my influence. You stood up to me way better than I expected so I dramatically upped my Game. Look at the phenomenal gift on your wrist that you've been offered! You *owe* me, Trent. You think you can just blow me off and walk away?"

"I don't owe you anything. You're like a predatory shark, aren't you, with your radar scanning the Earth for vulnerability. The way I see it, today has been a trade-off. I let you pick my brain all day and you've given me insights into my unconscious Shadow world. So we're even. Now, what I want is for you to disappear and take your *Cuff of Kosala* with you!"

He edged closer: "Get this, Jackson! When I leave, it's on my terms, not yours."

We just stood there glaring at each other. As I looked into his eyes, I saw fury. It was like a bonfire of anger, distilled down into a focused, laser-like ferocity. I took long, deep breaths to keep from being completely withered by his fierce gaze. With a razor's edge in his voice I hadn't heard all day, he said very slowly: "I'm warning you. You can't do this."

"Yes, I can and I'll tell you why. Free will, remember? And let's not forget, you gave me your word that I could end this conversation anytime I wanted."

"My word, like a lot of other things about me, plays by a different set of rules. To put it into language you can understand, 'my word' is based on what best serves my purpose."

Suddenly, like the sun breaking out of the clouds, Lucifer's face lit up with a deep rosy benevolence. "Jackson, Jackson, my friend, listen to me, now. Don't be foolish. Come into my realm! What a team we could make! We can creatively merge the two, my purpose and yours.

I'll make you into a heroic star! You can carve out a life beyond your wildest dreams!"

I wasn't biting and then, another insight flashed within. "I just realized something, Lucifer. I know what it is about you that I find so barren. Your world, it has no love in it."

The 'sun' disappeared. He let out a derisive laugh. "You think love makes a difference?"

"Yeah, it makes all the difference. Power without love makes for a dangerous force. It's the heart that you have no connection with. You don't really love anything, let alone anyone, do you?"

He scoffed. "Love … oh, please. It's far and away the greatest source of misery on this planet."

"Maybe so, sometimes. But love is what defines us as human beings. From what I can see, you're a loveless creature."

"By choice, I might add. I put my stock in much more potent qualities than such sentimental nonsense."

"You think love is nonsense? Well, let me tell you something. This afternoon, when I dissolved into the great Oneness, what I discovered is that the Universe is bathing in Love, infused with it. God, or The Universal Being, or whatever label we put on It, isn't just a loving Presence . . . it's Love Itself."

By the strange look in his eye, I knew I was on to something. Each time I spoke the word 'love,' Lucifer's anger went up a notch. I persisted:

"I think that love is the key that threatens you most in your role as the guardian of the Underworld. It's the secret you conveniently neglected to tell me, which guides me through the Shadowland. It's what generates compassion for my rejected selves. Love is the Awakened conscious heart that'll take me back to Wholeness, that'll pull me through the portal on the other side of the Shadow, isn't it?"

"You'll never get back to that Light, Jackson. Your Shadowlings will overpower you, mark my words."

Like an angry jaguar, Lucifer stood up and began slowly pacing back and forth in front of me, keeping his enflamed eyes trained on mine. And yet, I felt, remarkably courageous. There was something about sensing the Truth on my side that infused me with grit. I held my ground. Crossing my arms, I faced him squarely.

"I'm not afraid of you."

He stopped pacing and stood directly in my face.

"Really? Well, you should be!"

With that, Lucifer's energy field exploded outward. I was blown back a few steps from the sheer force of it. Then, like an eerie nightmare, the pupils in his eyes started to pulsate, in and out. The pupils kept slowly expanding outward until the entire surface of both eyes was solid black. *Holy shit!* My heart began pounding with hammer blows. If I was going to do this. It had to be right now. Closing my eyes tightly, I pointed directly at him, putting my entire focus onto creating the desired image . . . Lucifer gone!

What happened next, I'm not quite sure. I remember holding the vision vividly. The power surge began taking its natural course, rising up, gathering strength and blasting through me. But then, the flow of the surge that was flying through my arm thickened, slowly coming to a stop.

For the first time, it began to reverse its course, flowing back through my hand and up my arm! Lucifer was fighting me. I held steady, keeping the vision intact, which seemed to arrest the backflow of the energy. I had the Power of the Snake on my side. I was wearing it, so its allegiance was to me.

Then . . . *Whoosh*, the surge shot forward and out. There was a flash of blinding light, like one of those phosphorous grenades. When I opened my eyes, Lucifer had vanished. All that was left where he had been standing was a cloud of iridescent blue smoke. The air smelled like burnt hair.

As the haze cleared, I glanced at my left wrist. Damn it! The Cuff was still there. Lowering my arm, I stood, immobilized, not sure what to do. Slowly, I felt the pounding of my heart begin to ease as a flood of relief swept over me. I had just dodged the biggest bullet of my life! I had held my own and escaped from Lucifer! It'd been touch and go but, in the end, I hadn't taken his deal. And the Cuff? It may still be on my wrist, but I'd have it removed by a jeweler first thing in the morning. Relief, with the lightness it brings, is a beautiful emotion!

"Jackson?"

I spun around at the sound of my name. I knew that voice! Nalani had changed into a short, sleeveless silk dress. I felt a bit anxious, not knowing what to expect and looked, tentatively, into her lovely face. I figured her expression would tell me all I needed to know and it was soft and smiling.

"You mentioned you might come tonight. I'm so pleased you did." Lightly touching my shoulder she whispered: "I could use a drink! How about you?"

I hesitated, not quite believing the shift in her response. "Uh, Nalani, do you remember our conversation tonight at the *luau*?"

She gave me a quizzical look. "You mean this morning? I loved our conversation. I was so moved that you trusted me with all the heartbreak you've been through."

I exhaled slowly, realizing she had no memory of the fiasco this evening. I glanced down at the Snake and just relaxed. "I believe I see a *Haupia* in our immediate future!"

We made our way to the bar. As we waited for our drinks, I had a fleeting memory of the nasty exchange I had had right in this exact spot with Milton, just a few hours earlier. How fortunes can change! Now it was me who had the full attention of this belle of the ball. Nalani seemed so at ease and comfortable. Any lingering guilt for having manipulated this situation was disappearing from my mind.

Finding a couple of chairs, we took a seat, sipping our drinks and watching the gathering. What I found so lovely was that we were both quiet, yet there wasn't the slightest discomfort in this silence. The easy, peaceful flow between us that we'd experienced this morning had, like the tide, naturally returned. I recalled a line my mother had taught me years ago: *Silence gives the proper grace to women.* Yes. Just show up fully and be real for her, which may or may not mean having much to say. Finally, I murmured quietly: "Your *hula* touched me deeply."

"Thanks. *Hula* makes me so free and happy. It's said that doing what you want is freedom, and loving what you do is happiness. I have both."

"As I watched you dance, I could see your grandmother in you."

Nalani's eyes opened wide with surprise. "You did? My sweet Tutu. God, I miss her! She'd be delighted to hear you say that. As a dancer, Tutu was a legend in her time. She poured everything she knew into teaching me."

"When you dance, you keep her memory alive, don't you?"

"It's actually much more than that. It's as though she and I are dancing together. This may sound strange, but I invite in her Spirit and she moves through me. So, when people offer me compliments, I simply give them over to her."

As I listened to Nalani, I was struck by the sharp contrast in our cultures. On the mainland, by and large, we worship at the altar of youth and everything is in a forward rush. In the traditional Hawaiian culture, there seems to be not only a deep and abiding respect for elders, but also a reverence for their ancestors, keeping alive the lineage, the thread of life backwards in time.

I could hear the irresistible sound of the surf calling. "Do you feel like getting your feet wet?"

Nalani's face lit up. "Sure! Let's go. The moon's full tonight!"

The *luau* was winding down as we meandered through the thinning crowd. We took off our sandals and set them at the base of a palm tree.

As we neared the edge of the surf line, I rolled up my pant legs. The ocean was calm, the sea breeze soft and serene. The saucer-edge of a huge yellow moon was peeking just above the treetops, beginning to bathe the beach in its silver luminosity. We strolled along the wet sand, letting the small, rippling tail end of the waves wash around our ankles. In a lovely gesture, Nalani quietly removed the *lei* that graced her neck and placed it around mine. Then she asked: "You're a writer, yes?"

I scooped up a shell and skipped it into the waves. "Yeah, these days I'm a blogger but I don't really want to talk about my writing. I'm feeling a little embarrassed."

"Embarrassed? How so?"

I paused. How to answer that?

"For me, writing's a peculiar experience. I kept asking myself, do I have anything to contribute that hasn't already been expressed by someone else in a better way? Ultimately, yeah, I really believed that I had something unique to offer. I hoped it would resonate with anyone whose interest is diving in, exploring their 'inner nature.' We all need good guides and solid information. So, after a lot of trial and error, my blog became a kind of map that I laid out, pulling together carefully selected jewels of what I considered to be invaluable, metaphysical information that I'd absorbed over time and could share."

"It sounds to me like you created a very cool offering. So, why would you be embarrassed?"

"Because I'm disappointed in myself. I launched my blog last year, before I lost my daughter."

"Yeah? So?"

"Lately, I've come to feel somewhat disingenuous. The theme of my writing's called *Snap Out of It.* I write about important things I wish I'd known about much earlier on my own path. Okay, great. But then, when disaster blindsided me and my own life collapsed onto itself, I wasn't able to follow my own map!"

Nalani stopped in her tracks and turned to face me. "But, so what? So you saw your own limitation. That's a good thing, yeah? Look, believe me, I know what it's like to get flattened, crushed. Given what happened, the fact that you actually got back up on your feet tells me a lot about you. Healing from a blow that severe, that tragic . . . it simply takes time."

"Time wounds all heels, huh?" I teased. "Actually, I had an experience this afternoon that brought such peace to my emotions."

"Really? Tell me."

I was quiet for a moment . . . remembering.

"I just surrendered into the hands of a blessed mystic on the island. This shamanic healer found her way deep into a carefully protected place in my heart to uncover my wound, tenderly easing it out of hiding and then lifting it up into the light of day, letting the warmth of the Sun of her loving kindness work its magic."

"Oh, how sweet is that? And now, with that release, you can forgive yourself, yes?"

"Can I?"

"Yes, you can. What I learned from my husband's death is that everything has its season. Pain is unavoidable but, at some point, suffering becomes optional."

Whoa! I stayed with that line for a moment, allowing the truth woven in those words to sink in. I wondered, have I been 'milking' my suffering? Nalani spun around in the soft sand, dancing in the light of the moon.

"Wow, Jackson. Sounds like you've had quite a day!"

"That's not even the half of it."

She stopped twirling. "Oh? So what else did you experience that could possibly match that?"

Tell her, said a voice within. *She can handle it.* I reached out and lightly held her shoulders.

"Nalani, look at me. I want to tell you the truth of what happened with me today, but I'm not sure I could describe it in a way that wouldn't sound bat-shit crazy. I'm so enjoying your company. I don't wanna take the chance of freaking you out. This is pretty . . . startling."

"Hey, don't worry about making sense. Just give it to me, straight up. And just so you know, I don't scare easily."

"Yeah? Well, I guess we'll see about that! Alright . . . what if I were to tell you I've spent the day with . . ." I swallowed hard. "With *Lucifer.*"

Whatever Nalani was going to say next seemed to have gotten stuck in her throat. Finally: "Lucifer . . . as in . . . the dev . . ."

"Yeah, that Lucifer. And I'm totally serious. He's nothing like what I'd have imagined him to be, at least the sides of himself he showed me."

She studied my face, waiting for the coming punch line to a joke. The look in my eyes said otherwise. My only thought was *please don't turn and run.*

Nalani's expression was hard to read, as she seemed to be trying to wrap her mind around this explosive revelation. "Right . . . sure. You were with Lucifer . . . today?"

"I was, and guess what? You met him! Remember this morning, that big boorish guy I was with on the deck by the banyan tree? He was the one trying to be cute and insulted you about the Moloka'i lepers?"

"That was Lucifer?" Nalani just shook her head, as it was all coming back. "What a jerk! I couldn't understand what a nice man like you was doing with such a . . ."

"Prick?"

"Exactly." Nalani looked somewhat dazed as the full impact was setting in. "Jackson, I've gotta sit down. This is a lot to take in."

She dropped to the beach and pulled on my hand to have me join her on the sand.

"I'm going to really stretch here and assume you're not kidding or playing me." After a long moment, she said: "Of all the questions that are swirling around in my head at this moment, there's one that outweighs the rest. Why you? What did Lucifer want with you?"

"He wanted a conversation and to make me an offer."

"Yeah? And did you take his offer?"

"To a point, yes I did." I glanced down at my left hand. "I took what he was offering for an incredible, mind-bending test drive. But in the end, I turned it down. I tried to give it back to him. Tomorrow, I'll be rid of it completely."

"And exactly what did you get out of your day with Lucifer?"

What did I get? How to answer that?

"It was quite a ride, a lot of highs and lows. Everything from terrifying moments to deep debates about human nature. But one thing's standing out as something very big. It's still percolating inside me but I'll try to explain if you really want to hear this."

Nalani spread out her palms. "Don't stop now."

"Okay, first, let me tell you a bit about me. For much of my life, I've been exploring ways to connect with Spirit. I'm not talking about the spiritual, which is such a vague term. I mean the quest, the discovery and the tangible deepening connection with Spirit in me."

"Yes. In our culture, what you're describing is the path of *Huna*, lifting into one's True Nature on the quest to discover God within."

"Right, Nalani. I'm sure that all true paths lead to the same place, no matter what it's called. It's our natural curiosity about the deepest essence of the soul. Well, long before today, what I discovered for myself is that Spirit isn't a 'thing;' *it's an alive Presence . . . a field of Beingness.* So how to make the connection with my Spirit? Is there a bridge? This question led me to the discovery of my own personal Presence. It's that awake state within me that becomes the lightning rod that allows for the possibility *of an alignment* with Spirit. *My Presence is the bridge that connects me to my True Nature. My personal awakeness attracts the deeper awakeness of my higher Self.* Am I making sense so far?"

Nalani took my hand, the moonlight reflecting in her eyes. "A mystic once said: 'What you seek . . . is seeking you.' I'm totally with you."

"Okay, so here's the point. This is the game-changer that I've learned from my day with Lucifer. Just as in my past, I was a mountain climber, always stretching to go up, my orientation to the realm of Spirit has been the same direction—'Wake UP'—always with the mindset of elevating to more Light, to a higher consciousness."

"That all sounds perfectly valid to me."

"It is valid, Nalani, but something happened tonight that changed everything. I discovered the intrinsic value of also going in a *downward* direction. Lucifer manipulated me into an experience that uncovered part of my Shadow World, an entire side of myself that I've been, more or less, unconscious to. I unearthed a whole pocketful of Shadow Selves that I've been denying. They've been totally disowned. My way of handling these unwanted Selves is by pushing them down and away: '*You don't belong to me.*'

"But Jackson, we all do that very same thing. It's how we manage to cope. All those parts of ourselves we refuse to own? We have to stick them somewhere, right? So, yeah, down they go . . ."

"Right. So, I knew intellectually, that I had some kind of Shadow buried in my psyche. I knew it but I didn't really understand it. And that's because I really didn't want to face it. So, by always stretching upward, I've totally neglected what was hidden below! By reaching for the Light . . . I abandoned the Dark."

Nalani shrugged. "Well, the Light is certainly much more attractive."

"That's for sure! But here's the huge piece of news I got today, the real kicker. Lucifer revealed that the path to our Authentic Self, the path to spiritual Wholeness, is through this Shadow World, which is the last place I'd ever have looked. It's through the Shadow World, not avoiding it that we reach the true Light. It's a question of balance."

"You mean . . . to hold the Light and the Dark together?"

"Exactly! Balanced. I'm already in touch with the Light in me. The question is, can I embrace my Shadow in a compassionate way?"

"Yeah, but let me ask you something, Jackson. This new realization today, did you actually experience your Shadow World and pass through it in some tangible way?"

"Somewhere in-between . . . I'd say that I definitely got in touch with elements of my Shadow. But no, I haven't yet experienced what it actually means to 'pass through' that underworld. Believe me, this evening at the *luau*, I got a real taste of parts of myself I've been sitting on. I'm just now getting a sense for 'who's who in the jungle' of my Unconscious. But I can't pass through the Shadow until I discover and own who's down there. But I get it . . . I now have a sense for the direction I need to go, carefully bringing these disowned energies up, out of the darkness and into my conscious awareness to be recognized."

"Well, then your inquiry awaits, yeah? I get it, too. It's the journey we take back to loving ourselves, actually loving all of our selves."

"That's it, Nalani. Lucifer called these deeply suppressed so-called 'flaws' of ours, Shadowlings. They're full of energy, unrealized potential 'life force' and power. But, like any living thing that's been kept hidden and locked up in the dark, they might be distorted or stunted in growth or worse."

"Well, for that reason, aren't these Shadowlings parts of oneself to be wary of?"

"Oh yeah. Definitely. But I think these 'character rejects' of ours can be uncovered and 'seen,' or even better, embraced, which, in time and with a bit of love, could defuse some of their negativity. Might even turn some into friendly allies!"

Nalani's face took on an impish expression. "Well Jackson, I read once that we're all searching for someone whose demons play well with our own! I do have a question about Lucifer. Why would he offer you such a key piece of information? I mean, if he's all about keeping the

Shadow alive and hidden, why should he be helpful to you? Doesn't that make you suspicious?"

"Everything about Lucifer makes me suspicious. He's a consummate Trickster. His entire M.O. is the art of skillful manipulation that we aren't even aware of. That's how he keeps us playing his Game. But one thing seems true. If I'm not integrating my Shadow, it's bound to be subverting my life. Can I approach my Shadowlings with eyes wide open and a fearless, yet, open heart? I don't really know. I guess I'll see. Why would he offer such a choice piece of information? I'm not sure, but Lucifer is nothing if not utterly confident. I think he also loves the challenge when someone 'ups their game.'"

As I toyed with a piece of driftwood, she snatched it out of my hands. "Hey, how about a beach fire? This is a good spot."

We had fun combing the stretch of sand together, gathering up a few armloads of sun-bleached and bone dry wood. I needed some paper to get the kindling started. There was nothing in my pockets, but I opened my wallet and found the receipt from Mama Kamea's place. Smiling to myself, I whispered once again, "Thanks, Mama."

Quickly building a small teepee of kindling on top of the wadded-up paper, I coaxed the tiny flame by gently blowing on it. Soon, we were seated around a roaring blaze. Toying with a fire stick to poke the embers, I kept stealing sidelong glances in Nalani's direction. I'm not sure there's any lighting that makes a woman look more beautiful than the golden flickering flames of a beach fire. I wanted to know more about her.

"So, with all the tourists passing through, I'm sure there are a lot of men interested in you."

Nalani rolled her eyes. "Yeah, men on vacation. Not my style . . . usually." She glanced over to me with a coy smile.

I felt my heart click its heels! "So what is it you're looking for in a man?"

Nalani stared up at the moon for a long moment. "Okay, bottom line? I want to feel met. I want a relationship where my partner and I are matched, where we're not straining to fit into some preconceived mold for each other. We just get each other effortlessly. To be honest, more than anything, I want a man who can be 'present' with me. Know what I mean?"

I grinned inwardly. "I think I know exactly what you mean."

"Really? Tell me what I mean."

I stirred the coals at the base of the fire with my stick. "What I hear is that you want a guy who's not in his head all the time, who knows that his heart is something more than the place where he gets excited about his favorite sports team. Someone who can continually 'see' you with fresh eyes . . . the real you."

"Yeah."

"And I'll bet you want a spiritual connection. By that I mean two Spirits consciously connecting, with love and fun and depth, like a couple of dolphins, swimming freely but choosing to be together, side by side."

"Right. Jackson, look at me. I'm not a 'half' looking for my other 'half' to make myself whole. I'm my own person. I want to be seen and loved for who I am."

Nalani rested her chin on her knee, staring into the blaze. "Is that too much to ask?"

"No, it isn't. You're not asking for too much. You're just asking for the right guy. I think any man worth his proverbial salt wants a woman who knows who she is within herself."

"Exactly! I'm a dancer, Jackson, so I'm very much 'in my body.' I find that your point is true about most men, disconnected from the neck down. Their body is just this thing that's carrying their precious head around! And what's going on up there within those constantly turning gears? Hello! Anybody home?"

Nalani looked at me with a kind of "I give up" expression. I understood her complaint all too well.

"Yup. I know just what you mean. I've been accused of that very thing myself. It's what we guys tend to do. We hang out in our heads, heavy on thinking . . . light on feeling and devoid of Being. And that just seems normal to us. In our 'heady space,' we don't realize we're constantly living one step removed from the real world."

She tossed a driftwood log on the fire. "Yes . . . as if life were some kind of movie instead of a magical unfolding."

That comment took me aback. I could hardly believe how much we were aligned. She continued:

"The thing is, I'm not asking for everything to be focused on me. I'm simply wishing for someone to actually, literally BE with me. Be awake with me. Everything else can be built atop that foundation. But without it . . . count me out. When I say I want a man to be 'present,' I don't mean, 'Hey! Pay more attention to me.' I mean I want him to be mindfully aware. When I look into his eyes, I want to see someone home. Otherwise, the relationship is all just a sleepy illusion."

"Right, a Web of Illusion."

"A what?"

"Never mind." I reached over and brushed some sand off her cheek.

"Nalani, you don't know anything about me, but what you're searching for in a man . . . it's not unreasonable."

"You don't know anything about me either, Jackson, but I'd like to believe that. It seems to me that love isn't complicated, people are."

Speaking of complicated, I suddenly, I felt an overwhelming urge to 'come clean' with her:

"Nalani, I gotta tell you something and you may not like it."

She said nothing but her brow furrowed, one eyebrow raised ever so slightly.

"I know this sounds strange but I did something seriously manipulative to make you choose to be with me this evening." I took her hand and placed it atop the Cuff.

"Can you feel that?"

She looked startled. "The bracelet. It's vibrating! What is this gizmo? "

"I don't know if you're going to believe this, but let me tell you about this thing."

With a deep breath, I now plunged into telling her the whole story, withholding nothing, about my strange and momentous day with Lucifer. I went into specific detail regarding the Snake, its astonishing powers, to the degree that I had experienced. I shared how the first two times I commanded this Cuff, it was to actually save lives, my own included! But then the next two episodes, both of which involved her, were totally self-serving and no doubt an abuse of its power.

Nalani's eyes narrowed. She was not amused. In a slow, ominously even tone she asked, "And so you're telling me that tonight you forced my date to make a complete and utter ass of himself, publicly humiliating me in the process, just so you could be with me?"

"Yeah, that was my doing."

Her eyes flashed with anger. I didn't see it coming but I sure felt the slap she whacked across my face. *Ow!*

"That's what I think about your 'seductive magic.'"

I found myself watching her hand to see if she was going to smack me again. "Please believe me; I have no excuse . . . . Wait, that's not quite true. I have a damn good one, given who was manipulating me but you don't wanna hear that. Let me just start by apologizing."

"You should start by apologizing to my date."

"I already did, as best I could. I caught him on the way out."

"You did? Oh . . . " She studied me, her lips pursed. "Well, that was decent of you."

"Nalani, please, cut me some slack and just let me try to get this out. Right now, I want very much to say to you I'm sorry for what I did, but the truth is . . . I'm not. When I first saw you this morning . . . you took my breath away. Something inside me lit up and said: There you are! I knew right then that I just had to get to meet you and spend time together, like we're doing now."

Nalani said nothing, her arms still crossed.

I plunged on . . . "But feeling, of any kind, to a heart that's been broken just hurts. So, in my emotionally crippled condition, I declined your gracious dinner invite. But all afternoon, I couldn't get you out my mind."

At this point, I turned away as my eyes had filled with tears. Nalani reached across and put her warm palm on my heart and left it there.

"Go on, Jackson," she said softly. "I'm listening."

"Okay, here I was spending my day with Lucifer! He goaded me into releasing my deeply buried *Eros*, my 'wild panther' he called it, which I had buried away for quite a while. And then, at the *luau*, there you were again and there went my breath. I'll bet there were a hundred lovely women at that gathering, but I only had eyes for you. Did I make a kind of 'pact with my Shadow' in a sense, to use this Cuff to turn you my way? Yeah, I did. I knew full well it was manipulative. Am I sorry? No, I'm not. Why? Because you're here with me right now. Would I do it again, given the chance? You bet . . . in a heartbeat. I'd do anything it took if it meant being with you, to share your sweet company like this. Will you forgive me even though I'm not a bit sorry?"

Nalani gazed at me for a very long moment, biting a fingernail. Finally, with a wry smile she murmured:

"Jackson, that was either the best line I've ever heard, and I've endured more than my share or you're actually a really decent guy. Which is it?"

I shrugged: "Let's go with option #2, shall we?"

We both laughed and Nalani scooted close. Reaching for my left wrist, she felt into the vibration of the Snake once again, studying the intricacy of the ancient design.

"Wow, this thing is incredible. Did Lucifer tell you where this Snake came from originally?"

"He told me of an ancient Kingdom in what's now northern India. A land called *Kosala*."

A silence settled in between us. Nalani seemed deep in thought. Then:

"Jackson . . . would you do something for me?"

"If I can. Sure."

"Would you show me what the Snake can do?"

Before I could object, she squeezed my arm imploringly. "Please? You can't tell me about something this stunning and not offer me a tangible example. It's not fair!"

I could see that 'no' wasn't going to fly. I stared down at the Cuff and then back at her.

"Okay, what would you like me to do?"

"Anything you want. Your choice."

I closed my eyes, leaving my mind open and empty of thoughts. Within that quietude, what emerged was a memory of what I'd just said . . . about two people connecting like a couple of dolphins. From that, an image arose in my Mind's Eye and, with a slight grin, I raised my left arm and pointed out to sea, commanding the Snake from within.

Whoosh!

When the dynamic flow finally ebbed, I turned to see that Nalani was scanning the direction I'd pointed. We both gazed out at the calm sea for a few minutes. I was just beginning to think: "*Oh great. Now it doesn't work!*" when, just beyond the small, curling waves, the placid water began to agitate. Suddenly, in a startling burst, two bottle-nosed dolphins rocketed out of the water together. They shot straight up, high into the air, their smooth silky skin glistening in the moonlight. As if choreographed, they performed an elegant, circular flip before landing gracefully back into the waves. If that wasn't spectacular enough, after a brief lull, the dolphins exploded upward again. This time, their ascent was in a 'corkscrew' motion, each spinning clockwise, as they arced upward. Reaching the apex of their leap, they touched snouts, as if kissing, and then back-flipped in a perfectly synchronized reentry.

Nalani whispered in an awed voice some Polynesian phrase I didn't understand and jumped up, racing to the water's edge. "That was magnificent!"

Hearing her say that set my heart aglow. Something was clearly shifting in me. I was 'feeling my oats' and quickly changing into a whole different mindset regarding the Cuff. Maybe I'm being hasty rejecting this thing. With it . . . anything was possible. Was I gaining confidence or was my vanity being fed, enjoying showing it off?'

As we sat together, watching the gentle swells rippling onto the beach, Nalani again dropped into a quiet space. Then, I felt her body suddenly go rigid. She grabbed my hand tightly.

"Jackson, did Lucifer make any mention of the Cuff in relation to Time? Can it change past events?"

I thought back. "Yes, he said, under certain conditions, this *Ouroboros* has been known to have the capacity to alter the past. 'Redirect history,' I think he called it. But, please . . . I don't want to relive the experience of you with your date tonight. Forget it!"

"No, that's not what I'm thinking."

Turning to face me, she took hold of both my hands in hers. Slowly, deliberately, she whispered:

"Why not command the Snake to bring your daughter back?"

If I live to be a hundred, I'll *never* forget that moment. For a few heartbeats, there was stunned silence inside me. Then, my entire body erupted in goose bumps. Redirect history!

"Do you think it's possible that I could?"

"Why not try? Yes! Lucifer said it himself, right? Alter the past! And, Jackson, will you ever have a stronger intention than this one?"

I was shaking with exhilaration! For chrissake, why hadn't this occurred to me? I knelt in the sand and Nalani did the same, facing me. We looked at each other, sharing this tense, extraordinary moment. I reached back and brought out my wallet. Unzipping a hidden side pouch, I slipped out a picture of Francesca, taken on that fateful day on Portuguese Beach. Over this past, calamitous year, I had never *once* been able to look at it, until now. I held the photo in front of me. There she was, my sweet angel, with that impish, happy grin! I glanced up at Nalani, her eyes gleaming with anticipation. In a flash of intuition, I realized what she, herself, must be thinking. If I could somehow bring back Francesca, perhaps I could do the same for her husband, Kekoa. With that, I felt a selfish pang of 'No!' But I realized, if I brought back Francesca, I'd have to offer her the same possibility.

Taking one more lingering look at my daughter's face, I closed my eyes and let this poignant intention gain strength. I've never wanted anything more in my entire life and it was building quickly in intensity. Like a swirling whirlpool, Francesca's image began to form. The intention gathered speed and force, infused with the power of my love for her. As it reached a crescendo, I leapt to my feet. Pointing the ancient, mysterious *Cuff of Kosala* directly at the sea, I cried out a command from the depths of my Being:

"Bring back my daughter. . . Bring back my Francesca!"

A bolt of Power shot up from my *Hara*, the surge literally blasted through my body. It passed through the crystal clear vision being held rock-steady in my Mind's Eye and flew down my outstretched arm. I stood, frozen, as the pulsating energy just kept firing through me, burst after burst. Finally, when it was over, I collapsed onto the sand, spent.

The only thought that managed to work its way through my frazzled brain was . . . now what? My head swiveled, looking up and down the long strip of sand, expecting to see my daughter walking along the water's edge towards us. We waited in a breathless, expectant hush.

Finally, in the distance, I saw her! She was way down the beach, her silhouette outlined by the moonlight. Jumping to my feet, I raced along the sand, shouting at the top of my lungs: "Francesca! It's me . . . Dad!" As I got really close to her, with my arms opened wide, I skidded to a stop. Who I thought was my daughter turned out to be a young surfer kid with shoulder length hair. His eyes were wide with fright and all he said was:

"Dude . . . you're scarin' me."

"Sorry. I thought you were someone else."

"Yeah. I got that." Keeping a wary eye on me, he gave me a wide berth and kept moving, now more quickly, on down the beach.

I returned to Nalani and our fire, feeling a little sheepish. We sat there for what seemed like an interminably long time, just holding our breathe . . . and waiting. But, no, nothing. Nothing! All I saw was the glistening reflection of the full moon on the waves as they washed ashore on an empty beach.

It's awful when 'hope' flips and turns into its opposite. That hyper-excited state of anxious expectancy slowly leaked away and, finally deflated, I conceded defeat. It hadn't worked. Francesca wasn't coming back. I felt shattered all over again as my 'grand intention' fizzled into a wrenching disappointment. I'd been so successful in wielding the power of the Snake that I'd become convinced of my invincible ability to make my command materialize. Now, absorbing this cruel blow, I withered inside, sinking into the morass of a heavy funk. My head drooped down as if my neck couldn't support it. Then, right on the heels of this huge emotional downswing, I sensed an incoming tsunami of something else. Anger. I was suddenly so pissed! The bitter taste of Acrimony was flooding in. I was becoming ablaze in the fiery, high-octane, combustible fuel of Rage.

Storming off, I muttered to Nalani: "I'm sorry. I need to be alone for a bit." Heading up the beach a little ways, I was lost in a swirling cloud of dark emotion. Blame was rising up in me and I was furious at myself for my own limitations, for having failed miserably. At the same time, I was now filled with resentment towards the Snake and Lucifer. If it was true that it had the capacity to alter time, why had it come to naught for me, refusing to give me what I wanted most? Grabbing the Cuff with my other hand, I pulled and twisted, trying to rip it off, but it just seemed melted to my skin. In an outburst of frustration, I knelt down on the sand and tried beating the Snake on a rock to break it off, but all I did was hurt my wrist.

I just let the anger build, unchecked. And as this potent vehemence circulating within me, it gathered momentum until it boiled over, becoming volcanic. As the 'cone of the mountaintop blew off,' I suddenly felt, rippling through me, the desire to destroy! The Snake seemed to sense my state of fury and vibrated accordingly. It appeared to be saying:

"Sure! Why not? What would you like to annihilate?"

And standing there, at that moment, I felt, full on, this unbridled force of my own Shadowling of Destruction, this treacherous capacity to want to obliterate something. Power, frustration and rage blended together, creating a kind of white-hot noxious inner fission. I then got a jolt of how readily and dangerously agreeable the Snake seemed to be to feed my wish to strike out at something. *Let's do it!,* it seemed to suggest.

In the midst of that state of an all-consuming eruption, and to my surprise, the root cause of this seething emotion broke through the surface of my heart. I looked down and opened the tight fist I had made with my right hand. In my palm was the crumpled picture of my daughter, smiling back at me with all that lost promise of her youth. It was then that my anger began to liquefy, to morph and transform into what had been hiding behind it, a crushing, abysmal despair.

Holding Francesca's picture in my shaking hand, I kissed her forehead and felt my legs collapse. I dropped to my knees in the wet sand, the waves rolling in and washing all around me as my heart just cracked open, allowing the full impact of this profound letdown. Instead of my arms being wrapped tightly around my returning little girl, I wrapped them around my own shoulders, as I swayed back and forth in the swirling surf, my tears mingling with the ocean's salty waters.

And there, immersed in my dashed hopes, something quite extraordinary began to open up! I felt the emergence of my Presence gently enshrouding me. Slowing my breath, I allowed this expansion to stretch out and bloom. There was the sense of 'me' in all my dejected sorrow. And then, enveloping all around me was a palpable, pulsating field of Awareness; so clear, calm, rational, soothing, loving and fully imbued with an infinitely deep, merciful understanding. As I shifted into this Presence, I recognized myself not through my memory of my own life, but by my Awakeness, in this moment, to my True Self.

With exquisite empathy, my Beingness held my pain with such tender loving-kindness, not attempting to fix anything, just allowing deep compassion and a penetrating supportive consolation. It seemed to convey: "Yes, Jackson, be fully with your grief and I'll be fully with you." And within this beautiful collaboration between two dimensions of my own soul, my heart had its way with me. I felt, full on, the piercing pain when towering expectations collapse into the rubble of failure. And there I stayed, with this despondency wrapped in the tender field of Being, allowing the emotion to pass through me like a mountain stream and run its course.

Then, as the sadness dissipated, the Presence remained. And as the need for loving-kindness diminished, the Awareness spontaneously filled me with a different kind of energetic quality... *Lucidity.* I felt like clarity itself. I was suddenly 'wide *WIDE* awake.'

I stood up, dripping wet, and faced the sea. I became acutely aware of this new perception I was developing today regarding my Light and my Shadow. I could now actually experience them both, together. I could feel the Light, the positive side of my nature that I so identified with. I invited this energy to come forward and I fully stepped into it. This was the state I was always reaching for. As I stayed with this Light energy of mine, I could sense its good intentions. I looked down at the Cuff, feeling the intense vibration. This part of me was full of affirmative resolutions of ways in which the Snake could be directed towards the highest good for all concerned.

With this state of lucidity intact, I then shifted my inner gaze and invited my Shadow side to emerge, without censoring or any judgment, allowing it equal time. *Whoa!* Well now... what a different cast of characters! Rejected and disowned aspects gradually came up the 'inner staircase' and began to reveal themselves. I permitted them to come alive. Once encouraged, these Shadowlings weren't shy. Some, I had already encountered at the luau. My Jealousy and Revenge reappeared to me, among others.

As I was dialing in to these energies, I could feel the presence of another, a deeper 'Shadow self' still unrevealed, as if it was staying hidden off to the side. I sensed that it was a powerful entity and I invited it to step forward. *Come on out!* And what warily came forth out of hiding was my 'spiritual Ego.' Some traditions call this entity the 'False Jewel.' This Self of mine represented the dark side of all my metaphysical training. Having wrapped himself in the cloak of 'The Path' and absorbed the knowledge, he could 'talk the talk' of awakening with great authority, but was not going to ever allow the actual transcending of my egoic self, the shift from the 3rd to the 4th dimension. His bottom line? To block, at all cost, any real awakening! *Sure! Work on yourself all you want. I'll be right there, too, to make you look and sound good to others. But get this! I'm not about to actually let Presence dissolve my iron grip of the 3rd dimension. Ever.*

"So," I murmured, *"we finally meet."* I had sensed this influential and slippery entity within me, but never came close to breathing life into him like this. Here was Lucifer's great ally, carefully concealed deep in my Shadow world, totally committed to fostering and protecting my egoic consciousness. I recalled a comment Lucifer had made earlier: *"Maybe I'm just talking to the wrong part of you, Jackson."* I realized now who he was referring to.

I let this False Jewel open up so I could really feel him. He lifted the Cuff to eye-level and studied it with gleaming eyes. The sense of his mindset was: *Oh yeah . . . Let's take this Snake for a ride!* Waves of temptations and images of fulfilled desires flooded my imagination. I had instinctively been so wary of the Power within the Kosala Cuff. Now I understood why. Corruption, skillfully camouflaged behind a 'spiritual persona' was just under the surface, whispering, *Trust me with the Snake. I'll be a great steward of its incredible capabilities.*

The False Jewel slowly withdrew and melted back into the darkness within. Having made contact with that powerful Shadow Self had been so revealing and liberating. I was now free to move forward, without being blocked by its resistance.

And now, as I stood there at the water's edge, holding both the Light and Shadow at the same time, a compelling 'state of equanimity' arose. How empowering it was to have the capacity to contain these opposites simultaneously, in a kind of metaphysical balance; both sides acknowledged, integrated and loved as a vital and legitimate part of the whole of me yet neither running the show. I could sense that, followed further, this powerful balance, based on strength and love, and held together by my awake Presence, could conceivably lead me through the Shadow World and into the dimension of Wholeness itself. This was the tricky map Lucifer had left behind, the key to the pinpoint of Light on the backside of the Shadowland that he thought I'd never really be able to reach and pass through.

Basking in this new, fresh place of inner symmetry, I felt so settled. I smiled as I looked down and realized that my right hand had, once again, clasped itself onto the Cuff on my left wrist, so drawn to its magnetic pull. I wondered . . . *Now that I was more acutely aware of who's who within my dark side, perhaps I could actually entertain the idea of keeping the Cuff, using it wisely, judiciously.*

Suddenly, I felt a jolt of emotion. Nalani! All I wanted was to be back in her sweet company. I could see our beach fire a short distance away that she had kept stoked. I turned to make my way back to her when I heard a Voice in my head, clear as a bell, that simply said:

"Get rid of it. "

I stopped in my tracks, stock-still. *What?* Then again:

"Get rid of it."

At the sound of those words, I felt the Snake begin to pulsate more intensely than ever before, now agitated in alarm, like an angry hornet. My entire left arm seemed to be buzzing from the intensity."

"Ask the Snake...how many have failed."

Okay. . . I followed the dictate of the Voice, demanding of the Cuff an answer, having no idea what to expect. Then, as if by some decree, my eyelids drooped shut, closing tightly. And in my Mind's Eye, with stunning clarity, the strangest of visions opened up. In a single file parade, the faces of men and women from vastly different historical eras and, by their diverse clothing, apparently from all parts of the Earth, began appearing to me. The Voice said:

"These are the wrecks that litter the path of Kosala. Get rid of it."

With this inner vision, I gazed directly into the faces of these beings as they, one at a time, passed before me. Some of these individuals held such Light in their eyes.

"Ask them! This Power devoured them alive . . . and in ways they least expected.

They never saw it coming. You never do.

He lied. No one who willingly takes on Kosala escapes unscathed. No one.

Get rid of it."

I was both floored and mystified as the procession within continued, the line stretching on and on. At some point, I heard myself say: "Okay. Enough!" Instantly, the vision vanished and my eyes fluttered open. I was horrified. Now I knew the truth and I wanted this thing off of my body immediately! I pulled and tugged but, try as I might, it came to the usual result. I just couldn't budge it.

I cried out: "I can't get it off!"

"Command the Snake to remove itself."

For chrissake . . . of course! I did just that, and within moments, the Cuff was like a hot stone in the palm of my other hand. I held it up in front of my face to peruse it one last time. It never looked more dazzling! And now that it was off of my wrist, the vibration had ceased. Something about its constant humming had been giving it a sense of weightlessness. Now, I could feel its true heft. The solid gold made it heavier than a ball of lead.

As I brought it close and marveled at its intricacy, the Cuff seemed to whisper to me, *"You're not really contemplating what I think you are."*

I whispered back, "Yeah, I am."

In the most soothing, hypnotically soft murmur, the Snake began to telepathically ever-so-delicately paint a picture for me of my future life, drawing in refined, intimate brush strokes the extraordinary range of pleasures that I would revel in, the beguiling possibilities that would be all mine to obtain and possess at will! It gracefully guided me through a vivid visualization of all the 'good' that I could secure for this desperate world so in need of my assistance. Omnipotence? Phew! "Not you, Jackson," sighed the Snake. "You're so much stronger than that!"

It portrayed with such clear-cut precision, my forthcoming command and expertise of the Power inherent in the Cuff; how I would be able, with competence, to govern with equanimity, handling and harnessing with true authority this *tour de force* that I held in my hand.

As I listened with rapt attention, the swell of superiority was slowly inching its way into my soul but it was cleverly camouflaged as a sense of clean, strong Power . . . the Power representing the Light! Oh . . . so soothing . . . so exciting . . . righteous . . . juicy . . . controllable!

Way off in the distance, over some yonder hill and dale within my inner landscape, came a clarion call echoing back to me:

"Jackson, snap out of it!"

As that alarm registered, my head jerked, and my eyes opened with a start! I hadn't realized they were closed. There I was, with the Cuff now carefully, lovingly pressed to my ear, the Snake having been whispering to me. Damn! I'd been lured and seduced down some captivating rabbit hole. All my sucker points had been so skillfully touched upon that I was practically drooling!

I slapped myself to shake off the idyllic fantasy. So Lucifer had lied! No one escapes the Cuff. Bastard! I shuddered with the realization of how frighteningly close I'd come, once again, to being sucked in, duped by my own naïveté and hubris, just like the Snake eating its own tail.

With the bracelet now tightly held in my fist, I whispered to it: "Thanks but count me out, *Kosala*."

From where I stood, I now walked with measured strides four feet deeper into the ocean, the water now up to my chest. *Okay, do it now!* In a state of calm, dispassionate clarity, I took a deep breath, reached back and heaved the Cuff as far as I could out to sea. Watching it soar, the gold glinted in the light of the moon. I heard the distinctive 'plop' as it hit the ocean and disappeared. I just stared at that spot on the water's surface for a while. Now with a huge grin, I turned back towards the fire and lovely Nalani.

Flopping down onto the sand alongside her, I was so thankful to be back in her company again. I thought of apologizing for disappearing like that. Instead, I said nothing, just opting to not disturb this sweet, easy feeling between us. I was still abiding in the profound state of Beingness. Nalani sat up and looked me over with alarm.

"You're soaking wet and shivering, Jackson!"

Throwing some extra logs on the fire, she stripped off my shirt and hung it on a stick to dry close to the flames. Then, she studied my face and with an intuitive grasp, seemed to sense that a major shift had taken hold within me. In the flickering light of the blaze, we just became like two magnets, slowly repositioning until we sat facing each other, our legs lightly straddling one another. Whatever it was she perceived in me at this moment, I could see reflected back to me. Nalani was aglow with a presence all her own.

I silently held up my left arm, and she immediately perceived that the Cuff was gone. A look of wistfulness cross her face for a moment, but was replaced with that of a deeper 'knowing.'

"For the best . . ." is all she said.

Feeling an alive closeness, we began to exchange what was in our minds and hearts. I told her about what had just happened to me, how my towering rage had revealed the depth of my disappointment, which had, in turn, transmuted and lifted me into this state of Presence. I shared with her what it felt like to hold both the Shadow and the Light, together, honoring the two sides . . . maintaining that balancing middle ground that transcended both. She spoke of how impacted she had been by the spectacular display of the dolphins, how elated she was to experience being 'met' like this, to be truly 'seen' by a man. I related my inner vision of the parade of the wrecks of *Kosala,* of the Voice that had emerged from within to warn and guide me out of danger. I described how I had flung the Snake into the sea. Lucifer could, no doubt, somehow retrieve the Cuff, but me? I was now free and clear of it.

Nalani held my hands and soothed any lingering regrets I may have been feeling about that decision. I expressed my innermost thoughts regarding my experience of spending the day with the Shadow Master, himself. She listened closely to all that I had gleaned from him, yet how relieved I was to have eventually won out: I made him disappear! Back and forth we went. I spoke . . . she listened. I listened . . . she spoke. It was evolving into a beautiful communion . . . a sacred space, two hearts opening wide, sharing the secrets of our souls.

At a certain point, we both fell silent . . . as if our connection was now deeper than words could touch. Our arms entwined, we closed our eyes. Magically, the feeling of separation, of there being two of us, began to soften and dissolve. A genteel message from my Wisdom Voice passed through my mind and down into my heart with one word: Surrender.

And again, with each breath: Surrender.

Yes . . . let go. Let go of doing, of thinking, of holding on with the grasping of all the sticky attachments . . . Surrender.

And then, sprinkling down from above, like a soft, divine mist, there descended upon us a form of spiritual fairy dust . . . Grace. We were gently enveloped in a state of bliss.

I leaned her head back until it rested on the soft beach. Slipping my hand behind her head, I let my palm get lost in her long, flowing black mane. The rich texture of her silky hair sent thrills through my sense of touch. And in the sweetness of the moment, there we were, animated spirits, in true contact . . . gazing through the windows of our eyes, into the depths of the other. Touched by this heavenly state of *Bhakti*, Presence as Love, our two hearts began to melt, creating a pooling together of liquid gold.

Passion is often a misconceived, unexplored emotion. When it comes to romance, the word tends to conjure steamy images of clothes flying in the air and two naked bodies pouncing on each other, caught up in a heated jumble of flailing arms and legs, racing towards an orgasmic climax. For me, in this exquisitely affectionate moment with Nalani, passion opened up ever so slowly, as if it was simply not to be hurried. Just holding her in my arms was so incredibly fulfilling and erotic! I was aware of sweeter subtleties like the sensual electricity in my fingertips by simply grazing the soft skin on the back of her neck. Our shared, tender intimacy was a space of enchantment, not an experience to go racing past. You don't gulp an extraordinarily fine liqueur. It's to be sipped . . . savored.

Gently moving in, as Nalani's sensual lips beckoned, I was delighted that she met me halfway. The sparks I felt from that lovely, genteel embrace were more intense than those bursting off our fire. I heard myself whisper, "That same mystic you mentioned earlier also wrote: 'Lovers don't finally meet. They're in each other all along.'"

She flashed her dimpled grin. "That's lovely, Jackson. Do you think I've been in you all along?"

That made *me* smile. "Yes. I'm beginning to think that may be true for both of us."

As my fingers gently followed the contours of her face, I glanced at the purple bruise developing on the wrist that had worn the Cuff. From that visual image, a compelling realization dawned on me. Lucifer had it all wrong! It isn't Power that's my real heart's desire . . . it's Love. It's deep, authentic, true connection, the kind of love that generates an awakening Presence with another. The kind of love I'm feeling right now with her! Unbounded freedom of the heart . . . that's what I've always wanted. One thing Lucifer did get right . . . this woman *is* most definitely my 'Juliet.'

Nalani lay back on the sand looking skyward. Then, in a fluid motion, she reached up and pulled me to her. Our lips touched again, but this time the kiss was deeper, a juicy passion beginning to surge between us, one torch igniting the other. Now entwined together, our hands began to roam, freely exploring the hills and dales of each other's body. My God, at long last the full-on emergence of my buried panther was coursing through me! Running her fingers through my hair, Nalani gently, but firmly, cradled my head in her palms, an intensity developing in her gaze. I held this contact between us, scanning, with sheer pleasure, her loveliness, especially the light shining in her eyes!

Hmm. Well, that was interesting... and strange. For a moment, in this soft, defused moon glow, it seemed as if her irises were dilating in and out.

Whoa! There it was again! What in hell? I squinted, staring hard. Yes. It was the black pupils in the very center of her green eyes that were expanding and contracting, like they were breathing! I looked away and then back again for a double-take, thinking I was hallucinating! Something was definitely...

Bloody hell!

My head instinctively snapped backwards. Her pupils had now expanded outwardly, until the entire surface of her eyes was solid black!

"Hello Romeo," she purred, her razor sharp fingernails slowly, suggestively, scratching all along my cheekbone.

Diagonally Parked in a Parallel Universe

If the dream is a translation of waking life,
then waking life is a translation of the dream.

—René Magritte

I EXPLODED LIKE A GRENADE, SHOCK BURSTING ME APART like shrapnel. At the split second when I recognized those menacing, black eyes, I felt my shoulder being shaken. Wild with confusion, I ripped my gaping stare away from Nalani and whipped my head around to see who was trying so hard to get my attention. And now, the bizarre sound of *"Zaddy, Zaddy"* was reverberating in my ears.

What Polynesian word was that?

Again: *"Zaddy, Zaddy."*

Wait! That voice . . . it was calling out: "Daddy, Daddy."

Blinking and squinting, I bolted upright, drenched in sweat. I was sitting on the couch in my den, and there, standing next to me, was my daughter, Francesca, hands on her hips, and a look of concern on her brow. My eyes must have looked like saucers, as I gawked at her sweet, freckled face!

"Daddy, wake up! You're yelling and having a nightmare."

"Francesca!?"

Grasping her hand, I let my head fall back onto the couch, allowing my massive confusion a chance to organize itself. What? Just a dream?

As bewildered as I was, one fact towered above all the rest . . . *Francesca was here!* My heart was spilling over with joy that my daughter was alive and standing in front of me! I reached up and snatched her into the tightest embrace of a loving bear hug, smothering her with pure, reckless affection.

"Stop. I can't breathe!" She giggled and squirmed, then got very still, staring at my arm. "Dad . . . what'd ya do to your wrist?"

I've never had the experience before of cresting a wave of pure elation . . . then feeling instantly paralyzed, all in the same breath.

"Which wrist?"

"This one. How did you hurt yourself?"

I forced myself to look down. What I saw made me gasp so loudly that Francesca dropped my arm and took a step back.

"You're acting weird, Dad."

Encircling my left wrist was an ugly deep-purple bruise. Managing a strained smile, I placed my hands on her slight shoulders. "Don't worry, honey, I'm not hurt. Go back to bed. Sorry for waking you up like this. I'll see you at breakfast."

With an effort, I turned her loose. As Francesca was leaving the room, she spun around and gave me a long, dubious look. I managed a reassuring wave until the door was shut. Leaning back heavily on the couch, my mind felt like it was locking up, with so many conflicting thoughts simultaneously spinning their wheels. Tumbling off the couch, I straggled to the bathroom sink and splashed cold water on my face. One peek in the mirror at the wild look in my eyes gave me an indication of how rattled I was.

Fresh air! That's what I needed. Throwing on a jacket, I stumbled out of the house, dropping into a lawn chair in my backyard. I glanced at my watch: 4:15 a.m. The neighborhood was in a deep hush at this early hour, with just a few early birds starting to chirp at the approaching dawn. The air felt cool, yet I was still perspiring.

As I sat there, inert, my emotions were spinning like a whirlpool, sideswiping each other, trying desperately to connect the dots. Consternation, relief, loss, skepticism, fear, wonderment and my sanity were all up for grabs. The memory of that last frightening moment—Nalani's eyes—kept reappearing. Instead of the brisk air calming me down, the whirlwind inside only grew with each passing minute.

Okay, Jackson . . . for chrissake, *pull it together!*

Tiptoeing back into the house, I showered to clear my head, changed into a bathrobe and made a beeline for my den. Flipping on the light, I fired up my laptop. Writing always gave me focus and I just began jotting down the fragments of thoughts shooting through my frazzled brain:

What happened to me?

Had Francesca really been swept away?

The Snake!

Did my command actually bring her back . . . in this way that I least expected?

Impossible? No. I was there. I know it! I think . . .

I've had lucid dreams. They feel so real, but I always know when I'm dreaming.

This was entirely different but what then was it?

A wormhole to another realm?

An out-of-body experience? Yet I had felt so completely in my body!

I'm struggling here.

Does it matter?

Francesca's alive!

I got up and paced, back and forth, across my small den. It's said that sometimes confusion is a high state. The point being, if your world has been turned upside down, you can suddenly find yourself 'out of the box.' Conventional answers come up empty . . . and that space can create an opening for some new realization. Well, I must be very high right now as I've never felt more discombobulated and fractured, a foot in two different worlds. My island experience was so palpable and vividly fresh, and yet here I sit in my own home!

But the bruise? I shivered as a fleeting image arose of me, kneeling on the beach, pounding my wrist on a sharp rock, trying desperately to break off the Cuff. Looking down at my chest, I could see my heart was now thumping wildly. Bending my arm, I brought my injured wrist up close to my face to inspect it. Slowly, with my other hand, I wrapped my palm around the bruise, closed my eyes and gently squeezed. Then:

BOOM!

As if lightning had struck the back of my head, I was bowled over with blinding flashes of crystal clear images that now flooded back into my awareness: crisp, sharp waves of memory.

Hawai'i . . . Mama Kamea . . . the cliff . . . And what of Nalani? Oh no! Did you evaporate with my dream? Or were you a premonition?

And there, in the midst of all the vivid recollection, who emerged front and center in my Mind's Eye? It was he, the Master of the Shadow Land. And bubbling up with remarkable recall, the flow of my entire conversation with Lucifer unwound in all its complex totality.

How long I sat there, eyes closed, reliving the complete thread of our dialogue . . . I'm not sure. But, when it finally came to completion, it left me with one clear realization: *We're all stuck on his Web of Illusion.* What a nefarious net!

I could hear Francesca stirring in her bedroom. Still rocked and trying to regain my wobbly equilibrium, I adjusted my robe and I walked out of the den. My feet shuffled their way into the kitchen. As I fumbled with the cappuccino machine, Francesca came bounding in.

"Morning, Daddy." As I turned in her direction, she scanned me, up and down. "You don't look so good. Are you sick?"

"Good morning, Sweetie. I'm just tired. I had a long night . . ." I pulled out a chair and took a seat. "Listen, Cesca, I know I'm running a little slow this morning, but I just need to sit here for a few minutes, alright? Did you have breakfast?"

"I'll have some cereal, but I'm almost too excited to eat!"

"Yeah? Why's that?"

"Why? Cause you're taking me to the ocean today! C'mon Dad, wake up!"

Francesca bent down, lifting her daypack and a small yellow beach bucket onto the kitchen counter. I literally jolted at the sight of it! Very deliberately, I said, "Cesca . . . I'm really sorry but we're not going to the beach. Not today."

Her voice immediately spiraled into a whine. "But Dad! You promised! Why?"

This time, it was my voice that had a tone I rarely use, one that conveyed: Don't argue with this. It's not negotiable.

"Why? Because sometimes, Sweetie, I'm the Daddy . . . that's why."

One look at her face told me that this disagreement was about to escalate. I quickly shifted into a mode I generally tried to avoid with her . . . bribery.

"Hey! You didn't let me finish. Instead of the beach, I'll take you into the city! We'll do a little shopping and then catch a movie! And you can invite any friend you want. How's that?"

Francesca was smart enough to know when she was being played, but the bait was very tempting. Shooting me a baleful look of disappointment, tempered by budding new thoughts of checking out clothes at *Forever 21*, she swung her pack and the bucket off the counter and headed, pouting, towards her room. She tossed me a comment:

"How can we go to a movie when Mom's picking me up at 5:00 for the weekend?"

Damn! I hadn't thought of that. "Okay, let me call her. Would you like to spend another night here?"

Sensing she now held the advantage, Francesca worked her angle: "Can my friend stay over, too?"

"Sure, why not."

Taking my cell phone into my den for privacy, I speed-dialed Chloe. She picked up on the second ring:

"Hi Jackson . . . funny you should call. I was just getting ready to call you. What's up?"

"Hey Chloe. Quick question. Sorry for the late notice, but can Francesca spend another night with me?"

Chloe cleared her throat, a subtle habit just before she had something important to say.

"Listen, Jackson, before we get into that, I have to ask you something, a big favor, actually."

"Yeah? What's that?"

Her voice suddenly went up a notch, tensing: "I couldn't sleep last night. Don't ask me to explain but would you consider not going to the beach today? Look, I assume we're going to have a big fight over this, but I'm asking you . . . don't go."

Goosebumps!

The room suddenly felt like it was starting to spin. As I slumped into a chair, I was hit with a powerful insight about an unconscious characteristic of mine . . . my Arrogance, that Shadowling that so often sneaks up from below and takes over my thinking, assuming it knows best. How difficult that must have been for my wife over the years.

"Chloe . . . I'm so sorry I never paid enough attention to your intuition."

Chloe was silent. Finally: "Well, thank you." Then, after another couple of beats: "Are you alright? You're sounding really weird."

"Yeah, that's just what Fran . . . never mind. I'm fine. It's just something I've come to realize. But hey, don't worry about the ocean trip today. I had a change of plans. We're not going to the coast. I want to drive Francesca and a friend to San Francisco to shop and take in a movie."

"What? You hate shopping."

"Yes but today, for once, I love it. So can Cesca stay over tonight?"

Chloe gave a big sigh. I could hear her drumming her fingers. "Okay. But she'll need more clothes. I'm about to head out the door to yoga. I have to pick up some woman in my class who needs a ride. I'll swing by on my way and drop off the clothes. I'll just be in and out."

As I hung up, I sat there for a while, lost in thought. Eventually, I just decided to stop trying to figure out the strange happenings that I was immersed in from my dream . . . my premonition . . . my altered reality. . . whatever it was. Sometimes, when tumultuous perplexity reigns and conflicting thoughts are tripping over each other, all one can do is simply let go. If there was ever a moment to 'pull the plug' on my disorientated mental blathering and get myself centered, this was it. I let my shallow breathing drop down deeply into my *Hara.* Slowly, I could feel myself connecting with the 4th dimension and the simple stability inherent within my personal Presence. It washed over me as I opened to it. With my internal chatter subsiding, however, one thought did remain: *Thank God, we were dodging the bullet of going to Portuguese Beach today.*

Wandering back into the kitchen, I made another latte and sat quietly at the table. Francesca walked in, talking excitedly on her cell with her best friend, as they discussed the movie they wanted to see and she poured a bowl of corn flakes. I still couldn't peel my eyes off her. As I sipped my coffee, I could sense my bewilderment gradually beginning to settle down. The sudden jangle of the doorbell made me jump!

I rose up and leaned against the refrigerator for a moment to gather my scattered wits. Steeling myself, I walked into the living room, but Chloe had already let herself into the front foyer. I could see someone else standing just behind her. As my 'ex' stepped into the room to greet me, our hug had the nippy temperature of an early autumn frost. It was friendly but with that one-step-removed coolness that comes with separation and guarded hearts.

"Hey, Jackson." She handed me a small overnight bag. As I reached for it, Chloe glanced down at my outstretched left arm: "Jesus! What'd you do to your wrist?"

I looked down at it and mumbled cryptically: "I'm not really sure."

She rolled her eyes. "You're not sure? You don't remember how you got something like that?"

Chloe motioned for her yoga mate to step into the living room and join us. Out of the shadow of the foyer stepped a woman—a bronze-skin Polynesian beauty with deep, green eyes. She had a lovely dimpled smile; raven-black hair cascading down her left shoulder.

I stood there like a block of ice, frozen.

"Jackson, I'd like you to meet Juliet. She just moved here."

Juliet smiled. "Hi, Jackson. I've heard good things . . . mostly," she winked. "Chloe tells me you're a blog writer, yeah?"

She extended her hand. I just stared at it. Finally, I slowly reached out and grasped it, shaking it lightly as I searched into her eyes. Still incapable of speaking, I motioned for them to come in and have a seat in the living room.

Chloe shook her head. "Sorry, we're running late for yoga. Gotta go. Are you sure you're alright?"

"I'm okay," I croaked, stealing another glance at Juliet. "I'm still waking up from the most astonishing dream."

The two women turned towards the front door. Juliet spun around on her heels with the graceful agility of a dancer. Fixing me with a level gaze, she softly said:

"Your dream . . . whatever it was . . . why not write it down? I'd love to read it."

Then, they were gone.

I remained standing at the front door for a long time, dazed, looking out at nothing. My profound disorientation was having a weird side effect. I felt like I was underwater, everything moving in slow motion. Juliet's comment: *'Why not write it down?'* was still ringing in my ears. I finally turned and made my way back to my den. Easing myself down in front of my laptop, I stared at the empty screen. One word kept escaping my lips:

Juliet . . .

Then, as if she had been patiently waiting off in the corner of my mind, the Muse chose this pivotal moment to pay me a visit. The Muse . . . that lovely spirit of creative inspiration whom every writer knows and courts like a lover. Like a flock of birds, words began to gather together, elegantly arranging themselves into a cohesive form. And, like a thin, graceful waterfall, a story . . . my story . . . began to pour down and through me as I typed:

Lucifer's Game

You're playing it, whether you know it or not.

Dawn was cracking open across the Hawaiian sky like a fresh egg, the golden yoke rising out of the sea to the east . . .